A Zappy
Little
Christmas

Books by Paula Charles

The Hometown Hardware Mysteries

HAMMERS AND HOMICIDE

AXE ME NO QUESTIONS

A ZAPPY LITTLE CHRISTMAS

Books written as Janna Rollins

The Zen Goat Mysteries

AN ESCAPE GOAT

GOATS JUST WANNA HAVE FUN

A ZAPPY LITTLE CHRISTMAS

A Hometown Hardware Mystery
Book Three

Paula Charles

This is a work of fiction. The story, all names, characters, organizations, places, and incidents portrayed in this novel are either products of the author's imagination or used fictitiously. No identification with actual persons (living or deceased), actual events, or locales is intended or should be inferred.

ISBN (paperback): 979-8-9913828-2-3 / ISBN (ebook): 979-8-9913828-3-0

Edited by Brittany Sumpter

Book Cover by Melissa Bourbon of WriterSpark

First edition: October 2025

To Dustin, Prentiss, and Mateo –
who took us on a walk through their neighborhood where the
inspiration for this story line was born.

Praise for the Hometown Hardware Mysteries

"Charles hits the nail on the head with this intriguing series debut." – Maddie Day, bestselling author of the Country Store mysteries

"This folksy mystery is loaded with captivating characters and small-town charm, with the perfect touches of humor and magical realism." – Angela M. Sanders, author of the Witch Way Librarian mysteries

"This fun and well-paced mystery has a sleuth that is sassy and smart...A fabulous debut cozy mystery." – Christina Romeril, author of Killer Chocolate mysteries

"*Axe Me No Questions* hits the bullseye! Paula Charles possesses a toolbox full of talent! Authentic small-town living, realistic family dynamics, humor with an intriguing mystery, all through five-star storytelling – the Hometown Hardware Mystery series is a keeper!" – Rosalie Spielman, author of the award-winning Hometown Mysteries

"*A Zappy Little Christmas* is a wonderful, twisty, funny tale of murder in Pine Bluff. Dawna Carpenter needs to use her ingenuity and years of experience in dealing with people to solve a murder. The author did an excellent job with the descriptions of the town, keeping the reader firmly rooted in the community, and doling out information on the suspects. The plot moves quickly, keeping readers guessing who the killer is. An excellent read!" – Rose Kerr, author of the Mia Reid, Archaeologist, mysteries

Chapter 1

"My mama always said kill them with kindness, but that woman is trying every last ounce of patience I have left." I glanced at Roxy after finishing jotting down an order I'd taken over the phone.

"Let me guess, Sheryl Capri again?" Roxy Dunsmuir, my new hire at Carpenter's Corner Hardware and Building Supply, asked with a grin. "What's she after this time? Please don't tell me she wants another pallet of bricks."

I laughed. "Not today, thank goodness. She did special order one of those ridiculous inflatable Christmas dinosaurs though, which isn't something I have any intention of ever having in stock. The monstrosity won't be in for a few days, but she did order a list as long as my arm she'd like delivered this afternoon."

Roxy flipped her thick, wavy red hair over her shoulder, extended her arm and wiggled her fingers. "Hand it over, Dawna. I'll get her order put together and deliver it on my way home."

If the gray winter light out the window hadn't been enough indication, a quick glance at the clock let me know the afternoon was already ebbing away. It was ten to four and would be fully dark within the next hour.

"After you get Sheryl's order together, go ahead and scoot out of here a few minutes early. Things are winding down anyway."

Roxy drew her eyebrows together. "Are you sure? I don't mind sticking around."

"Nah." I flipped my hand at her. "Once you get Sheryl's delivery made, it'll be time for you to knock off anyway. Go home and grab the kids. You are coming back downtown for the Christmas tree lighting this evening, I assume?"

"For sure. The high school choir is performing. Makayla would serve my head on a silver platter if I missed it."

I chuckled. "True enough. How's your little spitfire doing?"

"She's not so little. The girl is nearly as tall as I am now, and that's nothing to sneeze at."

"No, it's not."

Roxy towered over me by a good eight inches. I'd hired her in early November, shortly after she'd split up with her husband and moved herself and two of her three kids into a cozy bungalow in town. Makayla was a sophomore at Pine Bluff High, and Hunter was a senior. The couple's oldest son, Grayson, was away attending college at Boise State. Her soon to be ex-husband had ended up with the lion's share of proceeds from the sale of the hundred-acre cattle operation the two of them had built with blood, sweat, and tears out on Coyote Flat. And from the amount of time Brett Dunsmuir had spent at Timber Creek Saloon over the years, I would venture to say most of the blood, sweat, and tears exerted had been Roxy's. Life wasn't fair sometimes, but Roxy rarely complained.

"Anyway, Makayla's loving being a townie. I don't think she misses the ranch at all." Roxy answered my question about her daughter. "She's getting involved in all kinds of things at school since she doesn't have to catch the bus home anymore. She can stay for more after school activities than she ever could when we were up at the ranch. It's been a really nice change for her. Hunter's adjusting fairly well too, though he's been spending most weekends out at his grandparents' place with his dad."

"And you?" I questioned. "You always seem so strong, but are you honestly doing alright?" I knew firsthand what it was like to put on a good face for everyone during the day, then cry yourself to sleep at night.

"Eh, I'll be fine." She shrugged and waved Sheryl's list at me. "Better get busy pulling this order or I'll end up leaving here late instead of early." Roxy grabbed a rolling utility cart and rattled her way to the seasonal section where the strands of Christmas lights were shelved.

"There's a twenty-five-foot extension cord on the list. You'll probably need to pull it from the back," I called after her. "We've sold four this afternoon, so I'm fairly sure the shelf is empty."

"No worries. I'll grab extra and restock the shelf while I'm at it," Roxy hollered over her shoulder.

Half an hour later, Roxy had the delivery order boxed up, and I was stapling the invoice to a brown paper bag holding the smaller items. I handed the bag to Roxy who plunked it on top of the other items on the cart. Before she had a chance to push the cart out the door to load the items into her car, the bell above the door tinkled. Cold December air rushed into the store, along with a stick-thin woman with shoulder-length gray hair held out of her face by a clip on the top of her head. Her sad sack face had aged faster than her seventy-one years, and her brown jeans and extra-long taupe parka added nothing to her overall beige appearance.

"That better not be more supplies for Sheryl," the woman warned, shaking an angry finger in my face. "This nonsense has got to stop. I see your girl over there making a delivery to her several times a week, and nobody gives a flying fig that every single one of those deliveries affects me personally."

If she wanted a more accurate account, I could share with her how we'd been making a delivery to Sheryl nearly every day since late October. Wisely, I thought it best to keep that little tidbit to myself. "I'm sorry Marsha, but Sheryl's a paying customer. You know as well as I do small businesses like ours can't afford to turn away valid transactions."

Marsha Slabinski had owned Bright Whites Laundromat over on Walnut Street, just off of Main, for longer than I had been the proprietor of Carpenter's Corner. We were both members of the Pine Bluff, Oregon Women's Service Club, and both attended more than our fair share of city council meetings. Marsha, however, had the unfortunate circumstance of living next door to Sheryl Capri.

"I swear, if that crazy woman puts up one more Christmas light, I can't be held responsible for what I might do." Marsha set her jaw so tight I worried she might crack a tooth.

Then I won't mention the giant roll of Christmas lights Roxy's fixing to take to her, or the ten-foot-tall inflatable dinosaur on order. "Has it gotten that bad?" I asked, already knowing the answer. With Marsha's attention focused on me, I made eye contact with Roxy and nodded toward the door, indicating she should make her escape while she had the chance.

"Bad? Are you kidding me? There are so many lights on her place that I haven't been able to sleep for a month. And the racket coming from the Christmas carols she pipes out over the neighborhood has my anxiety through the roof. I thought things were terrible with all the wooden ornaments she nailed to my fence, but now she's declared a light war directed at my house. The whole thing is a complete nightmare. Did you know Sheryl broke the restraining order I had on her? Stupid woman. Now she's on house arrest and has been ordered to wear an ankle monitor." Marsha threw up her hands, her natural frown deepening. "Every bit of the troubles coming her way are her own fault."

Yep, not only did I know about Sheryl's ankle monitor, but all of Pine Bluff was aware of the ongoing feud between the two neighbors. I nodded. "I did hear. Sheryl's house arrest is why we agreed to make deliveries to her."

Marsha scoffed. "I hope you're wise enough to charge her gas mileage for all those trips back and forth."

Instead of acknowledging the comment, I plastered on a smile. "Is there something I can help you find today, Marsha?"

"The vent hose on one of my dryers burst this morning. What a mess. Dryer lint everywhere." She mimed an explosion with her hands. "Sorry I got fussy about Sheryl. I know you can't afford to turn customers away. I apologize for my behavior."

"You have nothing to worry about. Now, let's find you that hose you need." I led her to the correct section of the store. "Will we see you at the tree lighting this evening?"

"Not on your life. Sheryl has managed to rob me of any fondness I had for Christmas. I loathe every second of it, and I'm counting down every minute until it's over. As far as I'm concerned, nobody should be celebrating that wretched holiday. January can't come soon enough, if you ask me."

And I was sorry I had. Her Grinchy attitude seemed harsh, but I wasn't the one on the receiving end of Sheryl's relentless war on her neighbor. I thought it was sad Marsha had let someone else rob her of the joy of the season, but wisely decided to keep my unwanted perspective to myself.

"Will you add the vent hose to my account, please?" Marsha asked.

"Sure enough." I added her purchase to the ongoing invoice for Bright Whites Laundromat.

Marsha turned to leave, but had to step aside and wait while two members of the Pine Bluff Chamber of Commerce squeezed a pine tree through the door. They both wore flashing reindeer antlers on their heads.

"Knock, knock. Avon calling," quipped Holly Flynn, president of the chamber. "Delivery of one Giving Tree complete. Where do you want it?"

Once the door was no longer blocked, Marsha sidestepped around the tree and scooted out of the festive atmosphere as fast as her feet could carry her.

"Isn't it gorgeous?" I took a deep breath of the fragrant pine, then hurried around the counter to help them put the tree in place. "We've cleared a space right in front of the window. This spot has worked great the last couple of years. People see the tree before they even get in the door and it reminds them to grab an ornament or two."

"Perfect." Holly handed me a packet. "Here are your ornaments. We'll let you put them up yourself. Please remind people to make sure the recipient's number is clearly marked on the packages. Every year we end up with a pile of gifts we don't know who they were intended for. We always find them a home, but it's a nightmare trying to match the gifts up." She pulled one of the ornaments out to remind me how each one had a unique number assigned.

Each paper ornament included the age, gender, clothing size, and gift wish for a person in need. Most of the ornaments were for children and teens, but a few were for senior citizens in our community. This year's tags were cut from both red and white construction paper in the shape of bells.

"Sounds good. Remind me when the pickup date is, please?"

"December 18th. Chamber members will be around to collect all the gifts that day. It'll give us time to organize everything and get the presents delivered by Christmas Eve." Holly brushed off her hands. "We'd better get going. We still have a few more trees to deliver. I love your gift receptacle, by the way."

"Oh, thanks. It's just the box a dishwasher came in, but I thought it was the perfect size for folks to deposit their gifts into. Darn thing took two rolls of wrapping paper to get it covered." I laughed and thanked them for bringing the tree.

I already had the lights and garland ready to decorate the giving tree with, so made short work of it, then hung the paper ornaments, selecting a few to keep back for myself. I couldn't resist the eight-year-old boy who wanted a Tonka truck, or the ninety-year-old woman who was hoping for a new pair of house slippers.

A couple of other last minute shoppers blew through the door with my daughter April right behind them. The shoppers both looked like they knew what they were after, so I turned my attention to April.

"Hey, Mama. How was your day?" She peeled off her coat and tossed it across the chair behind my desk.

"Good. Business stayed steady until late this afternoon. Can't ask for more."

"Do you need any help now? If not, I'm going to go tidy up my workspace and get ready to start on a new project tomorrow."

"I'm fine. Go ahead."

April ran her business, Carriage House Designs, from nothing more than her phone, laptop, and a workspace we'd finagled in the warehouse of my store and lumber yard. It met her needs perfectly since she restored furniture in the space, but met with clients in the homes and buildings they were interested in having updated. In her spare time, which wasn't much these days, she helped me out in the store.

Between April, Roxy, and a teenage boy named Westen who worked a few afternoons a week, I finally felt like I could breathe again. Running the hardware store after the sudden death of my husband a few years ago had been one of the main things that had helped pull me out of my grief. The store had given me a reason to get out of bed every day, but now I was more than happy to share the workload with my daughter and small staff.

A customer brought a bottle of wood glue to the counter. With my mind elsewhere, I rang up his purchase. "That'll be $55.40, please."

The guy gave me a deadpan stare. "That's a little bit steep, isn't it? You better try again," he said.

I wanted to smack myself in the forehead as my gaze flew from the bottle of glue to the price displayed on my ancient cash register. I shoved my glasses up my nose and frowned. "Oh my gosh, my mistake. Looks like I hit one too many fives. How does five dollars and forty cents sound instead?"

"Much better." He grinned and laid a ten-dollar bill on the counter. "I'm surprised in this day and age you don't have one of those scanner guns. Seems it would make life easier for you."

Someone behind me snorted. I swiveled my head. April stood there with a look of amusement on her face.

"Welcome to Carpenter's Corner, where we live in the dark ages," she quipped.

If customers hadn't been watching, I would've smacked her. Lightly, of course.

"I'll have you know, I have plans to bring the hardware store into the twenty-first century come January. There's a whole new computer system I've got my eye on."

"Well, good. But let's hope your improvements don't change the store too much. I remember coming here with my grandpa when I wasn't even tall enough to see over the counter." The man tucked his change back into his pocket and left with a grin on his face.

Sounded like I was going to be darned if I did and darned if I didn't.

Next in line, a woman placed four boxes of multi-colored strands of Christmas lights on the counter. She pointed two fingers at her own eyes and then at me. "I'm keeping my eyes on you," she laughed.

"Don't blame you one bit." Might as well join in by poking fun at myself right along with them.

"Oh, hey. I just noticed you have your giving tree up." She handed me her debit card for her purchases. "I'll take a look before I go."

"Thank you. The entire community appreciates your generosity."

A few minutes later, the woman left with two paper ornaments tucked into her purse and a promise to bring the gifts in on time. Once all the stragglers were gone, I locked the front door and flipped the cardboard sign to "Closed." While I counted down the till, April quickly swept the floor and rinsed the remaining dregs of coffee from the pot. I shoved the day's proceeds into a blue bank bag and placed it, along with the cash drawer, into the safe, clanked the door shut and gave the handle a final spin.

"That's a wrap. Let's go fetch Smitty."

Chapter Two

I pulled my cherry red Jeep up to the curb in front of my house, then April and I made a beeline through the snowy yard to Smitty's carriage house, sitting twenty yards from my own front door. Before I could knock, Bertha Smith, my eighty-eight year old neighbor and tenant, eased the door open.

"My word, that's some outfit you've got there," I choked out, wanting to shield my eyes from the glow.

"Whoa," April said. "We shouldn't have any problem keeping track of you tonight, unless we mistake you for Christmas lights."

Smitty's tiny frame was bundled head to toe in the most psychedelic plaid snowsuit I'd ever laid eyes on. Every color in the rainbow, plus ten more, stood out, loud and proud, on the boldly patterned outfit. There was no way Smitty's attire could have come from anywhere other than the 1970s.

"I thought you two would appreciate my style." Smitty's watery blue eyes twinkled from underneath the matching fur-lined winter cap circling her face. The cap snapped under her chin. "I purchased this snowsuit at The Bon Marché in Missoula,

Montana in 1971 when I was training for the winter Olympics, you know. It was a lovely decade."

The Olympics? Did I hear her right? I shook my head to clear the clutter, but instead disco balls danced before my eyes from the bright colors. "Excuse me, what?" Smitty never ceased to flabbergast me.

"You trained for the winter Olympics? In what sport?" April demanded to know.

"Well the luge of course," Smitty answered as if we were a couple of dense donkeys.

Of course. Silly me. "And did you make the team?"

"Did I make the team?" Smitty scoffed. "You bet my sweet britches I did. And if it wasn't for fracturing my pinkie," she held up her gloved pinkie on her right hand, "during our last practice run in Sapporo, I would have led our women's team to victory."

"That must have been disappointing for you." April and I flared our eyes at each other over Smitty's head as I tried to calculate how long before I could get back home to Google Bertha Smith and the 1972 winter Olympics.

Smitty shrugged her thin shoulders. "Such is life. No use dwelling on the things that might have been. No indeedy. Tonight I'm looking forward to the hot cocoa and trolley ride you promised me instead of looking back at the past." She rubbed her gloved hands together. "You two are such dears for inviting me."

"Well, let's go then. Do you have everything you need?" I questioned.

Smitty patted down her pockets with her hands, which had a constant tremble noticeable even through her thick gloves. "Phone, check. House key, check. Banana, check."

"Banana?" April repeated with a slight snicker.

Smitty drew her eyebrows together and blinked at April. "Bringing a banana is not weird, my dear. What if I were to get hungry?"

"We can't have that," April agreed.

The tiny woman had an appetite to rival a hungry polar bear, so she made a good point. April and I both took an elbow and escorted our eccentric friend across the snowy yard and into the passenger seat of my Jeep.

As I drove back downtown, Smitty twisted in her seat and eyed April. "What are you doing hanging around with a couple of old crones like your mother and me?"

"Hey! Speak for yourself," I chided. At over twenty-five years younger than my elderly passenger, I was on the verge of taking offense at her comment.

Smitty ignored me and continued speaking to April. "I thought you'd be sharing this romantic evening with that hunky police chief of ours."

In the rearview mirror, I saw color rising into April's cheeks, and I smiled to myself.

"J. T.'s on duty tonight. With Pine Bluff's small police force, public events like this call for all hands on deck."

"Chief Dallas will be wandering around the festivities, then, it sounds like. Perhaps you'll find a moment to sneak a kiss under the lights of the Christmas tree. There's nothing more romantic than sweethearts at Christmastime."

"Maybe," April conceded before changing the subject. "Hey, Mom, why don't you pull up in front of the bank and let Smitty and me out? It's the closest you'll be able to get to Postage Stamp Square."

"You know why the town founders called it Postage Stamp Square, don't you?" Smitty asked, her eyes twinkling.

Even though I'd heard the story many times, I didn't want to take away Smitty's pleasure at telling it one more time. "Not sure I do. Why don't you tell us?"

"It was my own great-great-grandmother who inadvertently named the park. I was named after her, you know. Bertha Margaret Hodge. Pine Bluff was growing, so the city leaders decided they wanted to set aside a piece of land on Main Street where folks could gather and have picnics when they were in town to conduct business. The park was laid out and Grandmother Hodge bustled her family right down, wanting to be one of the first families to have a picnic on the grounds. When they arrived, she looked around and declared, 'Why, it's no bigger than a postage stamp.' The mayor heard her statement, thought it fitting, and immediately proclaimed the new park Postage Stamp Square. And that is God's honest truth." Smitty beamed as she finished up her story.

"And with that, we have arrived." I double-parked in front of the bank. City workers had already blocked off Main Street for the festivities, so I let my two passengers out of the car then headed through the alley to park behind the hardware store.

The city had done a good job of plowing the streets, but the alleyway was another story. I put the Jeep into four-wheel drive and crunched my way to the back door of Carpenter's Corner where my lumberyard was located. When I got out, the snow squeaked under my snow boots. I walked with care until I reached the bare sidewalks lining Main Street, then picked up my pace the final two blocks to the square. Despite the crowd, I had an easy time spotting Smitty in her vibrant snowsuit.

"Great turnout." April glanced around at the crowd. "Pretty sure the entire town came out tonight."

I held up my index finger. "Minus one Marsha Slabinski. She told me in no uncertain terms she wouldn't be caught dead down here."

"Shh," Smitty admonished us, "the tree lighting is getting ready to start."

"You need quiet in order to see the Christmas tree light up?" I teased.

Smitty frowned at me as the mayor started the countdown over the loudspeaker.

Apparently Smitty was right, because a hush fell over the crowd as we all waited for the tree to burst into light.

"Ten. Nine. Eight..."

Before the mayor got to seven, the lights up and down the street surged. In a heartbeat, all of downtown Pine Bluff plunged into darkness. A few shrieks of surprise split the accompanying silence before the gas generators at the food trucks grumbled to life. In a flash, the food trucks were the only thing left illuminating the dark evening.

A sharp whistle cut through the air, followed by the voice of my best friend, Evonne Ford, Pine Bluff City Manager, ringing out over the silent crowd. "Bear with us for a few minutes, folks, while we get this sorted out. Mayor Vargas has the utility company on the phone right now."

A few people around us grumbled and groaned, but most took the opportunity to chat with friends and laugh about the unusual circumstances. A light snow fell, adding fresh icing to rooftops and eyelashes alike. Less than ten minutes passed before the electricity snapped back on with an audible pop.

"Sorry about the delay, folks," the mayor's voice rang out once again. "Seems there was some sort of a power surge that affected the entire town, but we're cooking with gas now. Somebody remind me, what are we all doing standing out here in the cold?"

"Lighting the Christmas tree!" a boy no older than five shouted from his perch on his dad's shoulders.

"By golly, I think you're right. Thank you for your help, young man. Now, without further ado, let's give this one more try."

This time, when the countdown reached zero, gasps of delight filled the air as the sixty-foot-tall Douglas Fir standing in the center of the park glowed with thousands of twinkling, multicolored Christmas lights. The crowning glory was a golden star sparkling atop the tree.

Moments after the tree burst into light, the first strains of "O Tannenbaum" filled the air. To the left of the town Christmas tree, the high school choir, dressed in red woolen robes, black and white plaid scarves, and white knit beanies, stood on risers, while the choir teacher directed them in song.

"We have nearly an hour before we need to hop on the trolley. Would you like to sit and listen to the carols for a bit?" I asked Smitty.

"Yes, please. Carols are my favorite music, no matter the time of year." Her eyes glittered as she began to shuffle toward the seating.

April nudged me with her shoulder. "I'm going to see if I can find J. T. real quick. Back in a flash."

Glancing around, I spied an open spot in the front row of the bleachers the town had brought in for this occasion. Smitty and I navigated to the seats as the choir transitioned from the German version of the song to the English "O Christmas Tree."

Once Smitty got settled, I peppered her with questions. "Are you warm enough? Can I get you a hot drink? Something to eat? Shoot." I snapped my fingers. "I have a blanket in the car I meant to bring. Would you like me to grab it for you? It'll only take a minute."

"Could we simply listen to the music? Not to be mean, but I can't hear the songs over all your questions." Smitty patted my hand. "Heavens to Murgatroyd, there's no reason to fuss so," she mumbled, though loud enough for me to hear.

I couldn't help but laugh. "Fine. How about you let me know if you need something, and I'll zip my lips?"

"Sounds like a solid plan," Smitty agreed.

Someone tapped me on the shoulder. I twisted around to find Roxy frantically motioning for me to scoot over. Her hair was disheveled, she was missing one glove, and the knee of her jeans was ripped.

"What happened to you? Is everything okay?" I scooted closer to Smitty to make room.

"Just a mishap with the dang dog." She shook her head in disgust. "Never get a beagle. If there's even the slightest chance that dog can sneak between someone's legs and get out of the house, she goes for it. And she's as fast as the wind. Once she starts running, she forgets her name and every single manner she was ever taught. I swear she's going to be the death of me." Her phone dinged. After checking her messages, Roxy's tense face melted into relief. "Hunter managed to chase her down. The two of them are home on the couch now."

"Well, thank goodness. I was about to round up a search party to help you find the poor thing," I said.

Roxy frowned at me. "Poor thing, my patoot." She pointed to the choir. "Oh! Pay attention now. Makalya has a solo in this next one. Thank goodness our runaway dog didn't make me miss my girl's special moment."

If one more person told me to pipe down tonight, I might get my feelings hurt.

As the choir began "Silver Bells," Makayla stepped up to the mic and stole the show as her sweet soprano rang out into the night. The crowd whistled and cheered when she moved back into formation with the rest of the choir.

"Oh, my soul. She certainly has a heavenly voice," I gushed to Roxy.

"Isn't she amazing?" She waved tears away from her eyes. "Sorry. Proud mama moment."

Smitty tugged at my sleeve. "Yes, the girl sings like an angel. I could sit and listen to her all night if I wasn't so hungry. I don't mean to be a bother, but would it be alright if we got something to eat now?"

I chuckled. That didn't take long. "What happened to your banana?"

Smitty pulled something out of her pocket, then held up an empty banana peel. "Long gone."

"Then we better get you something to eat without delay. I could use a bite myself." I waved to Roxy. "Tell Makayla I thought she was wonderful. See you in the morning."

Smitty and I wandered through the vendor booths, debating the merits of steamed tamales, bowls of chili, burgers, pizza, and plates of barbeque. Once we'd perused all the options, Smitty chose a half-pound hamburger smothered in grilled onions, while I settled on two pork tamales in green sauce. We'd found a place to sit at one of the picnic tables set up in the middle of Main Street when April squeezed in beside me, a bowl of steaming chili topped with melting cheese in her hands.

"Did you find J. T.?" I asked.

"Yep. He's wandering around here somewhere. Said it's been a quiet night for crime." April tucked into her chili.

"Apparently he hasn't noticed the teenyboppers over there hiding forties under their coats," a voice from the far end of the table said.

I looked up from my tamales to find Andy Kravitz with an amused smile on his bearded face. A full plate of barbequed beef, beans, and a biscuit sat in front of him. Andy was a mechanic who worked at Ernie's Garage, catty-corner from my hardware store and owned by my best friend's husband, Ernie Ford.

Andy leaned forward on his elbows and waved his fork at a group of boys gathered halfway behind the tamale truck. I threw a quick glance their way, then did a double-take. *Wait a minute. Isn't that Hunter Dunsmuir?* But he'd texted Roxy no more than fifteen minutes ago with the news he'd caught their wayward dog and was home cuddled on the couch with her. I squinted into the dim light. Must be some other tall blond kid.

"Teenagers have forty-year-olds hidden in their coats? What is this world coming to?" Smitty wrinkled her nose and looked around in confusion.

"Forties are tall cans of cheap beer, Smitty," April clarified for her.

"Oh," Smitty's eyes widened. "Well, somebody better mention the booze to their parents. Those young rascals will get up to no good with a tank full of beer."

"Maybe Andy should mind his own business." Shilo, Andy's wife and local eccentric poet, admonished him. A forest green wool hat perched on top of her Peppa Pig Pink dyed hair.

"That's rich, coming from a nosy parker like you who spends half her life with her snout pressed to the window, spying on the neighbors." Andy laughed.

"I feel attacked." Shilo laughed along with him, while stuffing the last bite of pizza crust into her mouth. "Hurry up and eat, Andrew. I'm freezing."

"Nope. You should've dressed warmer."

If it weren't for the shared laughter, I would have thought the couple was about to rip each other's throats out.

Chapter Three

When it was time for the Christmas Light Trolley tour, we walked half a block up Cedar Street to where the red and green trolley bus, decked out in festive lights, was loading in front of the post office. As a fundraiser for the Emery Theater, our Women's Service Club sold tickets for the light tour. For a mere five dollars, tour goers took a seat under the glowing lights inside the trolley where Christmas music was piped through the speakers to add to the joyful experience. Members of our club served baked treats and hot cocoa and coffee while the trolley cruised through Pine Bluff neighborhoods in search of the best decorated houses.

"How are you tonight, Marvalene? Good to see you," I greeted the driver as I followed Smitty and April onto the bus.

"Great. I'm caffeinated up and ready to get this show on the road." She held up a pink travel mug as proof.

As Smitty, April, and I were all fairly small people, we easily slid together onto one bench seat, giving Smitty the window so she would have the best view. A rousing rendition of "Jingle Bell Rock" had the three of us tapping our toes and singing along, albeit off key, while the rest of the tour group scrambled into their seats.

"Dad, dad, dad! I wanna sit in the back row." An excited towheaded boy, about five or six years old, motioned to his family to hurry.

Amused, I smiled at the kid then glanced at the dad and mom trailing in his wake.

"Slow down, buddy," Oscar Rudolf, the route mailman for my house, called to his son. Oscar carried a toddler, with hair so blonde it was almost white, in his arms. The little girl clutched the remnants of a candy cane in her chubby hand. Her cupid mouth and the front of her pink coat had fallen victim to the sugary treat. As they passed, the little girl tapped me on the top of the head with her candy cane.

"Emma, no." Oscar jerked to a stop and gently pulled the toddler's hand back. "Dawna, I'm so sorry."

"No worries. What's a little stickiness between friends?" I pulled off the handknit beanie covering my hair. "She only got it on my hat, anyway."

Little Emma's bottom lip jutted out as tears threatened to spill at her dad's reprimand.

"It's okay, Emma. You didn't mean to." To cheer her up, I clapped my hands and added, "Are you excited to see all the pretty Christmas lights?"

Emma's face lit up as the Rudolf boy begged his dad to hurry up.

"It's okay, buddy. I promise we'll get the perfect seat." Oscar grinned at me. "Guess I better get a move on."

Freya, Oscar's wife, came up the aisle behind them. She had a diaper bag flung over her shoulder, but stopped to press a wet wipe into my hand. "This should help get some of the sticky off. Thank you for being so kind," she said before hurrying after her family.

As soon as the trolley was full and the door had been wrenched shut, two of the members of the Women's Service Club began making rounds with a cart similar to those used on airplanes to serve snacks. The trolley slowly moved through the streets as the women navigated the narrow aisle to hand out treats. When it was our turn, Smitty and I both chose hot cocoa, while April went for a steaming cup of hot apple cider. We were served a selection of baked goods on individual disposable plates.

"A Christmas party bus is a splendid idea," Smitty declared. She licked her lips while trying to decide which decadent treat to indulge in first. Decision made, she popped a piece of peanut butter fudge into her mouth. "Mmm. Delicious."

The chocolate cookie topped with a marshmallow was calling my name. I bit in and nearly groaned. The treat made the perfect accompaniment to my hot cocoa.

The trolley felt like our own one-horse open sleigh as it took us over the hills and through Pine Bluff's beautiful neighborhoods. We exclaimed with delight over both tastefully decorated homes and those a little more cheesy with a plethora of inflatable, cartoonish décor in their yards.

"I think this one might be my favorite so far." I pointed out the window to the craftsman bungalow just down the street from my own house. "It's simple and classic. Reminds me of an old-fashioned Christmas."

White icicle lights hung from the eaves of the house, while each window was framed with more white lights. Strings of red and white wrapped around the four pillars on the front porch, creating a candy cane effect. A large evergreen wreath, with vibrant pops of red poinsettia, was mounted on the gable. A fir tree in the snowy front yard was decorated in multicolored lights while a family of wire reindeer glowed beside the tree.

"Sure, it's nice, but I'm looking for something with a bit more pizazz," Smitty remarked.

"Oh, I like that one," April said as we slowed in front of a much more modern display than we'd seen thus far. A tall tree was made entirely out of strings of lights running from a center point at the top downward into a teepee shape. A variety of bushes in the yard were covered with lights, each in a different color. The lights on the tree and the bushes pulsed together like a well-choreographed dance.

"It doesn't impress me." Smitty frowned, then studied the remaining treat on her plate. "How am I supposed to eat this gingerbread?"

"With your fingers," I suggested.

She looked at me, appalled. "Gingerbread is a cake, young lady. You don't eat cake with your fingers. We're not animals."

I chuckled. "Hold on. I've got you covered." I rummaged through my purse until I found the folding metal spork I always carried in case of food emergencies. I unfolded it and handed it to Smitty. "Here you go, this should do the trick. Don't worry, it's clean."

Smitty took the utensil and held it up for inspection. "You carry a fork in your purse?"

"A spork," I corrected her.

"Fine. A spork. But by the looks of the Mary Poppins purse you have there, bringing a banana in my pocket isn't any stranger than what you tote around."

"Maybe not," I conceded.

By the time we got the gingerbread issue cleared up, the trolley had turned right and made its way several blocks north of my house.

"Now here's what I've been waiting for," Smitty exclaimed.

Even though a few houses on the block were decorated, the entire neighborhood was overshadowed by the sheer explosion of Christmas on and surrounding a ranch-style home. Every square inch of the house and yard vibrated with lights and every type of Christmas decoration imaginable. A ginormous Santa waved at us from his sleigh atop the house, while his reindeer appeared to be taking off into flight.

The trolley stopped and Marvalene shut off the engine, effectively cutting off the Christmas music playing inside the bus.

Even so, festive music still thrummed through the air all around us. I craned my neck to see if a live band was playing "Run, Run Rudolph" from the yard we sat in front of. It took me a minute to realize the music was coming from four speakers mounted to the roof of the covered front porch.

"We're going to pause here for a few minutes so you can take it all in," Marvalene informed her passengers. "This is Sheryl Capri's home, in case you were wondering."

I'd heard the rumors, but hadn't driven by Sheryl's house in the last couple of weeks. Since Roxy had come to work for me, she'd been making all of the deliveries to Sheryl for the last month.

"Holy fright. I didn't realize how lavish it had gotten. There's not an empty spot to be seen. Where's she planning on putting the dinosaur?" I asked no one in particular.

"The dinosaur?" April gaped at me.

I laughed and filled her in on the special-order Sheryl had placed earlier in the day, while Smitty continued to stare out the window in awe.

"I guess a giant inflatable dinosaur isn't any weirder than the huge Jack Skellington over there." April pointed to the grinning skeleton wearing a Santa outfit.

"Nope, definitely not," I agreed.

"Her poor neighbors." April nodded at the tan, modest, two-story home next door.

"Yikes, yes. That's Marsha Slabinski's house. It's no secret the feud between the two of them is the entire reason Sheryl has gone so over the top with her decorations."

Side by side, Sheryl's home resembled Lady Gaga at her most outrageous, while Marsha's house stood tall and plain, like a buttoned down business woman. All except for the left side where a projector mounted on Sheryl's side of the fence cast rotating Christmas scenes and lights against Marsha's house.

Large wooden cutouts of The Grinch, his dog Max, the Whos from Whoville, and pine trees in various shapes and sizes were nailed all along the top of the fence between the two houses. A hand painted sign proclaimed, "My neighbor is a Grinch."

"Good grief. She's so clever," I said pointing to the fake fireplace in the middle of Sheryl's yard. "I was wondering what she was going to do with the pallet of bricks she ordered from the store."

There was so much to look at, it had taken me a minute to see the fireplace display. With the bricks, Sheryl had constructed a living room scene, complete with a fireplace with glowing inflatable logs inside. Stockings hung over the makeshift mantle, and a rocking chair sat beside the fire.

"Good night, there's even a Santa stuck in the chimney." I laughed at the woman's creativity.

At the top of the brick chimney, Santa's legs stuck straight up in the air. The only body parts visible were his legs from the knees down—or up as it were—and his boots.

"Poor guy." April chuckled. "Looks like he got tangled up in a strand of lights."

Glowing multicolored lights wrapped around Santa's legs, trussing him up like a Christmas goose.

My amused glance landed on none other than Sheryl Capri, standing to the side of the fireplace and watching as the tour participants gushed over her decorations. In the glow of the lights, the irate expression on her face made it clear she wasn't happy to have everyone gawking at her home. She stood with arms crossed angrily over her red coat. Black smudges resembling soot smeared her face, and her hair was frizzled and sticking up every which way, as if she hadn't bothered to comb it in a week. I shrugged. *Don't make a spectacle of yourself if you don't want people to look, lady.* The waving snowman on top of the house drew my attention, and when I glanced back down, Sheryl was nowhere in sight.

The trolley started back up and the driver yelled out, "Has everybody seen enough? We have a few more neighborhoods to cover before the night's over."

"My stars," Smitty exclaimed suddenly. As the driver threw the trolley into gear, Smitty shrieked and flapped her hands as she pushed past April and me to get into the aisle. "No. Stop the bus. Let me out!" She raced down the aisle and off the bus when Marvalene threw open the door, allowing her to disembark.

April and I gaped at each other for a split second before rushing after our friend.

If I hadn't seen it for myself, I never would have guessed an eighty-eight-year-old woman could move so fast. By the time I jumped off the bus, Smitty was already through the gate and into Sheryl's yard. *Oh boy*. If Sheryl didn't like people looking at her display, she certainly wasn't going to be pleased about the three of us rushing into her yard like a trio of stormtroopers.

"Smitty," I called, "what's gotten into you?"

"The trolley's about to leave. We need to get back on or we'll have to walk home." April reached for her arm, but Smitty shook her off.

Smitty kept trotting until she was next to the fireplace scene. Once there, she pointed to the top of the chimney, then turned to April and me. "Look closely. Santa Claus doesn't wear an ankle monitor, but guess who does?"

"Sheryl Capri," the three of us said in unison.

Chapter Four

I stared up at the legs protruding from the chimney. "I'm sure that's a dummy. It can't be Sheryl. She was standing right here not two minutes ago. She's got a warped sense of humor if she thinks putting a fake ankle monitor on her Santa is funny." I glanced around in confusion. "Sheryl? Where are you? Come out here and clear up this nonsense."

When nobody answered, April pulled out her phone. "I'm calling J. T. just in case. Mom, will you go tell the trolley driver to go ahead and leave without us? We can get a ride home from J. T."

Marvalene pointed to her watch as I approached. "I can't wait any longer, Dawna. Got to get back for the next tour. Are you guys coming or not?"

Not wanting to upend the tour for everyone else, I made light of the situation. "No, we're going to stay behind and visit with Sheryl for a few minutes. Go ahead and carry on without us."

The driver gave me a skeptical look. "You sure? Even Smitty?"

"Yep. We've got it handled. No worries."

As soon as the trolley pulled away, I twirled around and continued my hunt for Sheryl. Calling her name didn't elicit any response, so I trotted onto the porch and rapped on the front door. Nothing. With a quick twist of the knob, I eased the door open and listened. It was hard to tell if any sound was coming from inside the house over the loud Christmas music pumping through the outside speakers.

I stepped into a small tile entry, pulling the wooden door closed behind me in an attempt to cut down on the noise. The entry gave way to an open living room and a kitchen space beyond. "Sheryl," I bellowed into the house. "Are you here?"

The only answer was the lively chorus of "Grandma Got Run Over by a Reindeer" playing over the speakers. My debate with myself over venturing farther into the house was cut short with the arrival of Chief J. T. Dallas in his police cruiser, lights flashing. Though it was hard to differentiate between the police lights and the Christmas lights flashing all over Sheryl's home.

I rejoined April and Smitty in front of the fake chimney as J. T. marched into the yard, placed his hands on his hips and tilted his head back to study the legs in question.

"Smitty's correct. Santa is indeed wearing a police-issued ankle monitor," J. T. announced, raking a hand through his thick, dark hair. He glanced at the three of us. "Any luck finding Sheryl?"

"No," I answered. "But when the trolley first pulled up, she was standing right where we are now. She looked as mad as a wet hen over something. I swear to you, I saw her plain as day."

April raised her eyebrows at me in a question.

"Don't look at me like that. I'm not crazy."

My daughter moved closer to me, leaned in, and turned her head so she was whispering in my ear. "It wouldn't be the first time you saw a...non-alive person."

I sucked in a sharp breath, flaring my eyes at her. Could it be possible I'd seen Sheryl's ghost? Maybe she looked so irate because she was dead. Since my family moved into town when I was a young girl, leaving my childhood best friend behind—whom I was convinced had been a ghost—the only spectral visitor I experienced on a regular basis was my cat, Lilac. The little white cat passed away years ago, but had appeared in the house this past summer and hadn't left. She slept curled up on my bed most nights. Sure, I caught the sawdust and coffee scent of Bob, my late husband, from time to time, and had seen his Aunt Alta back in the fall, but it wasn't like I was a ghost whisperer or anything. I'd begged Bob to show himself to me, but so far, nada. Was it possible my sensitivity was getting stronger?

J. T. circled the makeshift fireplace while the three of us tagged along like baby ducks. Behind the chimney, a ladder leaned against the bricks. What appeared to be drag marks coming from the side of the house and ending at the ladder marred the newly fallen snow. The police chief climbed the ladder and used a flashlight to peer at the Santa upended in the chimney. He swallowed hard before radioing into the station for an ambulance.

Once the call was made, J. T. looked down from his perch. "It's Sheryl Capri alright. I need you ladies to step back. This is a crime scene. Deputy Everett is on the way. Once she gets here, she'll give you all a lift back home."

"Oh no. Oh dear." Smitty's normal tremor became more pronounced as she began to fidget and walk in small circles.

April helped me maneuver the tiny woman to J. T's cruiser and get her settled into the front seat. She sagged back into the seat, looking like a small rag doll. What was supposed to have been a festive light tour had turned dark and funereal.

Rummaging around in my purse, I found the water bottle I'd tossed in there earlier. I wrenched off the cap and handed the bottle to Smitty. "Take a sip. It'll help to calm your breathing."

Smitty did as instructed, then looked at me with sad eyes. "Oh, dear. Whatever shall we do?"

I patted her hand. "We don't need to do anything. The professionals will take care of everything. Chief Dallas has an entire team on the way."

She shook her head. "You don't understand."

"Then help me."

"Who is going to be our fourth player now?"

This time, it was my turn to shake my head in confusion. "Fourth player? What are you wanting to play?"

"Why bridge, of course." Smitty's eyes widened behind her thick, tortoiseshell glasses. "Sheryl was our fourth player at the Senior Center every Thursday afternoon. With her gone, we no longer have a full team."

Bridge? Unless Sheryl climbed into the chimney by herself, it was safe to bet someone had killed her, and Smitty was worried about her bridge game? Flabbergasted, I said the only thing that came to mind. "Sheryl was on house arrest. How was she playing bridge with you?"

"We were taking a hiatus for the holidays. The game was supposed to start again in January, and she was to be released off of house arrest on January first. If she behaved herself, of course."

I nodded. "I see. It sounds like you'll have time to find a replacement."

Smitty sighed. "I suppose you're right."

Officer Samantha Everett had arrived during our discussion. After she checked in with Chief Dallas, she helped Smitty to her squad car, then turned back to April and me. "Are you two coming?"

April shoved her hands into her coat pockets. "I'm going to stick around for a little while."

"Me too," I agreed. "It's only a couple of blocks back to my house. We'll be fine." So what if my Jeep was parked downtown? Sounded like a problem for future Dawna.

"Okay." Sam shrugged. "Suit yourselves, but the chief is not going to be pleased."

"Leave him to me," April said.

Officer Sam was right. The second J. T. noticed April and me still standing near the fence, a fierce scowl shadowed his face. "If you two insist on hanging around, you don't come one step closer than the sidewalk. Do you understand me? And stay out of the way." His fierce gaze softened when it landed on April. "Please."

April held up her hands. "We won't interfere. I promise."

The chief of police bounded over and left a soft kiss on my daughter's lips, before scowling and pointing a threatening finger at me. "I mean it, Dawna."

Sheesh. All I had done to deserve this treatment was to be in the vicinity of another dead body. How was that my fault?

"Turn that noise off," Chief Dallas bellowed over the strains of "Feliz Navidad."

A uniformed officer dashed into the house. It took a couple of minutes, but he must have finally located the source, because the Christmas party music came to an abrupt halt.

Despite my snow boots with a rating proclaiming to keep the wearer's feet toasty warm even in subfreezing temperatures, my toes were beginning to feel a bit frosty. I stamped my feet and tucked my gloved hands into the pockets of my winter coat.

An ambulance, and various other medical and law enforcement vehicles, screeched to a stop in front of Sheryl's house. April and I scooted down the sidewalk to allow them all room to enter the yard through Sheryl's front gate. We'd moved to the corner the property shared with Marsha's buttoned-up house. As I glanced over, the drapes on Marsha's window twitched, then parted six inches or so. I had a clear view of Marsha's pale face as she peered out the window, reminding me of the waiflike appearance of the Ghost of Christmas Past. When our eyes locked, she abruptly stepped back and whisked the drapes closed as she retreated into her home.

A good portion of Pine Bluffians were still downtown enjoying the live Christmas music and food trucks, but those people who were home on this particular street spilled out of their houses to keep vigil with us, and, in the spirit of nosiness, find out what was happening.

I nudged April. "If there were police cars, an ambulance and a fire truck at your neighbor's house, wouldn't you come out to see what was going on?"

April shrugged. "It depends. If I was in a ginormous feud with my neighbor, I'd probably just peek out the window like Marsha's doing. Not everybody is as nosy as you, Mother."

"Well, excuse me. When did being concerned for your neighbor's welfare start being viewed as being an intrusive busybody instead of somebody wanting to help?"

April's mouth dropped open and she blinked hard. "I guess you're not wrong about that."

"About time you saw things my way."

"Hey, what's going on?" A bright voice chirped in my ear. "Did Sheryl finally start a fire with all her crazy decorations? I keep telling Andy all those electrical cords plugged in have to be a fire hazard. And can you imagine what her electric bill must be? Uff da."

April and I both turned to find Shilo Kravitz standing behind us. Rotating lights from the display played over her features and glinted off the silver rings decorating each of her fingers as she gestured at Sheryl's house.

"What are you doing here?" I asked, surprised to see her again so quickly.

Shilo pointed over her shoulder. "We live across the street."

"I didn't realize you lived so close. And no, there hasn't been a fire, as far as I know," I told her. "But it appears something terrible has happened to Sheryl."

"No way!" Shilo's gaze darted to Marsha's house. "Marsha finally had enough, huh?"

Before I could respond, a car careened to a stop in the street. A woman flung open the door and jumped out of the driver's seat while the car still vibrated with the abrupt halt. Her red wool coat flapped open as she sprinted to Sheryl's front gate. "Sheryl!" she screamed, tearing into the yard. She barreled forward, slipping on the snow and nearly falling before making her way into the yard. "What's going on? Where is my sister?"

April sent me a questioning glance. "Isn't that Dr. Messina?"

I nodded. "Sure is. Laine Messina."

"I had no idea she and Sheryl were sisters."

"Neither did I," Shilo added. "And I went to Dr. Messina's chiropractic clinic for several years." She grimaced. "Didn't help me one bit."

J. T. gently guided the distraught Laine away from the chimney and the sight of her sister's demise.

I glanced around at the neighborhood people gathered in front of Sheryl's house. "How did Laine know something was wrong with her sister? She lives on the other side of town."

Before I could ponder Laine's quick arrival too much, I felt a sharp elbow in my ribcage. "Looks like they've got her out." April pointed to the now empty chimney.

The emergency professionals did a great job of shielding Sheryl from the sight of all of us looky-loos who had gathered on the street. In short order, they had her loaded into the ambulance. It left silently, no sirens blaring or lights flashing. The only sound was the wracking sobs from Sheryl's sister.

Officer Everett and her partner, Officer Pete Bowman, got busy stringing crime scene tape across the front fence and gate.

J. T. walked our way, weariness already showing in his gait. "Like I suspected, she's long gone," he said, stopping in front of us.

"An accident?" I asked, hoping for the best.

"Absolutely not. Sheryl was electrocuted before she was stuffed into the chimney."

Chapter Five

Neither April or I lived too far from Sheryl's house, so we both decided to walk home instead of wait for J. T. to finish at the crime scene. April went in one direction, and I took the other.

"Since your car's still at the hardware store, I'll buzz by and pick you up in the morning." April waved. "Does seven-thirty work?"

"Sounds good. See you then."

Lights still shined from Smitty's cottage when I made it home, sparkling across the newly fallen snow on our shared front yard. I knocked softly, not wanting to wake her if she was asleep, but feeling the need to make sure she was doing okay after finding Sheryl's body stuffed in the chimney.

"Yes? Who's there?" Smitty's small voice replied to my knock.

"Sorry to startle you. It's just me. Dawna."

"One moment, dear." The sound of shuffling footsteps came from inside, then the click of the lock. Smitty opened the door only a sliver to peer through the opening. Once she determined it really was me, she held the door wider and invited me inside.

I stepped into the toasty warm cottage that had been the carriage house to my own home when the two buildings were erected in the late 1800s. Smitty was dressed in a worn, but fluffy, light pink robe with matching slippers. She hurried to the vintage TV tray sitting in front of her flowered couch, picked up the remote control, and paused the show she'd been watching.

"Just wanted to check on you and see how you're doing. I know how traumatic situations like tonight can be. If you'd like, I can sit with you for a bit."

A steaming cup of tea and a plate with a stack of Nutter Butter cookies sat on the TV tray beside the remote. Smitty threw her treat a longing glance. "It's nice of you to stop by, but I'm perfectly fine. I've discovered many dead bodies, you know, in my years with Search and Rescue."

Another tidbit I hadn't known about Smitty.

"Death doesn't bother me in the least," she continued. "We all have to go sometime, but hopefully with a little more dignity than Sheryl was allowed. I'm trying not to dwell on our defunct bridge game. Things will work themselves out in that respect. They always do. Since I'm not sleepy yet, I'm getting caught up on my stories. They're a good distraction, don't you know."

"Glad you're taking it all in stride." I peered at the television, thinking how cute it was she called her shows stories. "What are you watching?"

"*Days of Our Lives*. It's my favorite. Monte bought me a subscription service so I never have to miss an episode. I simply turn it on and watch whenever I have the time. Isn't that clever?"

Smitty's son, Monte, had been a year ahead of me in school. He'd been trying to get his mother to move in with him and his wife for the last few years, but she liked her independence. I didn't blame her one bit.

I agreed with her about the cleverness of streaming subscriptions, wished Smitty a good night, and reminded her to lock the door behind me. Snow had begun falling in the few minutes I'd been with her. Icy flakes pelted me in the face, while a few slipped under the collar of my coat. I flipped the hood up to cover my beanie and protect my neck. Crossing the snowy yard at a quick pace, I climbed the stairs to the side door of my big brick house.

The door opened into the kitchen and was used far more often than the front entrance. Anytime someone knocked on my front door or rang the doorbell, it was a clear indication they weren't frequent visitors to the Carpenter house. The light I'd left burning over the sink welcomed me home.

Once inside the warmth of the house, I pulled off my coat and hat, hanging them on the hook by the door, then filled the kettle with water. Smitty's hot tea had left me craving a mug of my own to warm up my cold bones. While the kettle heated, I wrangled off my snow boots, then padded to my bedroom in the back of the house in search of flannel pajama bottoms, an oversized T-shirt and sweatshirt, and a pair of fuzzy slippers.

Lilac raised her head and greeted me with a soft meow from her perch on my bed.

"Hi there, sweetie." Once April's black lab, Thor, had started reacting to Lilac, I'd stopped feeling weird about talking out loud to the cat. Clearly if Thor knew she was here, she wasn't just a figment of my own overactive imagination. I only wished I could run my fingers through her soft fur, though just having her around the house was its own brand of comfort.

While I was pulling on my sweatshirt, the image of Sheryl glaring at me from beside the chimney housing her dead body worked its way into my brain. I glanced back at Lilac. Since I could see the cat, and it sure as heck seemed like I'd seen Sheryl's ghost tonight—if only for a few seconds—why had I only been able to catch glimpses of Bob in my peripheral vision? Sometimes in a half-sleep state, I swore I'd seen him clearly, but never while wide awake. There had to be something I could do to hone my ghost conjuring skills, but what? I was going to have to do some research.

With ghostly visitations on my mind, I strolled back through the house to fetch my tea, but as soon as I entered the kitchen, the swirling scent of sawdust and coffee enveloped me in a warm hug.

"Bob? Are you here?" I closed my eyes and let my departed husband's scent wash over me, providing instant comfort.

Bob had been a building contractor, and the same scents I smelled now had clung to him in life. In my mind, I pictured my handsome husband in the kitchen with me, leaning against the counter with his special teasing smile meant just for me. When I opened my eyes, I jumped and let out a startled yelp.

A wavering image of Bob stood, just as he'd always managed to do in the past, directly in front of the one cupboard where the mugs I needed for my tea were kept. He wore jeans and a soft, camel-colored wool sweater with leather slip-on boat shoes. The outfit had been his favorite and what he'd always worn when he puttered around the house. His striking blue eyes twinkled under pewter-gray hair. He leaned in and gave me a peck on the cheek. A tingling sensation warmed my face.

"I can't believe you're here." I tried not to blink so he wouldn't disappear when my eyes shut for a split second. "Is it really you?"

Bob slowly nodded, his eyes never leaving my face.

"Can you talk to me?"

He frowned and shook his head.

"Are you always here, just floating around the house?" The thought of him watching my every move was a little disconcerting to say the least. Did ghosts have the decency to turn their heads while you were taking care of your bathroom business?

Bob gave another negative head shake. *Whew*. What a relief. We were never the couple who needed to be in each other's pockets twenty-four seven. I certainly didn't want him stuck to me like glue now, either. Dead or not.

Seconds later, the edges of his body began to shimmer and became more transparent.

"No," I pleaded. "You've only been here a minute. Please don't leave yet. Can't you stay longer?"

His signature scent got stronger for a split second before slipping away as quickly as the ghostly visitation.

With emotions running high, I poured hot water into a mug, then added a bag of soothing chamomile tea. Instead of dwelling on Bob's welcome, but brief, visit, or Sheryl's death, I took a page out of Smitty's playbook and flipped on the television. A rewatching of one of my favorite Christmas movies with a big bowl of buttery microwave popcorn was exactly what the doctor ordered.

Chapter Six

"Can you scoot it back another foot or so?" April and Roxy moved a few of our display racks while I directed and supervised.

Carpenter's Corner's annual Santa's Workshop started in an hour, complete with a visit from the big guy himself. The workshop was open to whoever had the time to stop in and work on a project. We featured a different craft each year and had several regulars who never missed it. This year, workshop participants would be building, painting, and decorating wooden gingerbread houses. The three of us had spent numerous hours taking turns with the jigsaw to cut out all the needed pieces—fronts, backs, sides, roofs, and chimneys. We then used a laser cutter for all the small, intricate parts. Tiny gingerbread men, candy canes, snowflakes, reindeer, peppermints, gumdrops, and trees, all made out of wood, were only a few of the decorations that would adorn the completed projects. April had assembled one of the gingerbread houses as an example for people to look at as they created their own. The workshop was free, but we had also put together three dozen extra kits available for purchase

47

by anyone who either missed Santa's Workshop Day, or simply wanted an extra kit to construct at home.

After the display racks were pushed out of the way, the women wrangled the tables into place while I whipped out vinyl red and white tablecloths to cover them with. We arranged folding chairs up and down the tables, then went to work setting a gingerbread house kit at each place. As people finished their houses and left the store with them, we would set out a fresh kit at the vacated spot.

On the counter close to the cash register, I positioned a glass jar with a sign taped to the front: "Donations Welcome. All proceeds to support Pine Bluff Food Pantry." We managed to raise several hundred dollars each year. With the recent rise in inflation, more families than ever needed the groceries the pantry provided. This year, I was hoping for record breaking donations to help stock those shelves.

"Ho, ho, ho!" Bill Wilder, Bob's former business partner, pushed through the front door with his wife, Kim, right behind him. The couple was dressed as Santa and Mrs. Claus. On a typical day, Bill was more gruff than jovial, but he never failed to dredge up his inner jolly for the kids on Santa's Workshop Day.

"We're here with bells on." Kim shook her arm, sending the jingle bells on her festive bracelet tinkling. Decked out in a calf-length red velvet dress trimmed in white faux fur, black knee-high boots, and her long blonde hair fastened into a stylish chignon, she made a beautiful Mrs. Claus.

"Just in time. We've got your thrones ready and waiting for you." I gestured like a showman to the red and green chairs I'd repurposed as the Claus's thrones. Ten years ago, I'd found the two Mission-style armchairs at a yard sale. I'd mounted the backrest of a dining room chair to the back of each armchair, making them look like royal seats, then painted them in red, green, white, and a touch of gold, before reupholstering the seats and backrests in a royal green velvet. With a few touchups over the years, the chairs were still splendid thrones for Santa and Mrs. Claus, if I did say so myself.

"Perfect. We've got the kiddies' candy canes ready to go too." Kim held up a red velvet drawstring bag. She set the bag in the chair, then patted her husband's belly. "What do you think of my handiwork? Who ever heard of a skinny Santa?" Kim quoted a line from *Rudolph the Red-Nosed Reindeer*.

"Well, I was already far from skinny, but she managed to get me all fattened up anyway." Bill laughed. With a couple of well-placed pillows, his husky frame filled out the Santa suit well. To top it off, he'd been growing out his snow-white beard for the last two months just for this particular four-hour shift.

"You look like the real deal. The kiddos will be pleased."

"Did you hear about Sheryl Capri?" Bill stroked his beard. "That news was quite a jolt to hear first thing this morning."

"Shocking, to say the least," Kim added.

I shoved my glasses up my nose, licked my lips, and stared at them. "Are you two serious right now? Don't you think it's a little too soon for electrocution jokes?"

"We're not making jokes." Kim drew her eyebrows together and frowned. "The speed news flies around the circuit here, I was sure you would've heard by now. Word is, Sheryl died last night. I'm not sure what happened to her. A heart attack, maybe?"

"Yes, you could say I've heard." I sighed. "April and I took Smitty on the trolley light tour last night. Smitty is the one who noticed something was wrong when we were at Sheryl's house. She yelled and ran off the trolley. April and I followed her to find out what in the world the problem was, and unfortunately, found Sheryl."

Kim gasped. "That's terrible. Poor Smitty. Finding Sheryl must have knocked her for a loop. Do you know what happened, then?"

"Keep this to yourself, since I don't know what information the police are releasing, but she was electrocuted."

Our conversation was cut short when the bell over the door jangled again as a family of four entered the store, bringing a rush of holiday excitement with them.

Bill wiggled his eyebrows and whispered to Kim, "Are you ready to greet our first little rugrats, Mrs. Claus?"

Seconds later, the ponytailed young girl with the new arrivals yelled, "Santa!" She let go of her mom's hand and launched herself at Bill.

He chuckled heartily, placed the little girl on his knee, and asked if she'd been good this year.

By the time the family had visited with Santa and Mrs. Claus, taken pictures, and were ready to start building their gingerbread houses, a line had formed all the way to the front door. Four women without kids in tow skipped the Santa line and headed directly for the craft table. Westen scooted through the door, grabbed his work apron from behind the counter, and jumped right in to help Roxy and April with the workshop while I took up my position behind the cash register.

"If I knew I was going to have to navigate a crowd just to get a furnace filter this morning, I'd have driven over to Greenwood for it," a man grumbled, as he placed the filter onto the counter.

"Why go to Build-It Barn when you can get what you need right here?" It chapped my hide that this guy had the nerve to reference the big box home improvement store in Greenwood while he was standing in my hardware store. I snorted to myself. *Like there wouldn't be a crowd there. Please.* "Sorry about the inconvenience. Thanks for shopping local," I added with a plastered-on smile.

"For what it's worth," the next lady in line added, "I'd much rather shop here than at Build-It Barn. Nine times out of ten, you have everything I need."

I rang up her bag of de-icer and a roof rake. "I can't tell you how much I appreciate your loyalty. And if we don't have what you need, you know we can always special order it for you, right? We get a shipment every couple of days, so you never have to wait long."

"I had no idea, but now that I do, you can bet I'll be taking you up on that offer. In fact, I need some specialty light bulbs I didn't find on your shelf right now. Can you order me a couple of packs?"

"Absolutely." I took the details for the exact bulbs she needed, jotted down her name and phone number, and promised to call the minute her order came in.

As I attended to the next few customers, the noise level in the store rose as the line to visit with Santa continued to grow. I loved the energy and excitement of Santa's Workshop Day. Ornaments were flying off the giving tree like they had wings. I grinned, knowing the drop box would be filled to the brim with wrapped presents in no time.

With no one else ready to cash out yet, I checked on the workshop participants. Each spot at the table was full, but the crew had everything under control. The first four women were finishing up, and each requested an extra kit to take home. I rang up their purchases and was tickled to see them each shove a twenty-dollar bill into the donation jar.

"Morning, Dawna."

I swiveled around as Chief Dallas strolled into the store. He touched the brim of his black cowboy hat as he greeted me.

"Good morning, J. T. I figured we'd see you today. Are you wanting to get statements from April and me?" I sucked in a breath and glanced around the busy store. "We're really jamming right now. Santa's Workshop goes until four this afternoon, and the store is open until six. Can we get with you this evening instead?"

He nodded. "Not a problem. Unfortunately, I am going to need Roxy to come to the station with me now, though."

"Roxy?" I asked, appalled. "Why Roxy? What does she have to do with anything?"

"Me?" a voice squeaked.

I hadn't noticed Roxy walk up next to me. I glanced her way. Her normal ruddy complexion blanched as white as the snow outside the window at J. T.'s request.

J. T. nodded. "Yes. An eyewitness has come forward who places you at Sheryl Capri's house around the time of her murder."

"Her murder?" Roxy's eyes nearly popped out of their sockets.

"Yes. Her death was not an accident," J. T. confirmed.

"Of course Roxy was at Sheryl's house," I protested. "I sent her there myself with a delivery from the store."

"Nevertheless, I need to take you in for questioning." J. T. didn't divert his gaze from Roxy's face.

She bit her lip and her eyes watered, but she pulled on her coat and grabbed her bag without complaint. "I'm so sorry to leave you in the lurch, Dawna. I promise to be back as soon as I can and make up the time."

Chapter Seven

For the gazillionth year in a row, Santa's Workshop was a rousing success. A little exhausting, I had to admit, though it was the good kind of tiredness, coming from a day well spent. Once the workshop wound down, Bill helped me move the Santa and Mrs. Claus thrones back to their final resting place—until next year, anyway—in the warehouse. We covered them with tarps held down with bungee cords, then Bill and Kim took their empty candy cane bag and went on their merry way.

At six on the dot, I locked the door to the hardware store, and we all fell into chairs around the workshop table as if our legs would no longer hold us up. All of us except for Westen, who grabbed a broom and went to work sweeping the floors.

"Look at all his youthful vigor. I could use a smidge of his energy right now. I'm dead on my feet," I lamented.

"You and me both." Roxy had finally come back to work in the middle of the afternoon after spending three hours at the police station, her face blotchy and her eyes red from crying.

"Do you want to talk about it at all?" I asked.

Before she had a chance to answer, Westen interrupted. "The floors are done. Is it okay if I get out of here?"

"Got a hot date?" April teased.

The teenager blushed to the roots of his hair. A toothy grin was his only reply.

"Go on. Get out of here," I answered. "Thanks for all of your hard work today. We couldn't have done it without you."

I followed Westen to the door, re-locking it after him, then turned back to Roxy with a questioning look. "I was surprised J. T. kept you so long."

"Which reminds me," Roxy said. "Chief Dallas would like you to bring copies of the last four or five orders we delivered to Sheryl."

"Easy enough, but why?"

Roxy sighed heavily. "The main reason he interrogated me so long was because one of her neighbors said they saw me with an orange extension cord."

I threw up my hands. "Well, yeah. There was a twenty-five-footer on her order yesterday." I jumped up and went behind the checkout counter to retrieve Sheryl's order form. I rattled the paper in the air. "Here it is. This should clear everything up."

"You would think, but that's not really the case." The corners of Roxy's mouth pulled down.

"Why not?" April and I asked in tandem.

"Because apparently a brand-new twenty-five-foot electrical cord was purposely frayed."

"Like frayed how? With a pocket knife or something?" April fiddled with a leftover wooden gumdrop form that had been left on the table.

"Your guess is as good as mine." Roxy shrugged. "Anyway, Chief Dallas said they think the combination of the frayed wiring and Sheryl standing in the wet snow caused a power surge and electrocuted her when she plugged the cord in."

A chill tickled the hairs on the back of my neck and I shivered. "That poor woman. I wonder if the surge was what caused the power to go out downtown during the tree lighting?"

Roxy nodded. "According to what the Chief said, yeah. They think it caused a transformer to blow, and then the whole town went dark for a few minutes."

"If that's the case, we also know exactly what time Sheryl died."

"Crazy." April stood and started to gather up the workshop supplies left on the table. "Well, we know you didn't tamper with the cord, and J. T.'s smart enough to know it too. He's just making sure all of his t's are crossed."

"You're probably right, but since I'm the one who delivered the cord to Sheryl's house not long before the incident, I'm the cherry on the top of the suspect list." She shook her mane of thick hair back and stared up at the ceiling, blinking hard to keep the tears at bay. "Mostly I'm worried for my kids and how they're going to react to this. Lord knows they've already been through a lot with the divorce. The last thing they need is for their mom to go to prison for murder."

I reached out and cradled her hand between mine. "We're not going to let that happen. Are we, April?" I glanced at my daughter.

April shook her head. "No, we absolutely are not. Get it out of your mind right now. Not gonna happen."

"Thanks for all the support, but I'm not sure how you can stop it," Roxy replied.

"We have our ways." I winked. "Leave this to us."

"Mom will be like a dog with a bone until your name is cleared," April assured her.

I stood, pushed in the chair I'd been sitting in, and picked up a handful of paint bottles from the table. When Roxy rose and reached to help clean up, I threw out my arm to block her. "April and I have this. You go on home and be with your kids."

Tears welled in her eyes again. "I don't mean to act like a baby—"

"You're not," I interrupted. "It's been a rough day for you. You need to go home and relax. I suggest a bubble bath and a good book."

"Okay, as long as you're sure."

"I am."

"I think I'll order a pizza and watch some stupidly funny comedy with the kids, followed by the long bath. Good suggestion."

"Sounds like a great plan. See you tomorrow."

"You're off tomorrow," she reminded me.

"I know, but I'm still going to drop by and check on you. Make sure you're doing okay."

"If you feel the need, but after a good night's sleep, I'll be back to normal." Roxy zipped her coat and pulled on a knit beanie before heading out into the snowy evening.

April and I scrambled to finish the clean up, then drove the block and a half to the police station.

"He's waiting for you." Del Williams, gatekeeper of the station, nodded his head toward J. T.'s office, his bulldoggish jowls swaying. Del pushed a button, the door buzzed, and just like that, we were through to the inner sanctum of the Pine Bluff Police station. "You know where to find him."

April led the way, rapping on the doorframe to J. T.'s office to announce our presence.

The police chief stood, arched his long back in a stretch, and ran a hand down his tired face. "Good. Just the break I needed." He gave April a quick peck on the lips, then waved us into the guest chairs placed in front of his desk.

"Not much of a break for you, since we're here to give our statements." I swung my purse off my shoulder and dropped it onto the floor between the chairs, before handing J. T. the purchase orders from Sheryl's most recent transactions.

"True, but at least you're a couple of friendly faces." He pulled a yellow legal pad of paper out of a desk drawer, turned on a voice recorder, and we got down to business.

After we finished our statements and the recorder was turned off, I circled around to the topic of Roxy. "She seems to think she's your top suspect at this point. Is there any truth to her thinking?"

J. T. rotated his neck like an owl to stretch it. "There's a couple of people we're looking at right now, but the investigation is still early. I wouldn't say any of them have risen to the top yet. But yes, Roxy is on the suspect list."

"Because she delivered the extension cord?" April asked, clearly unconvinced. "It could've just as easily been me or mom."

"Seems like a pretty big stretch to me," I added.

"It's not only the extension cord that's the problem." J. T. tapped his pen against the paper, not making eye contact with either one of us.

"Then enlighten us," April pushed. "What other reason do you have?"

He rubbed a hand down his face and sighed. "You know I shouldn't be sharing this with either one of you, but..." He hesitated. "Roxy and Sheryl Capri have some history...well, present history, actually...which has nothing to do with someone from Carpenter's Corner making a delivery to her house, and is possibly a strong enough motive for Roxy to want Sheryl gone."

April and I gaped at him like twin goldfish.

"Present history? What does that even mean?" April demanded.

Another sigh. "It means there are current things in both of their lives that tie the two of them together."

"What kind of things?" I asked. "Why are you being so vague?"

"Because it's an active investigation. I can't divulge anything else." He shook his head. "If you want to know so bad, go ask Roxy."

"You bet your sweet britches I will." I stood and grabbed my purse.

J. T. blew out a frustrated breath. "How did I know you were going to say that?" He looked at April with a sorry expression. "See you tomorrow?"

"Yep." She gave him a quick peck goodbye.

Back in my Jeep, I buckled my seatbelt and glanced at my daughter. "Hungry?"

"Starving," April replied. "Stage Stop Café?"

Chapter Eight

April and I slid into opposite sides of a red vinyl booth at Stage Stop Café. We both paused to read the specials board hanging behind the cash register. A scrumptious sounding crab mac and cheese caught my attention, making my taste buds water and my stomach grumble.

"I'm always a little concerned about crab this far from the ocean. Probably because I was spoiled with fresh seafood living in San Francisco all those years." April plucked a laminated menu out of the holder between the bottles of ketchup and mustard.

"You make a valid point, but I'm going to go for it anyway. Sounds too good to pass up. Besides, I trust Mitch. He wouldn't serve anyone iffy crab." I smiled and shot a quick wave to Mitch Nelson, who grinned back at me through the pass-through kitchen window.

"Hey, ladies. It's always nice to see you Carpenter girls. Need a minute or do you know what you want tonight?" DeAnn, Mitch's wife, slid two blue plastic Pepsi cups full of ice water onto the table in front of us.

"The crab mac and cheese for me, please, and a Pepsi with a slice of lemon."

DeAnn smacked her gum. "Good choice, and right on time. You get the last serving tonight. It's been flying out of the kitchen like gangbusters. April, what can I get for you?"

"Chicken pot pie, please. And a hot tea. It's cold out there."

"It sure is." DeAnn wore a long-sleeved turtleneck under her Stage Stop Café T-shirt. "Extra ranch with both of your side salads?"

"You know it," April answered for both of us without hesitation. Like mother, like daughter.

"Now that we've got that out of the way..." DeAnn slid her order pad and pen into her apron pocket, then pushed April over as she slid onto the bench seat beside her. She crossed her arms on the table, leaned in, and whispered to me. "Rumor has it the two of you were there when Sheryl was found last night. Is it true? Were you?"

I nodded. "I'm afraid so."

"If you ask me, it's no surprise somebody finally killed her." DeAnn grimaced. "That woman was trouble with a capital T."

"What do you mean? I never really knew her well." I took a sip of my water.

"She was a user." DeAnn nodded at her own words.

"A user? Like a drug user?" April asked with a frown.

"No, not drugs. I mean a people user. She'd shimmy up to anyone she thought might have something she wanted, then suck them dry before they could blink."

"Like who, for instance?" I wanted to hear as many details as I could from DeAnn before she had to get back to work.

"Do you remember a diner in Greenwood called The Little Red Hen?"

I nodded. "Now there's a blast from the past I haven't thought of in a while. Bob and I used to take the kids over there for breakfast every now and again. They made a French toast stuffed with berries and clotted cream I would have killed for. Jeez, it must've been twenty years ago. They weren't open very long, if I'm remembering correctly."

"Oh, yeah, I remember the Little Red Hen," April chimed in. "The buttermilk pancakes were as big as my head."

"That's the place," DeAnn said. "Mitch and I were just barely getting the Stage Stop up and running when they shut down, but I've never forgotten the reason why they had to close their doors."

I frowned. "Okay. Did it have something to do with Sheryl?"

DeAnn nodded again. "It had everything to do with Sheryl. She worked at the diner as a cook, but had only been there a couple of months when she slipped and fell in the kitchen."

"A wet floor?" April asked.

"I heard it was an overflowing grease trap on the fryer. Whatever the cause, she supposedly broke her back and then sued the business. She was awarded such a large settlement, the owner of the diner couldn't recover financially. He shut his doors for good only about a month after the court case ended."

"As terrible as the whole thing was for the owner of the diner, a broken back is no joke. In my opinion, she was owed some compensation." Though if something similar were to happen at Carpenter's Corner, the outcome would likely be the death of my business just like had happened to the diner.

"Sure," DeAnn agreed, "if she was truly injured."

April cocked her head. "What makes you think she wasn't?"

"The weekend after I heard about the settlement, Mitch and I were up at Wallowa Lake for his family reunion. Guess who was at the marina unloading a jet ski from the back of her truck?"

"No way," I breathed.

"Yes way. The one and only Sheryl Capri. I watched her bouncing across the lake on it with my own two eyes."

My stomach growled long and loud, reminding DeAnn she needed to get back to work.

"Listen to me rattling on while you're sitting here starving to death. You're not going to get a full belly on my gossip. Let me get your order in." She hurried away and hung our order on the turnstile at the kitchen window, then hustled back with our drinks.

When she set my Pepsi in front of me, I grabbed her hand. "Hey, do you remember the name of the owner of The Little Red Hen, by any chance?"

DeAnn scrunched her lips to the side as she thought. "It's on the tip of my tongue, dang it. I'll ask Mitch. He'll probably remember."

Ten minutes later, April and I dug into our dinners with gusto. Between the busy day and the visit to the police station to give our statements, it was already later than I usually liked to eat and I was starving. Half my dinner was gone before I came up for air.

I clunked my fork down onto the bowl and pulled a small blue notebook and pen out of my purse. Flipping it open, I wrote Sheryl's name down and underlined it. "Our mission is to clear Roxy's name, but I think the first order of business will be to find out whatever secret she's hiding that J. T. hinted at."

"For sure," April agreed. "Let's make sure our first topic of discussion in the morning is finding out what her connection to Sheryl is." She took a sip of her hot tea.

I sighed. "There is a little something else that's been bothering me about Roxy's story."

"What's that?"

"I know for a fact she wasn't downtown when the power went out, and J. T. verified they think the power surge might be the exact moment Sheryl was electrocuted."

"How do you know Roxy wasn't downtown?" April questioned.

"Because the choir sang after the tree lighting, which was delayed a few minutes for the power outage. Smitty and I were watching the choir when Roxy came sliding in sideways. She was nearly late for Makayla's solo, and she was a disaster. Her jeans were ripped, her hair was a mess, and she was missing a glove. She said the dog had gotten out and she'd been trying to catch her."

"She probably fell when she was chasing the dog, then. Doesn't seem mysterious to me."

"Except a few minutes later, she got a text message. She said it was from Hunter, and he told her he'd caught the dog and was snuggled up on the couch with her."

April frowned. "But Hunter was with the group of boys sneaking beer behind the tamale cart."

"Yep. Which means either Roxy lied to me, or Hunter lied to his mother." I picked a cherry tomato off my salad and popped it into my mouth. When I bit down, tomato juice squirted out of my mouth and hit April square in the face.

I nearly rolled on the floor laughing as she shot me a death stare before wiping tomato seeds off her face with a napkin. "Nice, Mom. And for what it's worth, my money is on the teenage boy being the liar, not Roxy."

"Like you said, we'll get to the bottom of it tomorrow," I added once I'd stopped laughing.

"In the meantime, I can think of two possible other suspects. The neighbor Sheryl was in a war with—"

"Marsha Slabinski," I interrupted, jotting her name down.

"And whoever owned The Little Red Hen."

I wrote "mystery diner owner" in the notebook. "I wonder if it was Marsha who told the police that she saw Roxy at Sheryl's house?"

"Maybe, but my money's on Shilo Kravitz. She told us that she and Andy live right across the street."

I pointed my pen at my daughter. "You're probably right. Remember how Andy was teasing Shilo about always spying on the neighbors with her nose pressed to the window?"

April nodded. "Yep. We need to talk to her."

"Ready to go?" I pushed my empty bowl aside.

"You want to go talk to Shilo now? It's been a long day. I just want to go home, put on my PJs, and pet my dog."

"No, I meant are you ready to go home? I'm too beat to do any more investigating tonight." I glanced at the time on my phone in horror. "Poor Thor. It's way past his feeding time."

"Since I knew it was going to be a long day, I had Eida babysit him today. She fed him this evening before she went home," April said, referring to a high school girl from the soccer team she coached.

"Smart thinking." I grabbed my purse and headed to the counter to pay for our dinners, shrugging into my coat as I went.

"Clay Hopkins," DeAnn said as she ran my debit card.

"Who?"

"Clay Hopkins. He's the guy who owned The Little Red Hen."

Chapter Nine

Since hiring Roxy, I finally had two full days off each week without having to close the store to get them. I took Sundays and Mondays off, while Roxy had Tuesdays and Wednesdays. My part-timers, April and Westen, filled in the busy times when a second person came in handy. I'd won the lottery the day Roxy had walked into Carpenter's Corner inquiring about work.

This morning, I lounged in bed an hour longer than normal, catching up on my reading. When the third book in Christina Romeril's Killer Chocolate cozy mystery series came out last month, I'd hotfooted it down to Literally to pick up my pre-ordered copy. It had tested every ounce of willpower I possessed to wait to dig in, but now I was glad I had. Christmas was the perfect season to read *Deck the Halls with Homicide*.

A soft squeak of a meow caused me to tear my eyes away from my book. Lilac padded across the bed and curled up by my side as I read. Two chapters later, she narrowed her eyes at me and disappeared through the wall when I tossed the quilt back and climbed out of bed.

After a cup of coffee and bowl of brown sugar maple instant oatmeal, I quickly showered, then pulled on a pair of jeans and a sweatshirt. Before leaving home, I shot a text to April telling her I was headed for the hardware store to check on Roxy like I'd promised. And hopefully get a few answers to our burning questions.

Meet you there in 10, she replied.

I parked in my normal spot in the lumberyard behind Carpenter's Corner, entering through the man door next to the large, roll-up warehouse door. As I came into the main part of the store, a customer exited through the front door. Even though we needed the business, I was happy to see the store was as slow as usual for a Sunday morning, because I needed to be able to have a hard conversation with Roxy.

"Good morning," I called out so as not to startle her.

Roxy raised a hand in greeting from behind the cash register. "Morning." Her usual cheerful smile was in place, and her long hair was clipped back with a shiny silver barrette.

"You look well rested. I'm glad to see color back in your cheeks today."

"No use wallowing in self-pity. With all I've dealt with over the years, I'm not going to let this be the thing that breaks me." She lowered her voice and leaned close. "I didn't kill Sheryl, and I'm not going to go down for it."

"You go, girl. That's the spirit," I said. "But why are we whispering?"

"Mom, I finished dusting the paint aisle. What's next?"

Makayla strolled up to the front counter, a cloth and bottle of dusting polish in her hands.

"Ah. Disregard my last question." It was obvious Roxy didn't want her teenage daughter to overhear.

"Makayla wanted to hang out with me today, so I put her to work dusting the shelves. I hope you don't mind."

"Mind? Of course not." I smiled at the girl. "I'm grateful for the help and am pretty sure your mom is loving the company."

Through the front window, I saw April pull up to the curb in her baby blue VW Beetle. I opened the safe and pulled two twenty dollar bills and a ten spot out of petty cash.

"Makayla honey, would you mind running down to Cookie Crumbles to get us all coffee and doughnuts? Pay for it with this and then keep the rest for yourself for helping out in the store today."

Her brown eyes sparkled. "Really?"

I nodded. "Really."

Makayla's grin turned into a frown. "But how am I going to carry all the drinks back here without spilling them?"

"They'll give you a carrier," her mom said. "You'll be fine."

"Makayla's running to get us coffees," I told April as she entered the store.

"A sixteen-ounce peppermint mocha for me, please," April said. "If you're taking orders."

"Yum. I'm going to get the same thing," Makayla agreed.

I asked for a hazelnut latte, while Roxy said she wanted a simple Americano with cream.

Roxy jotted down our coffee orders, tore off the paper, and handed it to Makayla before pointing a finger at her daughter. "Just a small for you, young lady. You don't need all the extra caffeine."

Makayla rolled her eyes, but grinned as she ripped the paper out of Roxy's grasp. "Yes, Mother."

As soon as the door shut behind her, I turned to Roxy, knowing we had about twenty minutes before the flapping ears of her teenager came back. "Like April and I said yesterday, we're going to do what we can to help clear you of any suspicion. We knocked our heads together last night to come up with a plan on where to start."

The three of us grabbed seats around the coffee klatch table.

"I really appreciate you two helping me with this, but I'm sure I'll be fine." Roxy grabbed a sugar packet and worried it between her fingers.

I patted her hand. "You don't need to face everything alone. We're here for you. Let us help."

Tears welled in her eyes, but she blinked them back hard, unwilling to let them spill. "Thank you. It's not always easy to remember people care."

"I get it. You're a strong, independent woman. I am too but have learned to accept help when I need it." I nodded, then cleared my throat. "We do have a couple of questions for you, and I want to get to it before Makayla gets back. Are you okay with talking about it?"

"No problem. Shoot."

"First, please remember I'm asking these questions to get a clear picture of what happened the other night. I'm not accusing you of anything, okay?" I made eye contact with her to let her know I meant what I said.

Roxy nodded. "Yep. Got it."

"Just a recap. The power went out right before the tree lighting. According to what Chief Dallas told all of us, it seems to be the exact time when Sheryl was electrocuted. Are we in agreement?"

Both Roxy and April nodded.

"Once the power came back on, the tree lighting continued, only a little bit later than planned, and then the high school choir performed. Now, you came barreling in, almost late for your daughter's solo, which indicates you weren't downtown when the power went out."

Roxy frowned. "Exactly. Our dog got out and I was chasing her down the street. Remember? I told you about it."

I nodded. "I do, but I wanted to hear it from you again. Right after you got to the performance, you said Hunter had texted to let you know he'd caught the dog and was at home with her."

"True again."

By the look on Roxy's face and her clipped tone, I could tell she was getting annoyed at my rehashing of events. I bit my lip, trying to decide whether or not to throw Hunter under the bus.

April had no such qualms. "Not long after you and Mom were talking, we saw Hunter downtown with a group of teenage boys."

"You couldn't have." Roxy frowned and shook her head. "Are you sure it was Hunter?"

"One hundred percent."

Roxy scowled. "That little..." She scrunched up her mouth and nose instead of continuing with the name calling. "He must've run out the door the second he got the dog inside. I guess he'll be grounded even longer than planned."

"Hunter was grounded?" I asked.

"The school called Friday afternoon. Turns out the little varmint skipped school again that day."

"Again?"

"Yep. It's happened a handful of times lately. Why he continues to think he can get away with it when he keeps getting caught is beyond me."

"Because he's a teenager. They think they're invincible." I leaned back in my chair and puffed my bangs out of my eyes. "Boy, I don't miss those days, and I certainly don't envy you one bit."

April threw up her hands. "Hey, I wasn't so terrible. At least you had it easy with Goody-Two-Shoes Becky. And I was way easier than Patrick," she said, referring to her older sister and brother.

I harrumphed. "You think so, do you? Tell my blood pressure and my gray hair."

April slid her eyes back and forth comically while biting back a grin.

To change the subject, I turned back to Roxy. "In any case, I'm glad it wasn't you fibbing to me, but I'm sorry your kid is being a stinker."

"Me too. With the divorce and everything, I'm trying to give him some leeway, but he's making it tough." Roxy crossed her arms over her chest. "Does this mean you believe me when I say I was chasing the dog, and not at Sheryl's house killing her?"

I nodded. "You're off the hook, though there is another thing we need to clear up."

"Can't wait to hear it."

April took the lead. "When Mom and I went to the police station to give our statements last night, J. T. hinted you and Sheryl may have had a connection which might give you a motive for her murder."

Roxy sucked in a sharp breath. "The police chief told you? He should have kept that information confidential."

April shook her head. "He didn't really tell us anything, just suggested we ask you about your relationship with Sheryl."

I reached out and grabbed Roxy's hand. "If April and I are going to be able to help you, you have to come clean with us about everything."

"Mom, tell them." Makayla stood behind us with a tray of our coffees and a bag of donuts. None of us had heard her come into the hardware store.

The girl had been faster getting our coffee and doughnuts than I'd predicted. I kicked myself for spending too much time talking about angsty teenagers and not addressing the issues surrounding the murder.

Makayla handed out the coffees, while April fetched paper plates and napkins for the sweet treats. A customer came in and began perusing the various sizes and grit levels of sanding discs.

I studied Roxy's stricken face. "We can continue this conversation later, when we have more privacy, if you'd feel more comfortable."

Roxy glanced at her daughter. "It's fine. Makayla knows all about it, but I better help the customer first." She started to rise from her seat.

April waved her back down. "I'll handle it. You talk to Mom." She stood and marched over to the man looking at the discs. "Good morning. What can I help you find?"

I turned my attention back to Roxy, but kept my mouth shut, waiting for her to pick up the thread of the conversation.

When she did, she lowered her voice so any customers who came in wouldn't be able to hear. "I'm pretty sure I haven't told you this yet, but Brett already has his new fling living with him."

I leaned closer and shoved my glasses farther up the bridge of my nose. "Living with him? At his parent's house?"

Roxy popped her lips. "Yep. His parents are cutting a fifty-acre parcel out of their two-thousand acres. They're giving the land to him in exchange for taking over the ranch duties from his dad. Brett plans on building a house, but in the long run, he'll inherit the entire place when they're gone. In the meantime, he's moved his new squeeze in with Mommy and

Daddy Dunsmuir." She spit the words out as if they caused her pain.

I glanced at Makayla, who wore a scowl to match her mother's.

"A barely divorced, fifty-year-old man moving a new girlfriend into his mom and dad's house? Call me crazy, but the whole scenario feels weird." It left a bad taste in my mouth, which I attempted to wash away with a bite of an apple fritter and a swig of coffee.

"It is weird." Makayla shuddered. "And Dad's girlfriend is absolute cringe. I'm not going to stay out there again. Not unless she's gone." She took a long sip of her coffee.

I glanced at Roxy. "What does this have to do with Sheryl though?"

Roxy's eyes widened. "Oh, I must've left out the best part. Brett's new girlfriend is none other than Sheryl's daughter."

"No way." My jaw dropped open. "Jazelle?"

"You know her?" Roxy raised her eyebrows.

"Let's just say her reputation proceeds her." I hooked a thumb over my shoulder, indicating the shop next door. "I'm pretty sure she's a good friend of Darlene's. They run in the same crowd at least."

"Now why doesn't that surprise me?" Roxy sneered. "They're two peas in a pod."

"I didn't realize Jazelle was back. Last I heard, she'd run off to marry a rancher from Montana who was twice her age."

Roxy scoffed. "She must have drained the life out of him already, because she's definitely back."

I frowned. "I guess I'm still not connecting the dots. Why would Brett dating Jazelle give you motive to kill her mother?"

Roxy jerked her chin at Makayla. "Scoot on out of here now. You have more dusting to do."

Makayla sighed dramatically, but tossed her empty coffee cup in the trash and obeyed her mother without an argument.

Once the girl was out of earshot, I leaned in. "Do you want Brett back?"

Roxy almost gagged on her coffee. "Not on your life. That ship not only sailed, but it's rotting at the bottom of the ocean."

"Whew. Glad to hear you haven't lost your senses."

"Thank goodness. But I do have a theory about Sheryl and Jazelle I shared with Chief Dallas yesterday."

"Which is?"

"Maybe this notion is half-baked since I don't have any solid evidence, but I think the two of them were up to no good."

"No good how?"

"I think they planned to scam Brett and his parents out of their property. The first time I made a delivery to Sheryl, she said she'd heard about my divorce and expressed her sympathy, but then started asking me all kinds of questions about Brett and his parents."

"Questions like what exactly?"

"She wanted to know how long they'd owned the ranch, how many acres it was, if there was a trust set up to pass it on to the grandkids, that kind of thing."

"Seems strange. I mean, I'm nosy enough, but those questions seem really probing and personal."

Roxy nodded. "Exactly what I thought. At first I assumed she was just being chatty, stuck in her house all alone, but after a few minutes, it felt like she was really digging for information. Less than a week later, Brett told me he'd started seeing Jazelle, and it was only another week before she'd moved in. I have no doubt mother and daughter were in on the plan together. Jazelle has already made snide comments to Makayla about how, as soon as she gets a ring on her finger, the Dunsmuir ranch is going to belong to her and the kids won't be getting a dime. Makayla says she only talks to her like that when there isn't anybody else around to hear her. My gut tells me Jazelle is as evil as her mother."

Chapter Ten

With the morning wearing on, more customers were coming into the hardware store. Westen arrived for his Sunday shift and got right to work restocking shelves. Roxy took over running the register from April, while I grabbed two cans of white primer, a three-pack of roller covers, and a new brush, then wrote them up on a ticket for myself.

"What's on the agenda?" April asked as I loaded my painting supplies into my Jeep parked behind the store.

I filled her in on the parts of Roxy's story she'd missed while she'd been helping customers, ending with the fact Jazelle was a friend of Darlene's.

"Those girls were seniors the year I was a freshman." April kicked at a dirty ball of snow clinging to one of my mudflaps. "They always hung around at the park, smoking cigarettes with the wild crowd during lunch."

"Sounds about right. Don't you need a new tube of your allergy-friendly mascara?" I asked.

"No, I think I'm alright."

"I beg to differ. You're almost out. We better go see if Darlene has any in stock."

"Mom! I just got....Oh," she said, picking up my meaning. "You know what? You're right. I could definitely use a new tube."

April tucked her hand through my arm as the two of us marched around to the front of the building and entered Lipstick and Lace, the high-end western wear boutique adjoined Carpenter's Corner Hardware. I owned the entire building, but had rented the space to Darlene Lovelace for the last handful of years.

"Well, well, well. If it's not the Carpenter women. To what do I owe this pleasure?" The fake smile Darlene flashed our way matched the one plastered on my own face.

While I loved her boutique and the business it brought to Pine Bluff, I'd never much cared for the airs Darlene put on. Since I'd run into money troubles with the bank a couple of months ago, Darlene had been doing her best to try to snatch the building out from under me. I'd threatened to not renew the lease on her retail space, but so far hadn't followed through. Our landlord/tenant relationship stood on shaky ground these days. We'd always sniped at each other a little bit, but since I'd chased her out of my store with a broom, things had gotten downright icy between us. The only times I'd been face-to-face with her recently were when she'd come into the hardware store to pay her rent on the first day of each month.

"Do I need a reason to stop by and say hello?"

"Please," Darlene scoffed. "We both know you haven't stepped foot in here for two months."

Before I could say anything more, April strode up to the counter. "I need another tube of Pure Eyes mascara, please."

Darlene reached into the glass-fronted cabinet where she kept the specialty makeup products and pulled out a teal tube. She flung her long dark hair over her shoulder. "I hear you two found poor Sheryl's body. I'm beginning to think you're the harbingers of death."

"To be clear, it was Bertha Smith who found Sheryl. April and I just happened to be with her."

"Like I said." Tears sprang to Darlene's heavily mascaraed eyes, and she sniffed hard. "Sheryl was like a second mother to me. I can't believe she's gone."

It was the opening I'd been hoping for. "Oh, gosh, I'd nearly forgotten. You and Jazelle were close growing up, weren't you?"

"We still are. Losing Sheryl is destroying her." Darlene hunched her shoulders, as a sob wracked her body.

"I'm so sorry for your loss." As I tentatively touched her shoulder, I found myself meaning the words. Just because the woman rubbed me raw didn't mean I didn't sympathize with her grief.

"Speaking of Jazelle, we heard she's back in town. I thought she'd gotten married and moved to Montana this past summer. Is she just back home for a visit?" April asked, as if she didn't know Jazelle had already made a local love match.

Darlene pulled a tissue from a box and dabbed at her eyes while shaking her head. "Poor Jazz. First her new husband dies, and now her mom. It's a lot for anyone to take."

April and I made holy-buckets-did-you-hear-that eyes at each other while Darlene was busy swiping at her tears. Or so I thought.

Darlene's demeanor changed from grieving to irate as she shook a finger at me. "Now hold on there. I know what you two are thinking. Don't you think for a minute my girl had anything to do with her sweet mama's death. How dare you! She loved her mom. And her husband. So what if he was forty years her senior? The age difference didn't mean anything to them. Henry adored Jazelle, and I'm sick and tired of everyone talking crap about her."

I held my palms up in surrender. "Neither one of us said a word about Jazelle harming anyone, so I'm not sure what you're talking about." Though I was super curious to know who was badmouthing Jazelle and just what they had to say about the whole affair.

"You didn't have to," Darlene snarled. "I saw the look you two gave each other. You're up to your dirty old tricks again, trying to find a killer and accusing everyone in your path. Well, do you want to know what I think?" She slammed her fists to her hips.

"Nope, but I'm sure you're going to tell us any second now."

"I think it's awfully suspicious we hadn't had a murder in Pine Bluff for a hundred years and suddenly there's been four in an incredibly short amount of time. And every single one of them has some sort of tie to you." She pointed a sharp, fire engine red fingernail at the end of my nose. "You're the common denominator. Death surrounds you." She wrinkled her nose. "I can almost smell the scent of rot on you."

April shoved in front of me, all five-feet-one-inch of her body on full alert. "You have no right to talk to my mother that way."

Darlene huffed and tossed her head. "Are you feeling left out, April? Don't worry. Everything I said goes for you, too."

"Everybody needs to settle down." I gently moved back around April, then pointed to myself. "We're not accusing Jazelle of anything. I know you're hurting, Darlene, so I'm going to ignore the accusations you just hurled at us. Now, let's all take a deep breath and try to act like civilized human beings."

Darlene shot me another glare, but rang up the mascara. April swiped her debit card through the reader before tucking the makeup into her coat pocket.

As we left the boutique, April turned back. "A nap always helps me when I'm feeling out of sorts. Maybe you should give it a try."

Chapter Eleven

"We need to find out if Jazelle was in town when her mother was killed." April propped her elbows on top of her open car door.

"Agreed. Maybe Roxy will be able to find out for us. I'll go ask her before I head out. Do you want to meet me back at the house to figure out a game plan?"

"Sure. I'm going to stop by my place to get Thor first, though."

April zoomed off and I went back inside Carpenter's Corner.

"What did you forget?" Roxy asked as I opened the front door.

"Nothing, but I do have a task for you if you're up for it."

"Sure. Anything you need, boss."

"Is it possible for you to find out if Jazelle was in town on Friday night?"

Roxy made a disgusted sound deep in her throat. "Except for that."

"I know it's a lot to ask, but there are reasons." I filled her in on Darlene's disclosure about Jazelle's recent marriage ending in the death of her husband. "I'm guessing she's probably the sole heir of Sheryl's estate. I doubt there's much more for her to inherit than the house, but people have killed for less."

"True enough," Roxy agreed. She pulled her cell phone out of her apron pocket. "Hang tight. I've been meaning to give Pam a call anyway. Let's see what I can find out."

I rearranged our small impulse buy items on the counter while Roxy made the call to her ex-mother-in-law. I swapped out the display of small tape measures in favor of a box of windshield ice scrapers.

"Pam? Hello, it's me. Just calling to check on you. Makayla was disappointed not to see you and Barry at the choir concert during the tree lighting the other night." Roxy paused for a minute to listen to her ex-mother-in-law's reply. "Oh, no. Well, I'm glad everyone's on the mend. Sure, I'll let Makayla know. Maybe you could send her a quick text if you have a minute. Okay, sounds good. You take care and get to feeling better. Bye bye, now."

I finished refilling the display of trail mix. "Well? What's the word?"

"Pam says they all came down with a case of the nasty flu that's been going around. Jazelle must've brought it home to them, because she went down first on Thursday night, followed by Brett the next morning, and then his parents by Friday afternoon. Pam said they're all barely starting to feel human again, and this morning was the first time any of them has left the house since it hit."

"Which gives Jazelle a solid alibi."

"Yep, seems so."

"And you trust Pam's word?"

"With my life."

"Nice work. I'm impressed. You didn't even have to pry it out of her."

"Pam makes it easy. She's a talker. I'm relieved. It was going to be weird for me to point blank ask where Jazelle was Friday night."

"Agreed. Welp, one person we can scratch off our dance card." I slapped the counter. "I'm off to follow the next thread."

Back at home, I unloaded the painting supplies from the Jeep and brought them into the house. I lugged the cans of primer through the house and up the back staircase. With April's help, I'd been working on giving the upstairs apartment, which had been sitting empty and gathering dust for nearly two decades now, a much needed refresh. Once the kids had all moved out, Bob and I rarely ever went up there at all. After he died, I'd closed the door at the bottom of the staircase and nearly forgotten the space existed. Until a ghostly visit from Aunt Alta, Bob's long-deceased aunt who lived in the apartment thirty years ago, sparked my imagination and gave me the answer to a problem I'd been struggling with.

I hefted the heavy cans onto my makeshift worktable, then shook my hands to get the feeling back into them. Back in October, I'd broken my left wrist. The cast had come off only two weeks ago, but my arm felt close to being back to full strength. I walked around the apartment, smiling at the gleaming new kitchen. Suddenly, the entire house shook as what sounded like a herd of buffalo charged up the stairs and into the small space.

"Thor! I've missed you so much. Good boy." I vigorously rubbed the black lab's huge head as the dog snaked around my legs, whipping me nearly to death with his ecstatic tail.

"Alright, that's enough. Settle down," April suggested as she topped the stairs.

April's not-so-stern tone had little to no effect on the dog, so I pulled out my mom voice. "Thor. Sit. Gentle," I commanded.

The dog sat, though his tail continued to sweep the floor.

"What are you doing? Are you getting ready to paint?" April asked.

"A little bit later. For now, I was simply admiring all the shiny new surfaces. Have I mentioned how grateful I am for all of your hard work on this project? With my broken wrist, I wouldn't have managed to get anything done if it wasn't for you coming to my rescue." I ran my hand over the granite kitchen counter-top, admiring the blue and gray swirls running throughout the stone.

"Hey, this was my space when I was a teenager. There's no way I was going to let you have all the fun making it all spark-ly and pretty again. Besides, you wanted to go with that aw-ful bright yellow. Somebody had to veto your bad decisions." April's throaty laugh filled the air.

"Fine. I'll admit this soft, sage green was the way to go. It's cozy and, I don't know, welcoming, I guess. It feels good in here." I nodded. "But since we're on the subject of awful paint choices, how many coats of primer do you think the angry red in the bedroom is going to take before it stops bleeding through?"

April grimaced. "A couple, at least. Sorry. I was an angsty teenager when I painted it. In my defense, Dad let me."

"Mmhmm." I frowned at her. "I don't recall either one of you running it by me."

"Because Dad was the pushover." She tactfully changed the subject. "When are the carpet guys coming?"

"Two Mondays from now."

Both the kitchen and bathroom were fully finished. My goal was to have the bedroom and living room painted by the time the carpet was installed in two weeks.

"Just in time for Christmas." April grinned.

"That's the plan. There'll be room for everybody to stay over Christmas, then hopefully I'll be able to find a tenant come early January."

Becky and Patrick, their respective spouses and kids, would all be descending on Pine Bluff for Christmas week. I couldn't wait for the sound of the grandkids' voices to be ringing throughout this old brick house. My heart overflowed, imagining all the fun we were going to have.

"I can't wait." April's eyes glimmered as brightly as I imagined mine were. "I'm going to beat the snot out of my siblings at Scrabble and toast the kids in a snowball fight or two."

Okay. Maybe her eyes were gleaming with evil plans, as opposed to pure joy.

Thor, who had been following us around and bumping his nose into the back of my knees periodically, thumped his huge body onto the floor and sighed like the world was coming to an end.

"Okay, buddy, I know. I've made you wait long enough." April squatted down and rubbed his belly, then glanced up at me. "I promised him a walk. Are you up for it?"

"Yep, and I already have a destination in mind."

"Let's go."

Chapter Twelve

Scraps of bright yellow crime scene tape stuck to the fence in front of Sheryl's house and fluttered in the light breeze. Without stepping past the barrier and into the yard, I craned my neck to scope out as much of the property as I could manage. With the generators and Christmas lights all turned off, the blow-up style Christmas decorations were deflated and laying in heaps around the yard. What had been magical all lit up and dancing after dark, looked like a hot mess in the stark light of day. I walked to the far corner of the fence, trying to see as far into the side and back yards as possible.

"What are you doing? Hoping to see Sheryl's ghost again?" April held onto the leash and stretched her arm out as far as it would go so Thor could sniff out all the best smells.

I gave a slight shrug, a little embarrassed she could read me so well. "Maybe. I guess I was half hoping she'd show herself again. If my paranormal ability is improving but doesn't include a ghost being able to tell me who killed her, what good is it?"

"Give it time, Mom. It's a miracle you saw her to begin with. Until now, the only ghosts you've seen are people you cared about." She bobbled her head. "Well, and a cat you cared about."

I raised my eyebrows. "You seriously believe me, then? You're not just placating your crazy old mother?"

"No. We've talked about it. You know I saw Dad that night, too, right?"

April was referring to a night back in August when an unhinged person entered my house and threatened the two of us. We were both convinced Bob's ghost came to our rescue.

"I know you did, but I'm still coming to terms with the whole seeing ghosts thing myself. Lilac seems like she belongs curled up on my bed now, and it's comforting each time your dad's scent swirls around the room, but seeing Sheryl standing in her yard and then learning she was dead? Whole different ball game." I turned and leaned against the fence. "Since we're on the subject, I guess I should tell you what happened the other night."

"You mean here, with Sheryl?"

"No. The same night, but after I got home."

"Okay. Spill it." Thor tugged on his leash, nearly pulling April's shoulder out of the socket in the process. She reprimanded him, then planted her feet solidly apart to anchor herself better.

"I walked home from here and stopped to check on Smitty before I went into the house. She was fine, so I didn't stay long. It was freezing, so I started the tea kettle, then went into the bedroom and changed into my pajamas. When I came back into the kitchen to get my tea, Dad's sawdust and coffee scent filled the room. Honestly, I was more than a little miffed about seeing Sheryl but never being able to see your dad, except peripherally sometimes, or when I've been half asleep. Anyway, I closed my eyes and concentrated hard to try to conjure him up, and when I opened them, he was standing right in front of me."

April gasped. "Actually standing there? In the kitchen?"

"Yep. Right in front of the cupboard I wanted to get into for the tea and a mug."

"Of course he was." April laughed. "You're sure you weren't sleep walking?"

"Positive. I'd been home for less than fifteen minutes. Maybe even closer to ten. It was a super short time. I hadn't even sat down yet."

April chewed on her bottom lip as she considered my revelation. "Did he talk to you? What did he have to say?"

"Nothing, unfortunately. I asked him if he could speak to me, but he shook his head no. I guess I can only see ghosts, not talk to them. At least not yet."

April frowned. "Except for Karen. You used to talk to her, didn't you?"

"You're right. Definitely. Karen was my best friend. We laughed and played and talked all the time." I screwed up my face. "I wonder what the difference is?"

"You were a little kid and didn't realize she was a ghost. From what I've read, kids are much more open to sensing spirits. We get closed off in our beliefs as we get older."

"You've been reading up on mediums?"

"After seeing Dad this summer? You bet I have. It's fascinating."

"I wonder what would have happened if my family had stayed in that house. Would I have continued to see her, or would I still have lost my abilities anyway?" I mused.

April shrugged. "Hard to know."

I studied the neighborhood and blew out a long breath. "On another note, what do you say we go across the street and have a little chat with Shilo? Find out if she knows anything that could help us figure out who killed Sheryl."

"We need to start somewhere, and Shilo seems like a good choice." April tugged on Thor's leash and we moved across the street.

I only had one foot onto the walkway leading up to the Kravitz's house when the front door was yanked open, giving meat to Andy's joke about Shilo spending her days with her nose pressed against the window.

"Hey there. What are you two up to?" Shilo pulled the door closed behind her as a white French bulldog yapped at the window.

"We were out walking the dog and thought we'd stop by to see if you had a few minutes to chat. I'd like to pick your brain about your neighbors, if you have a few minutes."

Shilo's eyes lit up. "There's not much I like better than juicy gossip." She laughed and then pointed at Thor. "Elvira loves to play, but I'm a nervous mama. Is your guy good with smaller dogs?"

"Totally. He's a great big teddy bear." April patted Thor's head and told him to sit. "But we don't need to come inside. He'll destroy your house with his tail in under two minutes flat."

"Ack. I'm not worried. We're dog people." She cracked open the door and yelled inside. "Andrew, put a shirt on. We have company." Mumbling came from inside the one-story ranch house. Shilo rolled her eyes, then peeked back inside. "Okay, everybody's decent now." She held the door open, skillfully scooping up Elvira as the little dog tried to shoot out into the yard.

"You've done that a time or two." I laughed.

"Or twenty million. This little girl's an escape artist, and she's super fast. Once she gets running, it's hard to shut her down."

"What's up?" Andy flicked his eyes our way and tipped his chin at us in greeting before turning his attention back to the television screen. He sat on the dark gray, U-shaped sectional couch, with a game controller in his hands and a pair of noise cancelling headphones over his ears. On the screen, Vikings thrashed each other with battle axes.

Similar to the way Thor was thrashing me with his tail as he executed a perfect downward dog yoga pose while getting to know Elvira. At Shilo's urging, April reached down and let him off his leash.

A six-foot-tall, pink tinsel Christmas tree stood in the corner next to the television set. The shimmering tree was decorated with a plethora of sweet, whimsical ornaments interspersed with what looked like vintage, blown glass ornaments. A fluffy white faux fur tree skirt cradled the bottom. The fanciful tree lent a playfulness to the home, a stark contrast to the Viking war taking place on the screen.

Shilo went through the small living room and opened the sliding glass door in the kitchen just enough to let the dogs squeeze out into the surprisingly large back yard. She left it open so they could come and go at will. The two dogs zoomed around the snowy yard in a swirl of black and white, Elvira yapping for Thor to keep up.

"Can I get you some water? Tea maybe? Or I have some tangerine bubbly water." Shilo indicated we should sit on the couch.

"Thanks, but I'm fine," I answered, taking a seat on the opposite U from Andy.

"I'll take you up on the offer." April plopped down beside me. "The tangerine bubbly sounds too good to pass up."

Shilo came back with two orange cans. She handed one to April, then sat in the middle of the couch, and popped the top. "She wasn't my favorite person, but what happened to Sheryl is still terrible."

A round wooden coffee table sat between the extended ends of the couch. The base was painted mist blue, with a white top. The table had been distressed in a shabby chic farmhouse style.

A half-finished jigsaw puzzle, showing a cozy rabbit den with a Christmas tree and snow outside the window, took up the middle of the table. The puzzle scene reminded me of something from a Beatrix Potter book.

April ran her finger over the tabletop. "Hey, this is one of my pieces." She glanced at Shilo. "You bought it from my booth during the fourth of July."

Shilo grinned. "Yep. From your booth at the park. The second I saw the table, I knew it would be the perfect fit for this room, and I was right."

"Well, it's super fun to see it out in the wild." April grinned, then leaned back on the couch and crossed her feet at the ankles.

Shilo agreed, then turned to me. "Now, what is it I can help you with?"

"Ever since Sheryl's been on house arrest, she's been ordering all kinds of supplies from my hardware store. It's been a daily occurrence for the last several months, and because she was such a good customer, we'd agreed to deliver to her. Roxy, the woman who works for me, has taken over the bulk of that task. Do you know who Roxy is?"

Shilo nodded. "For sure. I've seen her here almost every day."

"Right, and because Roxy dropped off a delivery on Friday, the police have hauled her in for questioning in conjunction with Sheryl's death. Have you heard exactly how she was killed, by any chance?" If it wasn't a known fact yet, I didn't want to be the one to blabber Sheryl's cause of death all over town.

"From what I understand, she was electrocuted by an extension cord someone had tampered with. That's what everyone is saying anyway."

April nodded. "I have it on good authority that what you heard is true."

"You must get the inside scoop when you're dating the police chief." Shilo eyed April. "Have to admit I'm a little bit jealous. Though Andy does bring home some good gossip now and then from Ernie's Garage."

I cleared my throat to get us back on track. "Since Roxy delivered the cord to Sheryl, her fingerprints are all over the thing, making her one of the top suspects. Needless to say, she's beside herself about the whole thing. I know Roxy. She didn't do this. April and I promised to help clear her name."

"Okay. What can I help with?" Shilo took a sip of her sparkling water.

"We were curious to find out how much you may have noticed about the comings and goings of people in the neighborhood." April leaned forward and picked up her drink.

Her comment must have penetrated through Andy's headphones. He let out a loud "Ha," followed by, "Everything. Miss Nosy Buttinski here doesn't miss a thing."

"Hey." Shilo protested with a laugh. She good-naturedly backhanded him in the chest. "I'm a writer. A girl's got to get inspiration where she can find it, and this kooky neighborhood provides me with some good fodder."

Andy chuckled and went back to fighting Vikings.

"So, yeah," Shilo said. "I saw Roxy making the Carpenter's Corner delivery Friday afternoon. Chief Dallas asked, so I had to tell him. Sorry if it got her into hot water."

I shook my head. "Nothing to be sorry about. You were absolutely right to tell him what you saw. Is there anything else suspicious you can think of? Anybody else who was at Sheryl's house on Friday?"

Shilo shoved a strand of pink hair behind her ear and grimaced. "Roxy must've mentioned to you how she didn't just drop the delivery onto the porch and leave like she usually does, right?"

I frowned and pushed my glasses up my nose. "Uh, no, she didn't. What do you mean? Did she stay and visit with Sheryl for a few minutes?"

"Sheryl wasn't outside when the delivery came, as far as I know. I only saw Roxy. She always takes the delivery in through the gate, leaves it on the front porch, and skedaddles out of there like somebody's chasing her. This time, though, she stood on the porch for a minute or two, and then crept around the side of the house."

"Crept? Crept how?" The question came out harsher than I meant.

"Like, stealthily." Shilo stood and demonstrated a hunched over posture and swiveling head. Her charade reminded me of a robber in a cartoon. "Like she was trying to make herself small so no one would notice her."

"But you did."

"Didn't you hear Andy? I notice everything." Shilo tipped her chin coyly. "Roxy disappeared down the side of the house where I couldn't see her anymore. It was probably, I don't know, a couple of minutes before she came back out to the front yard."

"Which side of the house did she sneak down?" April asked. "Left or right?"

"My left, if you're watching from our window."

"Which is the side nearest Marsha's house." I turned to look out the front window and across the street to study the houses in question.

"And the side of the house where the outlet is located where Sheryl plugged in the dodgy extension cord," April added with a grimace.

I blew out a breath, making my bangs flutter. "Not good." I frowned at April. Seemed like Roxy still was keeping a thing or two from us. I was going to have to have another heart-to-heart with her, and she'd better come clean this time, or I was out.

"But Roxy wasn't the only one in Sheryl's yard on Friday," Shilo said with a sly look.

I jerked my thoughts back to the present conversation. "No?"

"Not by a long shot." Shilo started to tick people off on her fingers. "Roxy, yes, but also Marsha from next door, Dr. Messina, Oscar the mailman, and some rando with a bushy mustache."

"A rando with a bushy mustache?" I opened the notes app on my phone. "You didn't recognize him?"

"Nope, I'd never seen him before until a few days ago, but I've noticed him driving slowly down the street, like, three days in a row this past week. Pretty sure he's not from Pine Bluff."

Elvira ran into the house, then sprinted around the coffee table, Thor hot on her heels. April and Shilo lifted their legs and rolled back onto the couch, but I didn't have the quick dog owner reflexes. Both dogs smacked into my knees and Thor whacked me soundly in the face with his tail on the way by. His big body knocked the table a foot sideways and an unlit candle went flying, landing on the other side of the room.

"Ahh!" I yelled. "Watch the Christmas tree."

"Thor! Out!" April commanded.

The dogs zoomed back out into the yard, narrowly missing destroying the tree. Visions of heirloom glass blown ornaments shattering on the hardwood floor still played in my mind.

Shilo simply laughed and picked up the candle. "It didn't break. The tree's still standing. All good here. Now, where were we?"

"The rando dude with the mustache. This guy was in Sheryl's yard at some point? Along with all those other people?" I asked.

Shilo nodded vigorously. "Yep, he sure was. It was like Grand Central Station around here Friday afternoon."

"What was he driving? Do you remember?"

"A burgundy pickup. I'm not sure of the make."

Andy glanced over. "Chevy Silverado. 2002."

We all gaped at him.

"What? I'm a car guy." He shrugged and went back to his game.

I typed the information into my notes app. "Okay. Do you mind giving us a rundown, one by one, starting with Marsha Slabinski?"

"I'd love to. Did I mention juicy gossip is my favorite thing?" Shilo laughed.

April and I couldn't help but join in.

"You mentioned Marsha. Was she actually *in* Sheryl's yard?" April questioned once we'd settled back down. "Seems like it might be a violation of the restraining order she had against Sheryl. Doesn't it kind of go both ways?" She looked at me for confirmation.

"That's always been my understanding, though I don't have any working knowledge of them." I shrugged. "The restraining order would have been protecting Marsha from Sheryl, but I would think Marsha would also have been obligated to maintain the distance, right?"

"You would think," Shilo interjected, "but Marsha snuck around over there quite a bit. Friday, I'm pretty sure she slashed the Santa in the hot air balloon blow up. She messed with something different every day, just to get Sheryl's goat."

I shook my head slightly, trying to remember all the decor. "I don't remember seeing a hot air balloon Santa the other night, but I could've missed it. There was so much to look at."

Shilo shook her head. "You wouldn't have seen it. Sheryl hadn't had time to patch Santa back up yet."

"So Marsha snuck around sabotaging the decorations, and Sheryl fixed them back up?" April asked. "Sheryl was on house arrest, which means she was always home. She must've known what Marsha was doing. I would have bet money Sheryl would have had a hissy fit over the whole thing."

Shilo nodded. "You'd think so, but I'm pretty sure it was some kind of diabolical game between the two of them. I never once saw Sheryl come out of the house and confront her. She just let it happen, then would go out and fix whatever it was Marsha had broken."

"What a strange relationship." I hesitated for a minute to let the weirdness sink in. "Okay. Moving on. You mentioned Laine—Dr. Messina—was there also. Not surprising, since her and Sheryl are sisters."

Shilo held up her index finger. "Which I didn't realize until you said so the other night. Dr. Messina has only been over at Sheryl's a couple of times over the eight years we've lived here. That's why I was shocked when you said they were sisters. I mean, my sister and I hang out every chance we get."

"I don't know anything about their relationship. Some siblings aren't very close. Was there anything different about her visit on Friday?"

"Only if you count the two women screaming at each other."

"Screaming at each other?" *Now, that's interesting*. I shoved my glasses up higher on my nose. "Did you happen to hear what they were yelling about?"

"Something about Jazelle and money. I was leaving for the grocery store, so was getting in my car when the shouting started. Dr. Messina said she was fed up with being Jazelle's piggy bank. Which makes more sense now I know Jazelle is Dr. Messina's niece. I didn't hear anything else before she and Sheryl went inside the house and slammed the door."

"What time of day was this?"

Shilo tilted her head back and forth, thinking. "About two in the afternoon."

"Did you see Sheryl alive after you got back from the store?"

"For sure. She was out stringing up more Christmas lights when I pulled into the driveway. We waved to each other."

"Good. Who's next on the list?"

Shilo set her drink down on the coffee table. "Well, Oscar the mailman. Our mail always comes around three. Sheryl's box is mounted on her house, so him being in her yard isn't unusual."

"Not at all," I agreed. "He comes up onto my porch every day, too."

"Except," Shilo stood to scoot the dogs back outside again. "on Friday, Oscar was in and out of Sheryl's yard a handful of times. The first time was about six-thirty in the morning. I was sitting here having my breakfast tea and didn't see him arrive, but his face was as red as Rudolph's nose when he left."

"Red, like, mad red?" April asked.

"Yeah, like picture steam coming out of his ears. Then he was back a couple of hours later. Sheryl was working outside on her decorations. Oscar stormed into her yard and slapped what looked like a manila envelope down on her picnic table. They talked for a couple of minutes, and no, before you ask, I didn't hear what they were talking about. The third time he came back was for the regular mail route around three o'clock. Everything seemed normal by then."

I typed a few more notes out. "Alright, and what about the bushy mustache guy? What was he doing in Sheryl's yard, and when?"

Shilo pointed her index finger at me, on which she wore a silver ring shaped like Krampus, the dark counterpart to Santa Claus in Central European folklore. The gothic jewelry was in direct contrast to her Peppa Pig pink hair. "He was there later in the day. In fact, Andy and I were getting ready to leave for the tree lighting and it was already getting dark. He parked right in front of Sheryl's house and walked through the gate like he owned the place. He was pounding on the door, but we left, so didn't see Sheryl answer the door."

I raised my eyebrows. "Had you ever seen him enter her yard before?"

Shilo shook her head. "Never."

"I find it super interesting that whoever this mystery man is showed up not very long before Sheryl died, don't you?" April polished off the rest of her tangerine water and set the empty can on a coaster on the coffee table.

"Agreed. We need to find out who he is." I stood and grabbed my purse. "This has all been incredibly helpful, Shilo. Thanks for letting us barge in on you and interrupt your day."

April whistled for Thor, clipping his leash back to his collar when he barreled through the house.

"No problem at all." Shilo caught Elvira as the small dog attempted to jump onto the couch. "No you don't, Missy. You're covered in mud. Andrew," she called, turning her attention to her spouse. "Look at your dog. You need to give her a bath."

Without complaining, Andy paused his game and reached for Elvira. "Come on, you silly little mutt." He gave us a backward wave as he took the dog and headed for the bathroom.

April, Thor, and I were halfway down the sidewalk when the door to the Kravitz house opened back up and Shilo called out. "Oh, hey. There's one more thing I forgot to mention."

"What is it?" I trotted back to her gate so she didn't have to yell and share her thoughts with the entire neighborhood.

"When Andy and I left for the tree lighting, we passed Dr. Messina at the corner." Shilo pointed to the right, indicating the intersection of Alpine Drive and Jubilee Avenue. "She was driving back up the street in this direction."

"You're positive it was her?"

Shilo nodded. "Her metallic, tanzanite blue Beemer is hard to miss."

Chapter Thirteen

"Holy fright. My head's filled with all the information Shilo let fly." I shook my noggin in an attempt to clear some of the clutter.

"She's definitely a wealth of knowledge when it comes to the movements of her neighborhood." April blew out a breath that looked like smoke in the cold air. "I work with Roxy at the store tomorrow, so I'll try to ferret out what she was doing sneaking around in Sheryl's yard."

"Good. Right this second, I'm pretty frustrated with her for holding back on us, so I'm glad you're the one who is going to ask her about it. I'm afraid I might get a little harsh."

"Rightfully so. I want to help, but I'm about ready to tell her she's on her own."

I frowned and nodded my agreement.

Off his leash, Thor zoomed around in the fresh snow in my front yard. He lowered his head, burying his snout in the powder, and plowing it into a snowball as he ran.

The dog's antics made me laugh. "I don't know how he's not worn out from chasing Elvira for the last hour."

"Once I get him home, I guarantee he'll be a snoring heap for a few hours." April whistled for the dog. "What are your plans for the afternoon?"

"A big old mug of coffee and a paint brush. How about you?"

"J. T.'s cooking dinner for me later, but I was planning on vegging out with a few episodes of *The Great British Baking Show* until then. I'd be happy to stay and help if you want me to, though."

"Nah, I'm looking forward to the quiet time, but thanks for the offer. Think I'll put on some Christmas tunes and get cracking. The physical work should help me think and figure out what our next move should be."

"Sounds good." She wagged a finger at me. "But don't you dare head off to do any more poking around without me."

I held up my hands in surrender. "I wouldn't dream of it." Inside my boots, I attempted to cross my toes with little success. A promise like April wanted was hard to make when I didn't yet know what my snoop...I mean, investigating...would entail.

April opened the passenger door of her car and called for Thor to jump in. Three snowballs clung to his tail. April turned back to me, pointing two fingers at her own eyes, then at me a couple of times in rapid succession. She shot me a mock glare, then got in the driver's seat and skittered down the street, Thor riding shotgun.

Lilac met me in the kitchen when I entered the house, greeting me with a soft meow-ish squeak. I wanted to scoop her up and run my fingers through her soft fur, but, having tried the same thing a time or two, I knew it was impossible. On top of petting her not being a possibility, nothing made Lilac disappear faster than my hand passing through her ghostly form. I guessed it must be an unpleasant sensation for her. Instead, I settled for snuggling the sweet little cat in my mind.

"Hey there, little lady." She wound around my legs. "It's nice to see you, too. Did you get lonely being home all alone?"

I pulled turkey lunch meat, a head of romaine lettuce, mayonnaise, and mustard out of the refrigerator and made myself a quick sandwich. After eating, I started the coffee pot, then headed to my bedroom to change. Running my hand over Bob's old denim work shirt still hanging in the closet, I buried my face in the cloth, trying to breathe in any lingering scent of him. Over the past three years, the smell had faded to barely a trace. I pulled the shirt off the hanger, thrusting my arms through the sleeves and buttoning it over top of the cream-colored Yellowstone National Park T-shirt I wore.

"Why haven't I done this before?" I marveled. Wearing Bob's shirt gave me the feeling of being surrounded by his strong arms. Tears of gratitude for all of our memories together filled my eyes. I indulged myself, allowing a couple to fall before sniffing them back and wiping my eyes. "Alright, Bob. Enough sappy stuff. Let's get to work." If I didn't know better, I'd swear I heard him chuckle.

Grabbing a coffee mug the size of a cereal bowl, I splashed in a healthy dose of peppermint creamer, then filled the mug to the brim. Next, I opened the app I used to stream music on my phone, picked my favorite Country Christmas playlist, and headed upstairs. Lilac trailed behind me, padding softly up the aged and scarred wooden staircase. The risers could really use a good sanding and some new stain, but I loved the patina created from years of feet running up and down the stairs.

After flipping on the lights in the apartment, I pried open the first can of primer, gave the creamy paint a hearty stir with a wooden stir stick, then poured a portion into my plastic tray. Singing along with Dolly's "Hard Candy Christmas," I tackled the blood red bedroom first.

Two and a half hours later, the second coat of primer was doing a better job of covering the angsty red than I had expected. Bob's work shirt and my jeans sported a few extra spots of white primer, and my sore body cried out for a break.

I arched my back and stretched. "A visit to the chiropractor might be in order," I told the cat. Lilac blinked and washed her paw. I'd call first thing tomorrow to see if Dr. Messina was taking appointments despite her sister's recent death. And if she happened to want to talk about the argument she'd had with Sheryl the other day, who was I to deny a grieving woman the chance to get her feelings out? I'd be more than happy to listen.

Though right now I fancied a chat with my best friend. Evonne was always a great sounding board when I was trying to work out the details of a problem. We must have been on the same soundwave because I'd just finished cleaning my paint roller and setting it out to dry when my phone rang.

"Well, hello there, Evonne. Your ears must've been burning. I was just thinking about you."

"Were you also thinking about coffee and eggnog pie at the Stage Stop?"

"How'd you guess?"

"Meet you there in fifteen?"

"You bet."

Motivated by the thought of pie, I finished cleaning up in record time, changed into non-paint splattered attire, and slid into a booth opposite my best friend exactly thirteen minutes later. It was a personal best.

"Tell me everything." Evonne poured cream from a small stainless-steel pitcher into her coffee before ripping open three packets of sugar, dumping them in, and giving the concoction a quick stir.

To fortify myself for sharing my tale, I cut my fork through the pie. The first taste of the creamy eggnog pie caused me to close my eyes for a second to savor the flavor. Rich eggnog and the spicy combination of nutmeg and cinnamon exploded in my mouth. "Mmm. This is so good. It's like Christmas on a plate."

Evonne tasted her own. "Delicious. Now spill the tea."

"Fine." I set my fork on my plate. "You heard Smitty was the one who noticed Sheryl's body, right?"

"Well, duh. Not to mention, you and April were right there with her." Not only was Evonne the president of our local Women's Service Club, but she also served as the Pine Bluff City

Manager. There wasn't much her eyes or ears missed. "I know better than to hope you won't get involved this time."

"With Roxy a suspect, I don't have much choice."

Evonne shoved a bite of pie in her mouth, her eyebrows raised. She didn't have to say a word. After fifty-four years of friendship, we read each other's faces like a book.

I grimaced under her scrutiny. "If you were in my shoes, you would do the same. I can't just step back and let her deal with this on her own. The poor woman has had a hard enough time recently without adding the stress of being a murder suspect on top."

Evonne held up a hand. "Hey, I wasn't arguing."

"Maybe not in words, but your face sure showed your disapproval."

We both laughed, knowing Evonne had my back, whatever I chose to do. Which we also both knew was to jump into the investigation feet first.

"Changing the subject." Evonne cleared her throat. "Katherine Johnson called me this morning with a small request."

"What does she need? Is there a problem with the Christmas production?"

Katherine was the artistic director of the local Curtain Call Theater Company. Last week the group had started rehearsing for a production of *How the Grinch Stole Christmas*. It would be playing at the Emery Theater the week before Christmas.

"Not a problem, necessarily, just a small snag." Evonne signaled the waitress to ask for coffee refills for both of us. Even though I'd had plenty, I didn't argue. "The troupe is a few actors short for the Whoville choir. I signed us up."

My mouth flew open as if I was Cindy Lou Who watching the Grinch steal my presents. "Us? As in you *and* me? Are you nuts? You know I can't dance or sing to save my life."

"I know, but it's going to be a blast watching you try."

"No. No way." I shook my head adamantly. "I'd rather be shot in the foot with a nail gun than have to perform in front of people."

Evonne simply tilted her head and studied me. "Who is it that browbeats me into going to yoga three mornings a week? Against my will, I might add. And who talked me into taking a self-defense class I didn't want to take? You know, the one where I ripped out the butt of my jeans in front of twenty-five people. And what about the time you drank too much and ralphed all over the inside of my car?"

I threw my hands in the air. "Seriously? That happened forty years ago!"

Evonne shrugged. "I don't care, I'm never letting it go." She pointed her fork at me. "You're part of the Whoville choir, like it or not."

"Fine." I knew when I'd been beat. "But let the record show, I'm not happy about it." I glared at her over the rim of my coffee mug.

Evonne grinned. "You don't have to be. All you have to do is memorize the words to 'Welcome Christmas' and attempt to stay on the same beat as the rest of us."

"Mmhmm. Easy for you to say." The thought of singing on stage in front of all those people already had my palms sweating. My mind whirled with ways to get out of this predicament. *Lip syncing was invented for a reason.* And I planned to master the technique in record time.

"You'll be fine." Evonne finished her pie, scraping up every last bit with her fork. "First practice is Tuesday night."

"Oh, hey," I brightened up. "Is Marsha going to be part of the choir?" Play practice would be the perfect place to work in a conversation about her deceased neighbor.

"Marsha Slabinski? Mrs. Grinch herself? No. She wouldn't be caught dead celebrating Christmas." Evonne blew a raspberry and shook her head. "But speaking of Marsha, did you realize her and Sheryl were best friends when they were in school?"

"No way. They hated each other with a passion."

"Not always, from what I hear. They were as thick as thieves back in the day. As tight as you and I have ever been."

"How do you know? They're what, eight years or so older than us? Too much of an age gap for me to remember them in school."

"Gary mentioned it." Evonne referred to her older brother. "He was in the same class as they were. From what he remembers, Sheryl and Marsha both got married right out of high school and bought their houses next door to each other on purpose. They had big plans to raise their kids together. Not sure what happened, but I thought it was worth mentioning."

"So, you've been doing a little digging, too." I leaned across the table and smirked at my best friend.

"Maybe."

"I wonder what happened? How do you go from being so close," I motioned between the two of us, "to mortal enemies?"

"The same as any other relationship that goes bad, I would guess. I think a broken friendship can be as heartbreaking as a divorce. Even more so in some cases."

I nodded. "You're right. If something horrible happened between you and me, I would be devastated. I don't even want to imagine that kind of pain." I finished my second mug of coffee. "Divorced couples battle each other all the time, so I guess it makes sense that a broken friendship might cause a never-ending war."

"Think about a split like that and then the two of them having to continue to live next door to each other for all of these years. They had to see each other coming and going every single day. Can you imagine?"

"Which begs the question, why didn't one of them sell and get out of Dodge? Or at least out of the neighborhood."

Chapter Fourteen

After an energizing yoga session early Monday morning, I called Dr. Messina's office and secured an afternoon appointment. Next, I drove downtown and marched into Blue Mountain Community Bank where I'd had my accounts my entire adult life.

"Good morning, Dawna. What can I help you with today?" Sandy, a long-time teller at the bank, turned her sunny smile my way.

"Good morning to you, too. I have an appointment with Lisa at nine-fifteen. I'm a few minutes early."

"No worries. I'll let her know you're here." Sandy pushed an extension number on her desk phone. She hung up and motioned to the offices behind her. "Lisa said for you to go on back. You know where she is."

"I do. Thanks much."

Two doors down the hallway, Lisa Stauffer greeted me from the doorway to her office. She wore black pants and a blazer over a white and black polka dotted blouse. Her golden blonde hair, styled in a tousled shoulder-length bob, popped against the dark outfit.

"Hey, Dawna. Are you ready to get this finalized?"

A couple of months ago, I'd found out Bob had taken out a loan against Carpenter's Corner with a bank over in Greenwood before he passed. Way before. Like two years before. And for whatever whacked out reason, my darling husband didn't bother sharing that little fact with me.

To make matters worse, when the bank started calling, I had stubbornly insisted they had made a mistake. Carpenter's Corner had never had an account with Elkins National Bank. Their records were wrong. The loan they were trying to foreclose on was not mine. If they didn't stop calling, I told them, I was going to report them for harassment.

Then, lo and behold, while digging through Bob's old desk in search of something else entirely, it had shocked me to my core when I'd unearthed a loan document to Elkins National with Bob's signature scrawled on the bottom like he had good sense. It was a single payment loan in the amount of twenty thousand dollars that had come due some four months before. Foreclosure proceedings were already underway before I'd discovered the paperwork, so now I had less than two months to pay it in full, plus interest and penalties, before the bank stole my business out from under me. My fuse was still pretty short over the whole thing, so maybe it was good Bob couldn't actually talk to me. But he could hear me, and the next time he showed himself, I planned to give him a piece of my mind.

Hmm. I wonder if ghosts can read minds and that's why he's staying away? Good gravy. It was a terrible thought. To this day, I loved him dearly, but I didn't need him reading my mind.

"Dawna? Are you ready?" Lisa asked again.

I shoved the thoughts away and smiled at her. "You bet I am. I can't even express how ready I am to have this whole ugly episode behind me." I plunked my purse into one of the guest chairs in front of Lisa's desk, then slid into the second one.

"Taking out a home equity line of credit is a great solution, and I'm glad we're able to get this done for you in-house. I have a handful of items for you to sign, but it's nothing like the paperwork you get when you take out a full mortgage. We'll be done and you'll be out of here in a jiffy."

Lisa whisked a legal-sized document in front of me, pointing out the full loan amount, interest rate, length of loan, and monthly payment amount.

"Now, this payment amount is what it will be if you pull and use the entire amount available, and then only after the draw period is over. Until that time, you will only be required to make payments on the amount you've used. Interest only. The draw period is set for two years, and then your HELOC will be locked in. You won't be able to draw any more funds at that point, and your payment will then change to both interest and principal. Does all of this make sense?"

"Perfect." I nodded and added my John Hancock to the bottom line.

Lisa whipped a few more documents out in front of me. Once everything was signed, she straightened the stack of paper and fed them into the printer behind her desk to make me a set of copies. While the printer did its job, Lisa turned to her computer. She clicked around for a few minutes, then turned to me with a grin.

"Done. You're the proud owner of a new line of credit. What questions do you have for me?"

"How do I ask for a draw? Do I come into the bank each time? Can one of the tellers help me, or do I need to ask for you? Will I get a payment booklet?"

She waved a manicured hand. "Oh gosh, no. It's so much easier these days. Do you use our online banking program at all?"

I nodded. "All the time. I love being able to log on and check accounts whenever I think about it. I've set up several categories for various things."

"Perfect." Lisa grabbed the documents off the printer and placed my copies in a folder. "I've already connected your line of credit to your account. When you log in next time, you'll see it with your other accounts. When you want to draw funds, click the transfer button at the top of the screen, and you'll be able to move funds from the line of credit to your checking or savings accounts. You make your monthly payments the same way. I'm happy to walk you through the steps if you'd like. It's super easy."

"No need if it's the same as transferring between my checking and savings."

"Yep, exactly the same."

"You said you've already linked it, so the funds are already available?" I pushed my glasses up my nose, surprised at how quick and painless the process had been.

"Yep. You're good to go. Is there anything else can I help you with?"

I pulled a pink sticky note out of my purse and handed it across the desk to her. "Since we're sitting here, can I transfer this amount into my checking right now, and get a cashier's check for the same amount? It'll save me from having to come back today."

Lisa nodded. "Sure, I can do that for you." She turned back to her computer and tapped away at the keyboard. "The transfer is complete. Who would you like the cashier's check made out to?"

"Elkins National Bank, please." With the funds available, I wasn't about to waste one minute longer than necessary with the horrible foreclosure hanging over my head.

—◆—

Twenty-five minutes later, I wheeled my Jeep into the parking lot at Elkins National Bank in Greenwood. Even though the temperature hovered just under freezing, the sky was a brilliant blue. The sun reflecting off the pristine, snow-covered fields was blinding. I'd donned my sunglasses and blasted Gloria Gaynor's "I Will Survive" on repeat for the duration of the drive. The music pumped me up and got me ready to confront Frank Stockwell.

Pulling open the glass front door of the bank, I marched up to the receptionist behind the large wooden desk near the entrance and waited for her to acknowledge me.

The woman, close to my own age, glanced away from her computer with a sigh heavy enough to make it crystal clear I'd upset the balance of her entire day. She adjusted her glasses and graced me with a pinched smile. "Yes? Is there something you need help with?"

Sheesh. These people need to take a lesson on cordiality from the folks at Blue Mountain Community Bank. The two greetings I'd received this morning could've come straight from a training film on how and how not to welcome customers.

With the load I was about to release from my shoulders, my wide smile was genuine, despite the chill wafting off the receptionist. "I'd like to see Frank Stockwell, please."

The pursed lips again. "What time is your appointment?"

"I don't have one, but I'm hoping he can fit me in."

"Mr. Stockwell is a busy man. Why people assume they can waltz in here without an appointment is beyond me." A huff of breath and a subtle shake of her head let me know this woman was fed up with dealing with idiots such as myself.

I continued to smile at her. *I'll be hanged if I'll let her get under my skin.*

When I didn't turn and slink away at the sheer mortification of daring to show up without an appointment, she let out another overburdened sigh. "Name, please."

"Dawna Carpenter."

"One moment while I check." Theresa, according to the name plaque on her desk, turned away from me and spoke quietly into the phone. She shielded her mouth with a cupped hand as she talked. After hanging up the receiver, she turned back to me. "Mr. Stockwell will fit you in when, and if, he gets a moment. If you insist on waiting, you'll have to take your chances. Wait over there." She flung a hand toward a trio of chairs lined up against the wall. "Get comfortable. You'll be waiting a while."

"Got it." I started toward the chairs, but turned back, unable to help myself. "Thank you for your help. I hope the rest of your day treats you as kindly and pleasantly as you have treated me."

"You're....uh....welcome," Theresa stuttered. Her hand flew to her throat, grasping her beaded necklace while she blinked hard a few times, as if trying to decide if I'd given her a compliment or a curse.

I chuckled to myself as I sat down and wiggled my derriere around to show Theresa how comfortable I was getting while I waited for my nonappointment.

Not thirty seconds later, the banker called me into his office. I fought the urge to turn around and stick my tongue out at Theresa. *Have some dignity, Dawna. You're not five.* I clenched my fists. I so wanted to act like I was five.

Frank Stockwell, whose lanky form, long face, and heavy-lidded mortician eyes reminded me of Jacob Marley, ushered me into his office. He waved a long, thin hand at the chair placed in front of his desk. "Have a seat, Mrs. Carpenter." He breathed a heavy sigh.

Sheesh. Now I know the sighing is part of the training for Elkins National Bank employees. They've got it down pat.

"I assume you're here to beg for more time on your loan, but as I've explained to you, I simply cannot extend one single day past the final foreclosure date. My hands are tied. You must understand, if we offered leeway to every client with a sad story, the bank would be out of business in short order. There is no easy way to say this, but you have," he cleared his throat while consulting a document on his computer, "exactly fifty-five days before the bank officially takes possession of your building."

"You know what they say about assuming." It was all I could do not to slap the smug smile right off his horsey face. Instead, I resorted to slapping the cashier's check from my hometown bank onto his desk while I smiled and stared him dead in the eye. "I think you'll find this sufficiently covers the entire amount." I tapped my index finger on the total. "Penalties and interest included."

As the banker gaped at the check, I was half afraid his reptilian eyes would pop right out of their sockets. He spat and sputtered while clicking away at his keyboard. Frank glanced back and forth between the check and his computer screen, then swiveled to make a few more hasty calculations on his ten-key. Exhausting all options, he had no other choice but to give in.

"You've overpaid by twenty-eight dollars and thirty-seven cents," was all he said.

"I'll take it in cash." I plopped back into the chair and cradled my purse on my lap. "And before I leave here today, I will require the final statement showing my loan balance paid in full."

Frank scoffed. "Those documents take some time. We simply don't have the bandwidth at the moment."

"Good thing I have plenty of time." I sent him my shiniest smile and didn't budge from my chair. "Oh, and let's not forget, you'll need to call the Greenwood Searchlight and stop those terrible foreclosure notices you've been having printed in the daily paper."

"My administrative assistant will contact the newspaper. It will most likely take a few days to pull the notices."

I cocked my head. "No worries. I'm sure they'll be as quick to print my scathing letter to the editor about the less than upstanding business practices of Elkins National Bank. I've already written it up and have it with me, anticipating this moment. I'll stop at the newspaper offices the moment I leave the bank. It's not a problem."

Frank's face turned beet red, a vein throbbing on his temple. He loosened his black tie as if it were choking him, then punched an extension number on his phone. "Wendy. The business loan for Carpenter's Corner Hardware and Building Supply has been satisfied. Put aside whatever you're working on and prepare the final documents releasing the loan. I want them in my office in five minutes," he barked, then slammed the receiver down before lifting it again and hitting another extension. "Theresa. Get the ad manager for the Greenwood Searchlight on the phone for me. Now." He replaced the receiver with a clatter.

While he waited for the call back from his newspaper contact, Frank clicked around on his computer, refusing to make eye contact with me. I folded my hands over my purse and waited patiently. His extension beeped, and I listened as the banker insisted the notices of default on my business be pulled immediately.

"We're in luck," Frank told me after ending the call, "today's paper had not yet gone to print, so Neil was able to pull the notices effective immediately."

"I appreciate your quick response and am glad you were able to find the bandwidth to help me out."

A slight, dark-haired woman in her thirties breezed into the office and placed a manila folder onto Frank's desk. "Here you go. You'll find everything in order."

Frank cleared his throat but didn't make eye contact with this woman either. *Apparently, it isn't just me.*

"Thank you, Wendy," he managed. "Please bring your notary seal and join us."

Wendy smiled at me and nodded before leaving the room. *At least someone in this place is pleasant.*

Once Wendy returned, she took a seat in the guest chair next to me. Frank shuffled through the documents, signing a few, then handing one across the desk for Wendy to notarize.

When she finished, she showed me the notarized document. "This is the Certificate of Satisfaction on your loan. We will file and record it at the county courthouse this afternoon. It's the legal proof you've paid the loan in full and Elkins National Bank has removed the lien from your property."

I clapped my hands together once. "Excellent. What a relief." I already felt a hundred pounds lighter. While I'd love to know Bob's reasons for taking out the loan in the first place, and then not telling me about it, it was a mystery I might never solve. Better to put the whole ugly thing behind me and move on.

Wendy stood and indicated I should follow her. "Give me two minutes and I'll have a full set of copies for you, as well as the cash for your overpayment."

Before leaving Frank's office, I bestowed a thousand-watt smile on him. "It seems we've reached the end of our delightful association. May we never meet again."

Chapter Fifteen

With a satisfying thwap, I dropped the folder of loan documents onto the passenger seat of my Jeep. I'd been inside Elkins National Bank for less than thirty minutes. Between my appointment at Blue Mountain Community Bank and then here, it had been a highly successful morning, as far as my finances were concerned.

I glanced at the digital clock on my dashboard. Eleven-fifteen. My stomach growled. "Time for a celebratory lunch."

Two blocks down from the bank, I pulled into a diagonal parking spot on a side street. The temperature had warmed up to nearly forty degrees, so when I jumped out of my car slush splattered up the back of my jeans. I stepped up onto the sidewalk, brushed off the dirty ice, and continued on my way to The Nutty Goose. I'd heard good things about the small diner and was eager to give it a try. They had opened a few months earlier, but this would be my first time eating there. Since it was early enough to be a bit ahead of the lunch rush and a little late for breakfast, only a couple of the tables were full. I chose a smaller table for two which was placed against the far wall, leaving the booths and larger tables for bigger parties.

A server brought me a glass of ice water and a menu before I even got my coat off. "Need a second, hun?"

"A minute or two, if you don't mind." I quickly scanned the menu, looking for the soup section. I was ready when she returned. "How about a bowl of the beef stew and slice of cornbread?"

"Excellent choice. Clay's stew is my favorite thing on a cold day."

"Clay?" I pushed my glasses up. "Not Clay Hopkins, by any chance? The previous owner of The Little Red Hen?"

"The one and only." She placed her ink pen back into her apron pocket. "Do you know Clay? I'll send him over to say hello when he gets a minute."

"No, no. Don't go to any trouble. I don't know him personally. My family and I used to love the food at The Little Red Hen, that's all. I should have realized. The Nutty Goose isn't so different. Any chance he's going to have the delicious French toast with fresh berries and clotted cream I remember so fondly?"

She pointed to an item on the breakfast section of the menu and grinned. "We already do. Right there. We serve breakfast all day. Do you want to change your order?"

"Tempting, but no. The stew sounds perfect for today. I'll simply have to come back for breakfast another day." Besides, the stew was priced so reasonably that even after leaving a nice tip, I'd still have enough left of the cash from the bank to treat myself to a latte for the drive home.

When the server left to put my order in, I kicked myself for being so adamant about not talking with Clay. It would've been the perfect opportunity to find out if he was the man Shilo saw at Sheryl's house the day of her murder.

In no time, the server was back, sliding a steaming bowl of savory stew in front of me. I leaned over, whisking the smell upward as I inhaled the delicious aroma. I sliced open the hot cornbread and slathered it with the whipped honey butter served in a tiny dish on the side. The chunks of beef were melt-in-your-mouth tender, the carrots and potatoes done to perfection. I'd lost myself in my hearty meal when a deep voice addressed me.

"Glad to see you're enjoying your lunch."

Startled, I glanced up to find a tall man with a bushy mustache and wearing a white apron standing beside my table. Brown hair curled up from under his ball cap.

I wiped my mouth with a paper napkin. "This is so delicious I could swim in it. You must be the chef. Clay, is it?"

"Guilty." Happy crinkle lines formed around his eyes when he smiled. "I understand you and your family used to frequent my old establishment."

I nodded and introduced myself. "Dawna Carpenter. Nice to meet you. And yes, we did. We'd bring the kids over for breakfast about once a month or so. We loved The Little Red Hen, and I'm delighted to see that you're back."

"Well, thank you for your patronage. It's taken me a lot of years, but I'm finally back doing what I love." He cocked his head. "You said you'd come over. Over from where?"

I pointed northeast. "Pine Bluff. I own the hardware store on Main Street."

Something in his eyes flickered. "Ah. I don't get over your way too often. Usually just driving through when I do."

"No? I could've sworn I saw you in town the other night." A little white lie, but I wanted to gauge his reaction. "You sure you weren't around during our town Christmas tree lighting on Friday evening?"

He narrowed his eyes and studied me for a moment before answering. *Getting your story straight, are you?*

"Dang. You have sharp eyes. I'd been up Lost Canyon visiting a cousin. By the time I came back through Pine Bluff, the main drag was blocked off for the festivities. I had to weave through a few neighborhoods to make my way back to the highway."

"Sure. I must've seen you passing through. You didn't happen to park and stretch your legs for a bit, did you?"

Clay pulled out a white bar cloth he'd had tucked into his apron strings and slapped it against his thigh. "Nope. Just drove through, like I said."

"Interesting. I could've sworn it was you near Sheryl Capri's house. Tragic what happened to her. I'm sure you've heard about it, even over here in Greenwood. Do you remember her? I understand Sheryl used to work for you at The Little Red Hen."

"Must have been my doppelganger you saw. I wasn't any-where near the place." The happy laugh lines were gone, re-placed by a tenseness around his eyes and mouth. "Thanks for coming in. I need to get back to the kitchen. The food's not going to cook itself."

Feeling a bit of remorse for interrogating him, I smiled. "My bowl of stew is absolutely scrumptious. Thank you."

Clay sent me a tight smile, nodded, and headed back to his kitchen.

Even though I felt bad about questioning him in his diner, it didn't get by me that Clay had evaded my last question about knowing Sheryl. Or how he hadn't asked for my returning busi-ness. I crumbled the last of my cornbread into the stew and spooned it into my mouth. Before I paid my check and left, I attempted to stealthily snap a picture of Clay through the kitchen pass-over. I wanted to show the photo to Shilo to find out if he was the same man she had seen at Sheryl's. The bushy mustache most definitely matched her description.

Two men near my age sat at a neighboring table, plates of patty melts and fries in front of them. As I stood and pushed my arms into the sleeves of my coat, one of the men caught my eye and nodded. When I smiled back, he stood and walked my way. *Oh, lordy. I never should have smiled at him.* The last thing I wanted was a lunchtime flirtation.

"Sorry to intrude, but I couldn't help overhearing." He tucked his hands into the front pockets of his worn jeans, as if nervous. "You're Dawna Carpenter? You own Carpenter's Corner?"

"Yep, that's me." I studied him. He had a pleasant enough face, dark hair with streaks of silver running through. "I'm sorry. Do I know you? I'm usually fairly good at remembering names and faces."

He shook his head. "No, we've never met, but I knew Bob. Just wanted to say I'm real sorry about his passing. He was one of the good ones."

My breath caught in my throat, and I swallowed hard. "Thank you. I appreciate your kind words more than I can tell you." I cocked my head. "How did you know Bob?"

"CW Construction built my house. They did a fine job. The wife and I still love it. But not long after the house was finished, we discovered there'd been that problem with the shoddy work by the plumber. Bob must've told you about it. What a mess. We were going through a real rough patch, but Bob stepped in and made it right. He was an upstanding guy."

"What problem with the plumber?" Before I got the full question out, the man's cell phone rang.

"I need to take this," he said with a quick wave, "but it was real nice to meet you."

Chapter Sixteen

After swinging through a drive-thru coffee hut for my hazelnut latte, I headed back to Pine Bluff. I pulled into my normal parking space behind Carpenter's Corner ten minutes ahead of my next appointment, then hurried across Main Street. Messina Chiropractic was located on the second floor of the brick building directly across the street from my store. I entered through the street level door, then walked down the hallway flanked by an insurance agency and a computer repair service, to get to the stairwell.

Dr. Laine Messina herself greeted me in the lobby of her office. She wore navy blue slacks with a sky blue blouse and a pristine white lab coat. Despite her polished demeanor on the surface, Laine appeared to have aged significantly in the last few days. The lines on her face were deeper, her shoulders drawn in, and her eyes rimmed in red.

"Dawna, good to see you. Come on back. It's been a while since you've been in." Laine led me into the exam room. The calming space had mostly white walls with one painted a soothing sea glass green.

"A couple of years, I think. I haven't needed an adjustment in quite some time." I tossed my purse into the hard plastic chair in the corner, then peeled off my coat and threw it on top. "Before we get started, I want to say how sorry I am about the loss of your sister. I wasn't sure you'd be open this week. If it's too much for you right now, I can come back another time."

Laine dabbed at her eyes with a tissue, but then tucked it back into her pocket and waved away my concern. "No, it's fine. I need to work to keep my mind off of Sheryl's murder. It's the only thing keeping me sane." She patted the chiropractic table. "Hop up here and tell me what's going on."

"Nothing major. I spent the afternoon painting a room yesterday and am feeling my age. My shoulders are tight and I'm stiff and sore between my shoulder blades."

"Mostly upper back then?"

"Yes. And I probably made the appointment too soon. My muscles have already loosened up as the day has gone on."

"Well, let's take a look anyway since you're here. Go ahead and lie face down and I'll see what I can do for you."

As I rearranged myself, I mulled over a few questions I wanted to ask Laine. I decided to start with addressing her grief. I placed my face in the cradle of the table. "You'll remember I lost Bob a few years ago. I understand the grief, pain, and outright shock of such a sudden loss. It really helped me to have a sounding board. Someone to sit with you so you're not alone. I'm more than willing to be that person for you, if you'd like me to, since I understand what you're going through."

Laine felt along my spine with her fingertips, pressing harder in a few places as she approached the trouble area. "While I appreciate your offer, Dawna, I really do, right now I think I'm still in the denial stage. It feels completely surreal to think Sheryl's gone. Do you know what I mean?"

I nodded the best I could with my face pressed into the cradle. "Absolutely. I remember feeling completely disconnected from everything, like nothing was real. I had the sensation like I was floating almost."

"You described it perfectly." She paused and took a hitching breath. "Not many people know this, but Sheryl and I had a contentious relationship. We haven't been close in years, and I think having that distance between us is adding to my disconnect."

She'd left me with the perfect opening. "Maybe so. Funny you brought up how you and Sheryl didn't get along. One of her neighbors mentioned the two of you had been arguing on Friday afternoon."

Laine placed both of her palms flat on my upper back. "Breathe in."

When I obeyed, she suddenly pressed down with her full weight. Crackling ran up and down my entire spine and I yelped in pain.

"Nothing to worry about. It's a normal part of the process." She moved her hands a bit lower and repeated the same movement.

I yelped again.

"That neighborhood is full of busy bodies. Why can't anyone mind their own dang business these days?" She cracked my spine a third time, while finally addressing my comment. "Sheryl and I were like oil and water. If we were anywhere in the same vicinity, we always ended up yelling at each other."

"What was your argument about that day?" Laying on the table, I felt vulnerable, but asked anyway. It must be awful to have her last conversation with her sister be one of anger.

"My niece was begging for money again. She always needed one more favor. 'I promise, Auntie Laine, I'll pay you back in a couple of days. This will be the last time.' Yeah, right." Laine had worked her way down to my feet. She grasped my left foot in both hands and gave it a strong tug. I wanted to cry out again, but held it in this time so she would keep talking. "Those two were peas in a pod. Constantly using people until they bled them dry. I told my sister I was done. There was no more blood coming from this turnip."

"Rumor has it Jazelle is living with Brett Dunsmuir. Is she not working?"

"Jazelle work?" Laine scoffed. "The only work she's doing is entangling her next sugar daddy in her web." She let out a long breath. "You know how you always hear about people who are the black sheep in their family?"

"Sure. Sheryl and Jazelle are your family's black sheep?"

"Nope. My family is full of scoundrels. I'm the white sheep of my family. I'm the only one who went to college and makes a comfortable living under my own steam, without mooching off of anyone else. I hate to say it, but the world might be better off without my sister in it." A sob escaped her throat. "I'm sorry. That was an awful thing for me to say."

Laine moved up and placed a hand on each side of my head. With a quick movement, she jerked my head to the left. The crack from my neck ricocheted around the room like a gunshot. I screeched and jolted into a sitting position on the table, remembering exactly why I hated going to the chiropractor.

"That's all the adjustment I can take for the day." I massaged my neck and shoulders with both hands, a headache already pushing against my skull.

"You might hurt now, but your back has been out of alignment for quite some time. You've been compensating for it and now your body is adjusting to the correct position. Go home and use a warm compress on your neck and it'll all ease up soon. I promise."

I huffed. Weren't you supposed to have less pain when you left the chiropractor? I straightened my aching spine but remained perched on the table. There were still a couple more questions I was hoping to get answered. "Did you attend the town Christmas tree lighting the night Sheryl died?"

Laine crossed her arms and studied me. "No, I did not. If you're using a roundabout way to ask me if I killed my sister, the answer is no as well. Mel and I were home, having dinner together and winding down from the week. We were watching *Jeopardy* when the power went out. It's our Friday night ritual. Feel free to ask my husband for my alibi."

Maybe I will. "I'm sorry if I made you feel defensive. I'm not accusing you, just trying to understand what might have happened." I rubbed my neck some more. "I was there that night, you know, and I know you got there really quick. How did you know something was wrong at your sister's house?"

Laine grimaced. "Like I said, that neighborhood is full of busybodies. One of her neighbors called me." She frowned up at the ceiling. "Weirdly, I don't even remember who let me know."

"Funny how some memories fade into the background when you're dealing with trauma." I waved my hands in front of my face to indicate thoughts flying away. "You should just be able to check the call log on your phone, if it's bothering you."

"Great idea." Laine rubbed her arms. "I'll do that so I can thank them."

"Do you mind if I ask another question before I get out of your hair?"

She shrugged. "Go ahead."

"If Sheryl used people like you say, and I'm not doubting your word, there must be folks you can think of who might have wanted her dead."

"A handful, at least. You yourself mentioned Brett Dunsmuir. If I were the police, I'd take a good hard look at his ex-wife."

My mouth dropped open. Did Laine know the police had Roxy on their radar? Was she trying to play up that angle? "Roxy? Why?"

"Because Brett was their next victim. My sister and her daughter are...were...experts at reeling a man in, then emptying his bank accounts and sucking up any assets he might have. There won't be anything left for his kids when my niece gets through with him. Honestly, Brett will be lucky if he makes it out alive. Sheryl's last two husbands are prime examples of not paying attention to the red flags in a relationship. With Jazelle living at the Dunsmuir place, I can almost guarantee Brett's parents are on her list, too. Roxy would want to protect her kids' interests."

My mouth gaped open. Had Laine just accused Sheryl of murdering her former husbands? "You think Sheryl and Jazelle were planning on fleecing the Dunsmuirs? Or worse? Do you know all of this for a fact?"

Roxy's theory about Brett's new girlfriend going after the Dunsmuir land had struck me more as anger at her ex than anything substantial, but to hear the same thing out of Jazelle's aunt's mouth lent more weight to her speculation.

Laine rubbed the back of her neck. "No, but I've known Sheryl and Jazelle their whole lives. My educated guess is any assets the Dunsmuirs have will end up with Jazelle sooner or later. She finds any little area of weakness and worms her way in. My dear sister taught her well."

"Good night! I was surprised to hear Jazelle was back in the area after her recent marriage, but then Darlene Lovelace mentioned she came home because her new husband had passed away suddenly."

"Her new, nearly eighty-year-old husband, I might add." Laine shrugged and raised her arms to waist height, palms up. "I rest my case."

Chapter Seventeen

Instead of going into Carpenter's Corner like I'd planned to do after my chiropractic appointment, I snuck around the corner, climbed into my Jeep and headed home. My neck was already stiff from the terrible adjustment, and the headache had added another drummer to the band playing inside my skull. Since I'd managed to talk with two of my suspects today, I decided to give myself some grace and go home to relax for the rest of the afternoon. The warm compress Laine suggested was calling my name.

"It'll be the twelfth of never before I go to the chiropractor again," I told Lilac as she climbed onto my blanket-covered lap. I'd changed into my pre-pajama clothes—comfy sweats and an oversized sweatshirt—plugged the Christmas tree lights in, and brewed myself a cup of sugar plum tea before settling down in the sunroom. The tree stood in the alcove created by the turret on my brick house, decorated with all my favorite kitschy ornaments the family had made and collected over the years. The scent of sawdust and coffee swirled around me, indicating Bob was near, but he didn't materialize. Feeling safe and secure, I got comfortable and cracked open my book, nodding off before managing to read two pages.

"What? Who?" A bang jolted me awake, my thoughts foggy and my words not forming full sentences.

"What are you? An owl?" April laughed as she strode into the room. "We didn't mean to startle you. J. T. accidentally let the screen door slam." She hooked a thumb over her shoulder. "Not my fault this time."

J. T. walked into the room behind her, grinning sheepishly. He wore cowboy boots, jeans, and his taupe uniform shirt. "Sorry about disturbing your nap."

"What are you talking about? I wasn't sleeping." I rubbed the clouds out of my eyes and sat up straighter, trying, for whatever weird reason humans do, to pretend I hadn't been napping. "Aren't you supposed to be at Carpenter's Corner? Did you guys close the store early?" I glanced at April.

She wrinkled her nose. "Mom, it's almost six-thirty. We closed at the normal time. Well, I did. Roxy had to leave a couple of hours ago."

"Ow!" I tried to swivel my head to look out the window, but my neck caught, shooting pain into my shoulder.

"What's wrong? Did you hurt yourself? I should've carried those cans of paint upstairs for you yesterday." April hovered over me.

I waved her concern away. "I didn't hurt myself. It was Dr. Messina. She nearly killed me."

"Dr. Messina? Laine?" J. T.'s eyes flared. "What did she do to you?"

"Pfft. Adjusted my neck and back. A little aggressively, if you ask me. I thought I needed an adjustment after painting half the day yesterday, but boy was I ever wrong. Suffice it to say, I will not be going to the chiropractor ever again." I didn't mention how the catalyst for making the appointment in the first place was far more about trying to scope out information than it was about finding pain relief.

J. T. relaxed his stance. "Ah, good to hear. I thought maybe you were sticking your nose into my investigation again."

"Who, me? Don't be ridiculous." I played up the innocent act. "But are you saying Laine is one of your suspects?" I loved it when he inadvertently passed on tidbits about his investigations.

Without answering, J. T. mocked me by batting his eyelashes before he plopped down onto the couch. April had left the room, but came back moments later and handed me a rice bag she'd heated up in the microwave.

I pressed the bag to my neck, closed my eyes, and groaned in pleasure. Seconds later, my eyes flew open, my brain finally catching up with current affairs. "Wait a minute. Why did Roxy have to leave early? Did Hunter skip school again today?"

"No." April sat down next to J. T. "Her mother-in-law called..."

"Ex-mother-in-law," I interrupted.

"...to tell her Brett's dad is in the hospital."

"Oh, no." I levered the footrest down on the recliner with a thunk. "Pam told Roxy the other day that they'd all had the flu over the weekend. She made it sound like they were all doing better, but Barry must not have recovered as fast as the rest of them."

April nodded. "Sounds like Barry continued to get worse instead of better, so Pam was getting ready to take him into the clinic this morning. He went to put his shoes on and was gone so long that she went to hurry him up, but found him unresponsive on the bedroom floor. She called an ambulance, and they took him to the hospital in Greenwood."

"Have you gotten any updates from Roxy since she left?" My phone rang and I glanced at the screen. "Speak of the devil, there she is now." I answered the call, then hit the speaker icon. "Hey, Roxy. You're on speaker. April and J. T. are listening. They told me about Barry. Is there any news? How are you holding up?"

Roxy's voice sounded shaky. "He's not doing great. Still unconscious. He's having breathing issues, and his blood pressure is dangerously low. They're monitoring him closely and running a bunch of tests to try to figure out what's going on."

"Do they think his illness might be caused by the flu they all had?"

"The last doctor who came in said he isn't completely convinced. That's why he's running an entire panel of tests. He says it seems more like a toxin issue than a flu issue. They've been questioning Pam and Brett about what Barry has been eating the last few days, how he's been acting, if they've noticed any strange odors around the house or farm recently, stuff like that."

"The doctor thinks it might be poison?" I asked incredulously.

"Yeah. Maybe. They don't know for sure."

"It sounds like they're on top of things," J. T. said. "He's in good hands."

"I hope so. They should know more in the next day or two." Roxy sniffed.

"Well, keep us posted," I added. "Are the kids with you? Is there anything you need us to do? Does the dog need fed and walked?"

"The kids are with me, and I appreciate you offering, but we're going to go home for the night. He can only have two visitors at a time, and Pam and Brett are here so there's no point in us staying."

"No Jazelle?" April asked.

"No, thank goodness. Brett said she hates hospitals so chose to stay out at the ranch and take care of things there."

She's taking care of things alright, if any of the gossip can be believed.

"At least you don't have to deal with her on top of everything else," April said.

"No kidding. I can barely stand to be in the same room with Brett. Adding Jazelle into the mix would've been too much." Roxy sighed. "Alright. I'm going to go. I'll see you in a couple of days for my next shift, Dawna."

"We'll see. Depends on how things go with Barry. We'll touch base before then," I said.

"True enough. Talk soon." Roxy disconnected the call.

"Good night. I hope he'll rally and be okay." I tossed my phone onto the table beside the recliner and pressed the rice bag to my sore neck.

"Definitely worrisome," J. T. added.

"The whole thing reminds me of the conversation I had with Laine this afternoon."

J. T. raised his eyebrows. "Thought you went to see her for an innocent chiropractic appointment."

"I did. It's not my fault the good doctor was feeling chatty."

April chuckled while J. T. pinched the bridge of his nose.

"Spill the beans." He leaned back on the couch and pierced me with his steel-blue gaze.

I filled them in on Laine's disclosure about how she had a difficult relationship with both her sister and her niece. "She says Sheryl and Jazelle take advantage of everyone they come in contact with. Laine is sure the Dunsmuirs are their next targets. She went as far as to hint Brett might not make it out of the relationship alive, and how Jazelle may have been responsible for her late husband's death."

April's eyes bulged. "No way! You mean like a Black Widow?"

J. T. scratched at the five o'clock shadow on his jaw. "Seems a little far-fetched."

"I suppose it's possible Jazelle knew the guy was sick before she married him, instead of actually killing him." I stretched my neck, attempting to relieve some of the stiffness.

"Or she had some really bad luck," J. T. added. "It's not the first time someone has died shortly after their wedding."

April bit her bottom lip. "Yeah, but with her own aunt thinking she killed him, and now Barry Dunsmuir being poisoned, isn't that a little coincidental? I feel like there's something to the story."

"I'll tell you what, if it turns out Barry was poisoned, I'll look into this wackadoodle theory. Until then, let's put it on the back burner." J. T. stood and stretched.

"You've got a deal." April nodded.

"Not to mention, I think you two are missing the fact that if Jazelle is a Black Widow, and she and her mom were working together to get the Dunsmuir's land and money, it definitely gives Roxy a strong motive for murdering Sheryl."

"Wipe that from your mind. Remember how you said it was a wackadoodle theory? Roxy is not your killer." I clapped my hands together a couple of times to make my point, then changed the subject. "Oh, yeah! I forgot to tell you the best part of my day."

"Oh, right. I forgot you had an appointment at the bank this morning. How did it go?" April uncrossed her legs and scooted to the edge of the couch.

"Couldn't have gone better. I walked out of the bank here in Pine Bluff with a cashier's check in my hand and drove straight over to Greenwood. Walked into Elkins National Bank and slapped the check down onto Frank Stockwell's desk. I insisted on getting a copy of my loan satisfaction document before I left. You can rest easy tonight. The loan is paid in full, and Carpenter's Corner is safe and sound." I grinned like I'd won the lottery. Because I felt like I had.

"Mom! That's such great news. I can't believe you didn't call me right away." April exploded off the couch. "Darlene's knickers are going to be all in a twist when she hears the news."

"I plan to tell her first thing in the morning. It's going to be glorious."

April and I both grinned and cackled with joy.

"You two are diabolical. But I think this calls for a celebration." J. T. rubbed his hands together. "Should we go get a pizza? I'm buying."

"Yes, please. I'm starving." I kicked off my slippers and stood slowly to assess the pain in my neck and shoulders. Nothing seemed too bad, only achy, so I went to change back into my going out in public clothes.

Tucked into a back corner booth in Rocky Ridge Pizza Co. thirty minutes later, the three of us shared a thin crust supreme pizza with extra sauce and an order of breadsticks. I'd thought about adding a side salad but decided this was a celebration and I didn't need to guilt myself into a bowl of rabbit food. At least not tonight.

While we ate, April and I leaned in to quietly share with J. T. the various tidbits we'd picked up about the suspects over the last several days.

"The suspects?" J. T. nearly choked on his slice of pizza. "I was unaware the two of you were the ones building the suspect list. Silly me."

I eyed him over the top of my glasses. "So far, our instincts have been fairly good." If you didn't count the first murder I'd "assisted" with where the killer had given themselves away before I'd figured it out. Honing those investigating skills took time, and I was still leveling up my game.

J. T. took a large gulp of water, then set his glass back on the table. "You two are driving me insane. Why can't you leave things alone?"

"Trying to get us to stop is going to be as futile as trying to nail jelly to a tree." April blinked at him innocently. "We're Carpenters. Don't tell me you haven't noticed the meddling trait runs strong through our DNA."

"Oh, I've noticed alright." J. T. sighed, then propped his elbows on the table. "Fine. Please be so kind as to share your suspect list with me, and the intriguing reasons you've settled on said list."

April gave him a gentle whack on the arm. "There's no need for sarcasm."

I plopped my pizza back onto my plate so my hands would be free to tick off the suspects. "We came up with this list because each of these people were seen in Sheryl's yard the day of her murder."

"By whom?" J. T. interrupted.

April and I glanced at each other with toothy grimaces before she answered. "Shilo Kravitz."

J. T. ran a hand up and down his face, then let out a grunt. "Continue."

I held up my pointer finger. "First, we'll concede Roxy should stay on the list until she's been completely cleared. We're working on that."

April snapped her fingers. "Shoot. I forgot to ask her why she was creeping around Sheryl's house on Friday."

I kicked her under the table. There were some things we needed to keep to ourselves for the time being.

"Creeping around Sheryl's house?" J. T.'s interest perked up.

I waved a hand. "That's not the important part right now. I'm sure there's a perfectly reasonable explanation. Moving on." I held up the next finger. "Marsha Slabinski, for obvious reasons."

"Agreed." J. T. dipped his chin. "However, I don't see how Marsha could have done the dirty deed."

"Why not? She's as capable as anybody else."

"Because it took a whole lot of strength to haul Sheryl up the ladder and stuff her into the chimney."

"Strength or anger? This was like a Christmas crime. I mean, electrocuted, wrapped in lights, and then stuffed into the chimney in her own Christmas display? That's a whole lot of anger right there. And who was more angry about Sheryl's over the top Christmas house than Marsha?" I pushed my glasses up the bridge of my nose. "But you're right. I hadn't thought about the sheer amount of physical power it would have taken to get her up there."

"Which is why I get paid the big bucks." He smirked with a wink.

"Sheryl wasn't a big person, though. She couldn't have weighed more than a buck twenty-five. But Marsha isn't big either, and she seems kind of fragile. I really don't think she'd have the strength. Two people then, maybe, working together? Maybe Marsha had an accomplice." I wiped my fingers on my napkin.

"It's possible, but let's circle back to Roxy for a minute."

I glowered at him, but nodded for him to continue.

"Roxy is a tall, sturdy woman who is used to carrying heavy bags of animal feed and throwing around bales of hay. She's not somebody I'd want to tangle with." J. T. picked up a breadstick, broke it in half, and dunked it into the marinara sauce.

I huffed. "You make a good point. Roxy does have the strength to have been able to pull it off. The other day she picked up and moved a cast iron sink without asking for help. I told her she's going to hurt herself one of these days if she isn't careful." Realizing I wasn't helping Roxy's case, I doubled down on my belief in her innocence. "But mark my words, she didn't do it. She would never jeopardize her family. Her kids are way too important to her. You're trying to fit a square peg into a round hole."

"I'm just being practical. Laying out the facts." He chewed on his breadstick and stared at me.

"Let's table the Roxy discussion for now," April jumped in. "Next, we have Laine Messina, who we've already discussed. She was seen arguing with Sheryl on the afternoon in question."

"She told me they were arguing about Jazelle asking her for money again. Apparently, it's a regular occurrence that Jazelle acts like Laine is her personal banker, and Sheryl pressures her into handing over the money." I rotated my head in order to stretch the kinks out of my neck. "Laine isn't much taller than her sister was, but my sore muscles tell me she's strong enough."

"Seems like a weak motive to me. She could've stopped handing them money at any time. Problem solved." J. T. sat back and crossed his arms over his chest. "Who else are you looking at?"

"Later the same day, some guy with a mustache showed up at Sheryl's house. We haven't quite figured out who he is yet," April answered.

I held up a finger and fumbled around in my purse, looking for my phone. "I think it was Clay Hopkins. I forgot to mention I happened to run into him today. He owns a new little diner in Greenwood called The Nutty Goose. I had lunch there today. DeAnn at the Stage Stop Café put him on our radar. He used to own The Little Red Hen eons ago, and Sheryl worked there as a cook. From what DeAnn remembered, Sheryl had an accident at work and the lawsuit she won against him put him out of business. I snapped a picture of Clay and need to verify with Shilo that he's the same guy." I held up my phone to show them the picture I'd taken of Clay. "Pretty sure he could stuff someone in a chimney."

J. T. shook his head while he studied the photo. "I don't recall ever seeing him. How about you?" he asked April.

"Not that I know of."

"Anyone else on your radar?" J. T. pushed his plate back. "Or are you finished."

"There's one more. The mailman. Oscar Rudolf," I answered.

"Let me guess. Because Shilo saw Oscar in Sheryl's yard? Did you ever think he was simply delivering her mail. You know, doing his job?"

"Yeah, but I have a gut feeling there's a little more to it. Think about it for a minute. Who knows your business better than your mailman? He knows if you have any delinquent bills, what packages are delivered, everything really." I took a breath. "Granted, there's not nearly the amount of mail coming to our homes there was before email took over, but still, I bet he knows a ton about all of our lives. The guy spends far more time walking the neighborhood than the people who live there."

J. T. ran a hand through his dark hair. "Oscar's just a little guy, though."

"Sure, little but wiry, and I'd bet he's stronger than he looks. He packs those heavy mail bags all over town five days a week. If Oscar was determined to stuff Sheryl in the chimney, I'm betting he could do it. Or maybe he was Marsha's accomplice and helped her dispose of the body."

"Well, if they tried to dispose of her body, they failed miserably, leaving her in plain sight like they did." J. T. leaned back and took a sip from his beer mug. "I'll take your suspect list under advisement."

I nodded. "That's all I can ask for."

The Chief of Police didn't ask any follow-up questions to my many theories, so I followed his lead and chose not to elaborate.

"Hey, this is supposed to be a celebration. Who wants another slice?" I snagged an olive off a piece of pizza before sliding the slice onto my plate.

"Speaking of celebrations, Mom. With the loan taken care of and your line of credit available, are you going to be purchasing the software program for the store now?" April's eyes lit up at the thought of the point-of-sale program she'd been campaigning hard for.

"Come January first, getting a new system in place will be my top priority. Well, after finding a tenant for the apartment so I can make the payments on my new loan."

"Wahoo! Finally." April raised her glass of beer in a toast. "You're going to be amazed how much easier a new system will make your life."

I hoped she was right.

Chapter Eighteen

"Morning, Dawna. Ready to tackle the day?" Like usual, Ernie Ford arrived first at Carpenter's Corner for the daily coffee klatch. He was dressed in his usual workday uniform of heavy boots, jeans, blue-and-white striped long-sleeved denim shirt, and a dark gray canvas winter coat.

"Glad to see you braved the storm. The coffee's almost ready."

This morning, I'd woken to heavy snowfall and the wind howling around the eaves of the house like an angry polar bear. The forecast said the storm would ease up by the afternoon, but I imagined it would be a slow morning at the hardware store. Anybody who was able to stay holed up at home was wise to do so.

As Ernie lumbered over to fill his mug, the bell over the door chimed, announcing Bill's arrival.

"Good morning, Santa. Rudolph's nose must have guided you here, but I see you forgot your red outfit today," I teased.

He ran a hand down his tan Carhartt coat. "Thought this one was more appropriate for banging nails."

The door opened a third time, bringing in frigid winter air along with Rick Montgomery, a land surveyor and the third member of the coffee klatch. He stomped snow off his boots on the sidewalk before entering the store, then greeted the rest of us. "Brr. It's colder than a snowman's fart this morning. Glad I've got plenty of office work to keep me busy today." He rubbed his hands together and blew on them to warm them up.

"I hear you. Me and my crew are doing finish work for the next couple of weeks." Bill poured himself a steaming mug of coffee. "It's nice to be inside and out of the elements on days like this."

All three of them scraped back chairs around the table I kept just for them.

"Cold never bothered me when I was a young buck. Nowadays when the wind whistles through the garage, it puts a chill in my bones I can't get rid of." Ernie shook a couple of sugar packets, then ripped off the tops and dumped them into his coffee.

"Yep, same for me. This getting old thing sucks," Rick agreed.

On a number of levels. My sore back protested as I opened the safe, pulled out my cash drawer, and got the register set up for the day while the guys chatted and solved world problems. The ancient overhead heater roared as it worked overtime to keep the chill out of the store. Once I was ready for business, I wandered over, tossed my rice pack in the microwave, and leaned a hip against the coffee counter while I waited for it to heat up.

Ernie pushed his ball cap back and pointed his chin my way. "Evonne tells me you're getting tangled up in this new murder investigation."

"Imagine that." Bill snorted.

The microwave dinged so I opened it and pulled my rice pack out.

"For crying out loud, Dawna. Haven't you learned your lesson?" Rick shook his head.

I pressed the rice pack to my neck and glared at them. "Do you think I should ignore Roxy's pleas for help? Like I did for Kim, Bill, when you were cooling your jets in the city jail?"

Bill mumbled something under his breath, but didn't meet my eye.

"What did you say? I couldn't quite hear you."

He raised his voice to an audible level. "I said I 'spose not. You're pretty good at finding out the truth."

"We just worry about you," Rick added. "And speaking of worrying, what did you do to your neck."

"I know you worry about me, but I'll be careful." I pushed my glasses up. "My neck is fine. I had an adjustment yesterday and am still sore from it."

"I went to the chiropractor once." Rick shivered. "Never again."

Bill shot him a confused look. "I go twice a month. Makes me feel better every time."

"Glad to hear it. I won't be going back anytime soon," I said. "Now enough useless chatter. What can any of you tell me about Sheryl Capri?"

"Only that she was mean as a bag of rattlesnakes." Rick grabbed his coffee cup and started to stand. I waved him down and refilled all of their mugs before starting a second pot of coffee.

"What do you mean by that exactly? Did you have dealings with her?"

Rick nodded. "Marsha Slabinski hired me to locate the property line between their residences a couple of years ago."

"Before the fence was built?"

"Yep. Sheryl screamed and yelled at me to get off her property. Threatened me with a shotgun at one point. I had to bring law enforcement with me so I could complete the job. It was only corner locates and the line, so it should've taken me all of an hour to complete. Instead, the job took two full days because of all the trouble the old hide next door gave me. If Marsha hadn't of been so nice and apologetic about everything, I would've told her to find someone else."

"Good night! Makes me wonder how the fence ever got built."

"Marsha had it built two feet over on her own property. That way she can maintain the fence without having to get permission from Sheryl to go onto her property. It's not uncommon for homeowners to do it that way if they don't get along."

"Interesting. The two of them have been in this big dispute about the fence and Sheryl's yard décor for several years. She had all kinds of cut out wooden pine trees and characters from *The Grinch* nailed onto the fence, yet in reality, the fence belongs to Marsha since she paid for it and it's on her property. No wonder Marsha's been so angry."

"Their war goes back decades before the fence." Ernie leaned his chair back onto two legs, getting ready to tell his story. "If I remember right, I think Sheryl had an affair with Marsha's husband, or vice versa. Anybody else remember the details?" He thunked his chair back onto the floor and looked at the other guys.

"There were rumors going around about nobody knowing for sure which one of their husband's was the father of Sheryl's daughter." Bill tucked his hands under his armpits.

"Holy fright! That's quite the rumor. Why don't I remember hearing about it?" I eyed the guys, wondering what was based on fact, and what was simply pure gossip.

"It all happened about the time you and Bob got married. I'm guessing you don't remember, seeing how you were busy with your own stuff," Ernie said.

"That tracks. My mom and I were so caught up in wedding plans we barely came up for air. My poor dad." I laughed, remembering my dad shaking his head at our endless chatter and planning. I turned my thoughts back to the feuding neighbors. "Have both Marsha and Sheryl only been married once?"

Ernie shook his head. "No. Fairly sure Sheryl's had at least three husbands. All dead now."

"Marsha just the one time, though," Rick said. "Doug Slabinski."

"Right. I remember when he died in that horrific car wreck on the Greenwood Highway during a blizzard. Must've been fifteen years ago now." I shuddered and looked out the window where the snow was still coming down sideways and the wind was howling. The only thing I could see across Main Street was the faint glow of the Christmas star hanging from the light pole. I turned back to the guys. "Remind me again who Sheryl's husbands were, please."

Ernie scratched his jaw. "Let's see. First there was Roger Capri."

"Roger Capri. So she reverted back to using his last name after the other husbands died?"

"Maybe, though I think she kept it all along."

"Sure. Same last name as her daughter. I can understand the logic."

"Roger died a gazillion years ago in an accident up at the mill. He was about thirty," Bill reminded us.

We were all quiet for a moment, remembering the horrible accident.

"I'm trying to think what the next guy's name was." Ernie broke the silence.

"Wasn't it Phil Burke?" Rick asked.

Bill snapped his fingers and pointed at Rick. "Sure was. Phil worked for me and Bob for a few months. The guy was a piece of work. Talented enough builder, but lazy as the day is long. He took any opportunity he could find to do anything except work. Always claimed to not be feeling well. We let him go when it slowed down for the winter. Wasn't a big loss. Wonder whatever happened to him?"

"Dead. Like the rest of them." Ernie splashed a little more coffee into his mug. "Some random illness they could never really pinpoint. Seems like I heard lyme disease, at one point."

I nodded. "I remember now. Likely an autoimmune disease that was never diagnosed. They can be a bear to figure out." I pulled my cell phone out of my apron pocket, opened the notes app, and started a list with the names of Sheryl's unlucky husbands.

"Now I feel bad." Bill frowned. "Maybe the guy really was sick and not just lazy like we thought."

I looked up from my notes. "There's a strong possibility. Which is why I do my best to give people the benefit of the doubt, though it's hard not to judge and jump to conclusions."

"Especially when you're conducting a murder investigation." Rick looked at me with a grin.

"Or running a business," Bill added.

"True enough." I raised a finger in an "aha" gesture. "I remember husband number three better than the others. Jeff Creighton. He was a regular here in the store. Did a lot of work on upgrading their house."

"Jeff was a nice guy," Rick added. "We played on the community basketball team together. I was never sure why he got himself tangled up with the likes of Sheryl."

"He was a logger, right?" Ernie asked.

Rick nodded. "Yep. Met Sheryl somewhere along the line and moved here from Michigan when they got together. His death was a shock to all of us."

"Remind me what happened again?" I asked.

"Jeff was working on the light fixture at the top of the basement stairs. Fell and broke his neck. It was a terrible accident."

"Was it though?"

All six eyes swiveled my way.

"Think about it. Besides Roger dying in an accident at the mill, the other two could easily have been something else entirely." I was starting to think there might be something to Laine's suspicions about her sister.

Chapter Nineteen

When the bell above the door at Carpenter's Corner rang out, the guys all lurched to their feet, scraping their chairs back as if the bell was an alarm reminding them it was time to get to work.

"Luther, hello," I called out to the newcomer.

The tattooed plumber's Iron Horse Plumbing van was parked at the curb. He brushed snow off the shoulder of his black biker's vest and the arms of his long-sleeved T-shirt.

"Fine morning, isn't it?" Luther ran his fingers down his horseshoe mustache.

Bill approached the plumber and held out a hand. "Good to see you, man. I was going to give you a call, but in person is even better. We're ready for you to do the final hookups in both bathrooms in the Widmark house when you can fit it into your schedule."

"Great. I might be able to get there this afternoon. There's a slight emergency over at Bright Whites Laundromat. Shouldn't take me long to deal with, but if it ends up being more involved than I think, I'll get out to the Widmark place tomorrow at the latest."

"Sounds good, old friend. See you soon." Bill clapped him on the shoulder before he left the store with a wave to the rest of us, while Luther headed for the plumbing supplies.

Rick and Ernie finished cleaning up after themselves before leaving. I said my goodbyes, then wandered over to see if I could help Luther find what he was after. He held three valves in the palm of his meaty hand while he dug through another bin of fixtures.

"Which ones are you hunting for?"

"The three-quarter-inch brass fittings. I need six but am only finding three."

Together we sorted through every bin, but came up empty.

"Shoot. Let me check my order. Pretty sure I've got more on the way. The truck should be here later today, if they can make it over Meacham."

Luther gathered up a few other items he needed and brought them to the counter.

I flipped through my order, running my finger down the part numbers. "Aha, here they are. Yep, I've got a dozen on the way."

"Give me a call when they get in, will you? Marsha had a hose crack overnight that I still have to deal with, and a little flooding in the back room. I'm suspicious of a backup in the outside lines, so I may be over there most of the day, though I'm hoping for the best."

"I'll do you one better. April will be here shortly, so when...well, if...the truck gets here, I'll run the valves over to you. It'll be a good chance to stretch my legs."

Luther glanced out the door and looked back at me with a comical expression. "In this weather?"

I shrugged. "Sure. Why not? It looks like it's starting to let up." The wind howled in response, but it didn't faze me. I wasn't about to miss the chance to pop in on Marsha today.

"By the way, I want you to know I don't believe a word of the rumors going around about you Carpenter women." Luther patted the counter twice to make his point.

The blank stare I gave him must've resembled a bewildered dimwit. "I'm sorry, what? What rumors?"

"With the recent spate of murders in town, rumor has it you and April might have more to do with the killings than anybody realizes. They're dubbing them the Carpenter's Corner Murders."

He was referring to two terrible murders back in August, and another this past October. All the perpetrators had been caught and were behind bars.

"Wha...who?" A flicker of heat started in my belly, rapidly rising into my chest and turning my face into a ball of flames. I finally managed to untangle my tongue. "Who is saying this nonsense?"

Luther stuck out his bottom lip and shrugged. "Everyone. The rumor's spreading around town like wildfire." He thrust a thumb over his shoulder, indicating the shop next door. "Pretty sure Darlene Lovelace is heading the posse. I wouldn't worry about it none, though. Most of us don't believe there's any truth to it."

"Most. But some do?" I shoved my glasses up my nose.

"Well, sure, but they're idiots." He strode out the door and left me steaming in my own pudding.

As soon as I was alone in the store, I marched to the hallway and rattled the knob between the hardware store and Lipstick and Lace, ready to give Darlene a piece of my mind. When the door was still locked on her side, I gave it a little kick. Not enough to hurt my toes or damage the door, but enough to let off a little steam. Lucky for her, she wasn't in yet. Or unlucky, depending on whether I cooled off or got angrier before I was able to confront her.

As predicted, it was a slow morning in the store. To take my mind off my mad, I tore down an endcap display of painting supplies and began to fill it with gift ideas under fifty dollars. First, I loaded the bottom shelf with two different size tool-boxes, then added my best-selling cordless drill to the second shelf. Waffle irons and popcorn poppers went on the eye level shelf. Next, I hung screwdriver sets, various pocketknives, and a few of the extra gingerbread house kits on the pegboard above the shelves. I strung a red glittery garland across each shelf and around the top of the display, then added a silly motion-ac-tivated snowman between the waffle irons and popcorn pop-pers. Whenever anyone got close enough, he'd light up and play "Winter Wonderland." If it got irritating after a while, I'd take his batteries out and regulate him to the Island of Misfit Toys.

By the time April showed up, good coffee in hand from Rocking M Coffee Company, it was ten and my first endcap was finished.

"Before you take a sip, you need to know this is not your standby hazelnut."

I arched an eyebrow. Well, probably two since I've never mastered the one eyebrow raise, though I continued to give it my best shot. "Oh? What funky concoction am I about to try?"

April took a sip of her own and closed her eyes in pleasure. "Yum. It's a cardamom orange latte. Sounded too good to pass up."

Skeptical, I scrunched up my nose but took a tentative sip. My taste buds exploded with delight. "Holy buckets, this is pure delight! I'm going to need more of these."

"I told you. Expand your horizons. This is a seasonal flavor, so don't waste December on boring old hazelnut you can get any time." She grinned. "If you don't need me on the floor, I hear a vintage armoire calling my name."

I waved a hand in dismissal. "Sure. I'll call you if I need you, but before you go, let me tell you what I just heard."

"Did you glean any more information about Sheryl's murder?" She set her coffee down and shoved her bag under the counter next to my purse.

"No." I scoffed, before remembering the coffee klatch gossip. "Well, yes, but I'll tell you about it after I'm done with my first story. You'll never guess what Luther told me." I took a long sip of coffee to fortify myself before getting mad all over again.

"Don't keep me in suspense. What did he say?"

I pointed a forceful finger toward Lipstick and Lace. "He said Darlene is running around town shooting off her mouth about the two of us."

"By the two of us, you mean you and me?"

"Yep. She's trying to make people believe we had something to do with all these recent murders. She's calling them the Carpenter's Corner Murders."

April hee-hawed. "Sounds like a true crime episode," she said once she caught her breath.

I crossed my arms and frowned at my daughter. "I'm glad you're finding it amusing."

"Oh, come on, Mom. Nobody's going to believe her. The police have signed confessions from the murderers."

I shook my head. "You'd be surprised what people believe. Remember when Rick and Trisha got married and blended their families? Rick's youngest son and Trisha's oldest daughter were the same age. Suddenly people who had known both those kids their entire lives were asking if they were twins."

Aprils shook her head. "What a bunch of idiots."

"Which underscores my argument."

"Have you confronted Darlene yet? You were going to tell her about paying off the loan anyway."

I walked over and opened the front door, peering through the falling snow at the boutique next door. I shut the door and shook snowflakes out of my hair. "Lipstick and Lace is still closed. Miss Priss must be too dainty to get her feet wet."

April laughed again. "Well, if she shows up, or you need me up here, you know where to find me." She disappeared behind the swinging doors of the warehouse.

While she went to town with a sander on the armoire she was working on, I used the down time to continue rearranging displays and restocking shelves. I moved a display of snow shovels, ice scrapers, and pet safe ice melt crystals up front, placing it directly across from the checkout counter. A few hardy souls ventured in from time to time in search of various supplies. Every customer left with not only what they came in for, but also with an extra flashlight or two and a couple of packages of batteries, in case the power went out. Each time I glanced out the front window, the storm seemed to have eased up a little more.

As the morning wore on, my neck, shoulders, and back loosened up so much I was feeling like my old self when noontime rolled around. Over a lunch of heated up cans of chicken noodle soup and saltine crackers, I parroted the coffee klatch guy's gossip to my daughter.

"When I get a chance, I'll see if I can dig up anything more about each of Sheryl's husbands." April washed our soup bowls in the small sink next to the coffee pot.

"Good idea. So far, I feel like I'm spinning my wheels."

We both went back to work. By two in the afternoon, the wind had died down, the snow had stopped falling, and the sun was attempting to peek out from behind the heavy clouds. I kept peeking out the door, but the neighboring shop remained firmly locked up. Much to my surprise, the supply truck showed up only half an hour later than usual. I checked the order in against my original order sheet, then signed off on the invoice.

"Can I fill your thermos with coffee before you head out?"

"Gosh no. I've had your coffee. That stuff could strip paint off the walls." Dan, the truck driver, made a choking noise, then laughed heartily at his own joke.

I chuckled along with him. "Can't say I blame you. I don't drink the stuff myself. See you next week."

I tore into the box of washing machine valves and yelled for April. "Can you watch the front? I need to make a quick delivery."

Chapter Twenty

The city snowplow was already clearing Main Street as I hurried down the sidewalk. Several shop owners were out shoveling the walks in front of their stores. I made a mental note to clear my own once I got back to the hardware store. I greeted each person I came across with a hearty hello. Most returned my greetings, but I noticed a couple of people wouldn't make eye contact and stepped back to avoid me as I passed.

That darn Darlene. I'd always prided myself on having good relationships with the other downtown merchants, and the townspeople in general. *If she manages to ruin my reputation, I'm going to kill her.* Whoopsie. I glanced around, grateful nobody could read my thoughts. If they were buying into this whole Carpenter's Corner Murders thing now, they'd have a field day with that one.

Bright Whites Laundromat was two blocks up Main Street and half a block up Walnut from my hardware store. I made it there in less than ten minutes. Luther's van was still parked in front of the laundromat, but I didn't see either him or Marsha when I pushed through the door. Not a single holiday decoration livened up the place. A pregnant woman stood at one of the long well-worn tables, folding clothes from a wheeled laundry cart. An exhausted looking woman about my own age, wearing bulky knock-off brand suede snow boots, flowered leggings, and a lavender shirt under an open coat, sagged in an orange plastic chair next to a sloshing washing machine. An educated guess told me the two toddlers running wild, their squeals bouncing off the high ceilings and echoing against the concrete walls, belonged to the young mom folding clothes.

I walked through the laundromat to a narrow hallway where the restrooms and Marsha's office were located. A wooden door with a window taking up the top half stood slightly ajar. Through the clear glass, I had an unobstructed view of Marsha sitting at her old gray metal desk with the receiver of a landline telephone pressed to her ear. Her chair was swiveled so she faced the white painted cinder block wall. The top of her desk was cluttered with paperwork in three different piles next to a bulky desktop computer. A half-eaten peanut butter and grape jelly sandwich on white bread sat abandoned on top of a clear sandwich baggie. I thought about tapping on the door to announce my presence, but decided to wait until she finished her phone call, since I wasn't in a big rush to get back to the store. I leaned against the wall and patiently waited my turn.

"I wouldn't be surprised one bit. Sheryl never was one to use her own money." Marsha's voice floated out of the office.

Wish I knew who she was talking to. I scooted closer to the door frame, flattening myself against the wall, and strained my ears to try to hear better.

"You're right. Unless she finds a way to reach out of the grave, her days of using and discarding everyone she runs across are over. Though she might give the devil a run for his money. You finally got your revenge."

I covered my mouth to stifle the gasp. Now I really needed to find out who was on the other end of that phone call.

"I know it wasn't exactly how you wanted her to get her comeuppance, but I suggest you leave this whole nasty business in your rearview mirror now. Your new restaurant is going to be a triumph."

Good night! Could she be talking to Clay Hopkins? Whoever it was on the other end of the line, she'd just implicated them in Sheryl's murder. Was Marsha an accomplice? The theory I had that it took two people to wrangle Sheryl's body into the chimney was gaining traction, and Clay was the only one on my radar with ties to a new restaurant. What could the connection between Marsha and Clay possibly be?

"Dawna. There you are," a voice boomed in my ear. "You got those parts for me?"

My stomach tied itself into a knot as I jerked around to face Luther. The distinctive thunk of a phone receiver being slammed into its cradle echoed out of Marsha's office seconds before the woman herself stood in the doorway.

"Dawna? What are you doing here?" Marsha narrowed her pale eyes at me, her face devoid of any makeup. The gray striped sweater she wrapped tightly around herself reminded me of an old-school prison uniform. I wouldn't have been surprised to see block numbers written on the back. The drab color of her clothing washed out her complexion, causing her to appear sallow and sickly. Her posture, a hunched back and narrowed shoulders, didn't help. I straightened my own spine and vowed to rid my closet of any dull, washed-out clothing.

I held up the paper bag with my store's logo splashed on the front. "Making a delivery for parts Luther needed."

The plumber took the bag out of my hands. "Thanks. I appreciate you bringing them over. You were right. The storm let up just in time."

Marsha crossed her arms as if hugging herself. "Glad to hear Sheryl wasn't the only one to get special treatment from Carpenter's Corner." She huffed, then looked at Luther. "Are you making any headway?"

"We're nearly done replacing the damaged piece of pipe out back. Would've been a whole lot faster if the ground wasn't frozen solid. We'll finish up there shortly and I'll get these valves replaced before the end of the day."

"Today's going to cost me an arm and a leg," Marsha groused.

Luther clicked his tongue. "Just the cost of doing business." He headed out the back door to presumably finish the work outside.

When I didn't make a move to leave, Marsha finally invited me into her office. "Did you need something from me? Do I need to pay for those parts you delivered?"

I didn't waste any time sliding into the extra chair by her desk. "No, I've added them to Luther's account. I'm sure he'll invoice you for whatever he needs."

Marsha chuckled humorously. "No doubt about it."

"I thought it might be a nice time to catch up. See how you're doing." I thought fast. "It's no secret you and Sheryl were mortal enemies, but I also know you used to be best friends, once upon a time. Her death still had to have come as a shock to you." I gambled there must be some truth to the gossip that the two had once been close friends.

Marsha waved away my concern, but I noticed tears sprang to her eyes, nevertheless. "My friendship with that woman ended a thousand years ago. Not that I wished her dead," she added hastily. "Maybe I did at one time, but these days I just wanted to see her suffer for all the harm she caused."

Which explained the ankle monitor. Marsha seemed willing to talk, so I asked another one of the questions burning a hole in my mind. "What happened between the two of you, anyway? How did you go from best friends joined at the hip to hating each other with such passion?"

"It's a long story." Marsha heaved a sigh and leaned back in her rickety office chair, her thoughts a million miles away. "Even as kids, Sheryl was always coming up with a plan to get things the easy way. It was how she was raised. Her philosophy was, *why buy a soda if you could steal it?* Not me. I was raised on hard work and downhome values. While Sheryl's parents took every handout they could get, my family did without if we couldn't earn it ourselves. But she was my best friend and I loved her dearly, so I would turn a blind eye to her shenanigans. I always thought if I stayed on the straight and narrow, my values would somehow rub off on her. We were tight, as close as friends could be all through school. We even ended up dating boys from Greenwood who were best friends themselves."

"Doug and Roger?" I asked.

Marsha tore her gaze away from the ceiling and straightened in her chair to face me. "Yep. We met them at the skating rink when we were sixteen and the boys were seventeen. It wasn't long before Sheryl and I were making plans to rope those two into marriage."

"The plan worked out for you."

"Better than I could have ever dreamed. We had a double wedding the weekend after Sheryl and I graduated from high school. Doug and Roger both went to work at the mill, and not two years later we bought houses next door to each other and planned to raise our families together." She paused and stared at the floor with a faraway look on her face. After a moment, she picked the thread of her story back up. "A couple of years passed before Sheryl got pregnant and our carefully laid plans started to fall apart. As soon as she found out she was pregnant, she started hounding me every day to follow suit."

"But you didn't?" I prompted when Marsha fell silent.

She shook her head. "Not for lack of trying, mind you. It just wasn't in the cards for Doug and me. We were heartbroken over our lack of fertility, but what can you do?" Marsha lifted her hands in a shrug and let them fall back to the desktop. "While Sheryl's belly grew, Doug and I bought this building and started Bright Whites. She was furious I'd focused my attention elsewhere, and accused me of abandoning our plans. She didn't have any empathy for my suffering, but I smoothed over her anger and promised to be the best auntie I could be to her little boy."

"His name was Tony, right?" I did some quick math in my head. "He must've been five years or so older than Jazelle, if I'm remembering right. I'd nearly forgotten Sheryl had another child."

"She sure did." Marsha dug a tissue out of the front pocket of her pants and dabbed at her wet eyes. "Little Tony was such a doll. The second I laid eyes on the little guy, I fell madly in love. I wanted to be part of his life, so I tamped down my hurt feelings with his mother and embraced the aunt life. Losing him was the biggest heartbreak of my life."

Tears sprang to my own eyes. "What happened? I didn't realize Tony had passed."

Marsha jerked her head back. "Passed? No, Tony isn't dead."

I adjusted my glasses. "Oh, my mistake. I thought when you said you lost him..." I let my words trail off.

"No, he's alive and well, thank goodness, though the boy quit school at sixteen and got as far away from his toxic mother as he could. I meant Doug and I lost our relationship with Tony when Sheryl and I had our big breakup. Unfortunately, Roger wasn't strong enough to stand up to her either, so we were no longer allowed to be in Tony's life. After a while, the little guy didn't even remember us as anything more than the neighbors his mother was always feuding with."

"What did happen between you and Sheryl that caused the big split? There had to be more to the story than you not being able to get pregnant." While the backstory was interesting, I was anxious to get to the heart of the matter.

"Much more." Marsha nodded. "Doug was still working at the mill, and we had the laundromat up and running. Sheryl was a stay-at-home mom to little Tony, who turned a year old that summer—1979—and Roger was also still at the mill. Sheryl made all kinds of snide comments about how Doug and I were rolling in the dough since we had two incomes and no kids. While we were doing okay for ourselves, we weren't getting rich by any stretch of the imagination."

"But that's not how she saw it," I guessed.

"Not in the slightest." Marsha shook her head. "Doug always thought Sheryl was jealous she was tied down with a baby and I wasn't. I helped her out as much as I could, even bringing Tony to work with me every so often. But nothing was ever enough for Sheryl. We bought a new car, so she wanted two new cars." She sighed. "Anyway, I'm still not sure when it happened, but sometime that summer, Sheryl started buying nicer clothes and going on shopping sprees in Portland. Turns out, she'd used my driver's license and social security number to open at least four different credit cards in my name."

"She stole your identity?" I gaped at Marsha, stunned.

"Yep. She racked up several thousand dollars' worth of debt using my name. Doug and I spent years clawing out from under the mess she created. It was on me to try to prove my own identity with the IRS and debt collectors. All these years later, strange accounts still show up on credit reports from time to time."

My heart ached for Marsha at the thought of her best friend doing such a terrible thing to her. "I'm so sorry that happened to you. I can't even imagine how it must've torn you up."

Marsha's lower lip quivered as she swiped a lone tear from her cheek. "It felt like my heart had been ripped out of my chest, to be honest. The worst part was, had she ever even once said she was sorry or acted remorseful, I would have forgiven her in a heartbeat. But no, those words weren't part of Sheryl's vocabulary. Instead she acted like I was to blame. She kept saying I was worked up over nothing and how it wasn't a big deal. She wouldn't have had to use my identity to try to keep up with us if Doug and I hadn't been out there flaunting our wealth all the time. When I got upset, she told me I was crazy and that was why I didn't have any friends except for her. Said if I cut her out of my life I would never have friends again. And she was right."

"What? No she wasn't. She was gaslighting you."

"I know that now." Marsha nodded. "But she was right when she said I would never have friends again. Since her betrayal, I've never trusted people enough to let them in, so, like I said, she hit the nail on the head."

A ball of sadness welled up in my chest. I stood and rounded the desk, giving Marsha a one-armed awkward hug since I wasn't much of a hugger myself. "I want you to know, there are people in this town who care about you. You're one of us." Even though she did the bare minimum within the group, Marsha had been a member of the Women's Service Club for at least as long as I had. I thought back to the funeral for Doug Slabinski all those years ago. The church had been packed to the gills. "You have more friends than you think you do."

Ever stoic, Marsha took a deep breath and shrugged. "Sure, there's folks I can count on in a pinch, and that's all that matters. Sheryl was the only true friend I ever had, and our friendship turned out to be a web of lies. The woman used me up and never looked back."

I nodded. "When I first got here, I heard you say Sheryl never was one to use her own money. Put into context, your comment makes sense." As soon as the words were out of my mouth, I wanted to kick myself for revealing I'd been eavesdropping. Maybe she wouldn't notice.

Marsha cleared her throat and stared at me. "How long had you been standing outside my office? What else did you hear?" Her demeanor flipped from melancholy sadness to frosty rigidness in the blink of an eye.

Me and my big mouth. I shook my head. "Nothing, really. I'd just walked up and was waiting for you to finish your call. I didn't mean to listen to your conversation."

She frowned. "Well, whatever you think you heard, you are wrong. I wasn't talking about Sheryl."

I beg to differ, since I clearly heard you say her name. Before I could formulate an answer, Luther stuck his head into the office.

"Marsha? Can you come outside and look at something? I need your opinion. It'll only take a minute."

She reached for her coat and gestured for me to exit the office ahead of her. I said a quick goodbye and headed into the main room of the laundromat.

The mom and toddlers were gone, and the woman in the flowered leggings was transferring her wet clothes from a washing machine to a dryer. I turned and watched Luther and Marsha walk out the back door. When the metal door closed behind them with a click, I quickly tiptoed back into her office. There was one more thing I wanted to verify.

Lifting the receiver of the landline phone, I pressed the redial button. Two rings and a man's voice answered.

"Thanks for calling The Nutty Goose. This is Clay speaking. What can I do for you?"

Chapter Twenty-One

"You're sure it was Clay Hopkins on the phone?" April whispered so the customers in the Carpenter's Corner wouldn't overhear.

"Positive. I talked to him only yesterday. He's got a deep gravelly voice that would be hard to mistake. Besides, The Nutty Goose is Clay's establishment, and it was the last phone call on Marsha's redial." I kept my own voice low.

After leaving Bright Whites Laundromat, I'd hightailed it back to the hardware store and filled April in on how the war between the two former best friends had started. My story ended with the one-sided phone conversation I'd serendipitously been privy to.

"Maybe she called to find out the restaurant hours, or something else equally as innocent. Just because the last call Marsha made was to The Nutty Goose doesn't mean Clay was the person she was talking to when you were eavesdropping. Someone could've called the laundromat and their call wouldn't come up on the redial." April sat at my desk behind the checkout counter, her laptop open in front of her.

"True, but she clearly mentioned a new restaurant, and The Nutty Goose has only been open a couple of weeks." I turned to face a customer who was approaching the counter. "Did you find everything you need?"

The man placed a shower head with a bronze finish and a package of matching screws on the counter. "All set. For now, anyway. I always think I have everything I need but end up coming back a half a dozen times for one little project."

I laughed. "Isn't that the truth? If it makes you feel better, you're not alone."

Once the transaction was completed and the customer left, I turned back to April. She was hunched over her laptop, focused on something on the screen.

"What're you finding so interesting there?"

She waved me over and pointed at the article she was reading. "Did you know wills are public record in Oregon?"

I gave a half-shrug. "I haven't given it a lot of thought. It makes sense, though, since they are recorded at the courthouse after the person passes away. I do know that much. Why? Who's will are you looking at?" I pushed my glasses up and peered closer at the screen.

"Jeff Creighton, Sheryl's third husband." April scribbled some notes on a notebook page. "After what you told me about what Ernie, Bill, and Rick had to say this morning, I decided to spend the time you were gone seeing what I could find out about her late husbands. No luck finding anything on Phil, her second husband, but Jeff was a different story."

When April started to say more, I held up my hand. "Hold that thought, somebody is coming in. Oh, and thanks for shoveling the sidewalk while I was gone."

"No problem," April answered.

A customer who had called this morning had pulled up to the curb. "Hey there, Debbie. The wood pellets you ordered are ready and waiting for you. Did you need anything else before I help you load them up?"

"What do you have for propane heaters? Seth and I want to be prepared if the power goes out this time. Last winter we waited too long." She let out a self-deprecating chuckle. "Honestly, we're not doing much better this year. Glad this morning's storm passed without too much fanfare."

"No kidding. But you're in luck. We have a good selection still in stock." I led the way to the space heaters and showed her the propane options.

Debbie studied them for a minute, then glanced at me with a grimace. "Is there one you recommend over the others? I have no idea what I'm looking at here."

"It sounds like you're wanting something to use indoors in a pinch. Is that right?" When she nodded, I pointed to one of the heaters. "I recommend this guy over any of the others. It's rated safe for short-term indoor use, is lightweight, and you can't beat the price point. I have a couple of them myself."

"Sold!" Debbie pulled the model off the shelf. "Do you have any of your gingerbread house kits left?"

"I sure do. How many would you like?"

"Two, please. One each for my niece and nephew. My sister wasn't able to bring the kids in on Saturday, so I thought we could build them together during winter break. It'll be a fun project."

"That's exactly why we made extra kits." I grabbed two off the display, then rang up her transaction before hauling the cart, weighed down with a dozen bags of heater pellets, out the front door. Together, Debbie and I loaded the heavy bags into the back of her SUV. I waved and thanked her for her business as she pulled away from the curb.

"Back to where we were going." I walked over to the desk where April was still scrolling through documents on her laptop. "What did you find?"

She studied her notes. "Jeff was Sheryl's latest husband, but he's been gone a long time. He died in 2001. I found his will, his obituary, and an article from the newspaper about his death. Like the guys said, he fell off a ladder he apparently was trying to balance on the basement stairs to change a light fixture. He was only forty-four when he died."

I nodded, remembering back. "That sounds about right."

"Why would someone do that?"

"Do what? Die at forty-four?"

"Balance a ladder on stairs. It's completely idiotic. Makes him sound like a candidate for the Darwin awards."

"Good question. Jeff wasn't a dummy, but you know men. They think they're invincible." Needing an afternoon energy boost, I grabbed a Baby Ruth off the candy bar display next to the cash register and held it up. "Want one?"

"A peanut butter cup, please." April caught the candy bar I tossed her way, tearing into the crackling packaging. "According to his will, Jeff left his estate to Sheryl, except a thousand dollars he left to each one of his kids."

"His kids? I guess I never knew he had kids of his own. A thousand dollars each sounds reasonable. I don't recall what he did for a living, but they weren't a wealthy couple. You kids probably won't get much more than that when I kick the bucket, if you get anything."

"Except it looks like his estate was fairly extensive." April took a bite of her candy bar.

I frowned. "How extensive?"

"The will lists several properties he owned in Battle Creek, Michigan, one in Greenwood, a handful of stocks and bonds, along with three different savings accounts."

"No kidding? Does it list any dollar amounts?"

April shook her head. "No. It looks like the will was written up about five years before Jeff died. Not long after he and Sheryl got married. The value of things change so often, it wouldn't make sense to include a dollar amount."

"What about property addresses? Are they listed?"

"Good idea. And yes, they sure are."

April opened another tab on the computer. As I hovered over her shoulder, she typed the first address from Battle Creek, Michigan into the search bar.

I leaned in to get a better look. "Is that a house? It's huge."

"No, it's an apartment complex. And a nice one by the looks of it. Says here there's one hundred and twenty-five units. This property alone must be worth over a million dollars."

"Easily," I agreed.

The next search brought up a strip mall housing a craft store, a gym, a hair salon, a brew pub, and a coffee shop—all big chain stores.

I whistled. "This one has to be worth a pretty penny, too."

The third and last property in Battle Creek turned out to be a family home.

"That's a cute home," I said. "Modest. I really like craftsman cottages. Looks like it has elbow room."

"Modest, yes, but it sits on an acre right on the lake with its own dock. Look here." April pointed to the screen. "In today's market, its worth over half a million."

I crossed my arms and shook my head. "Crazy to think all of these properties were left to Sheryl. No wonder she had enough funds to purchase all the chainsaw art and decorations in her yard. She spent several hundred dollars a week with us the last couple of months, since she'd been going whole hog on her Christmas décor, and she certainly didn't get even a fraction of what she had on that house from me."

While I was contemplating Sheryl's cash flow, April did a search for the address in Greenwood. She grunted when it came up.

"What is it?" I turned my attention back to her computer screen.

"Those big storage units on the left-hand side as you're going into town."

"Holy cow. There has to be about three hundred units in there. They must provide a pretty decent income stream by themselves." I tapped my foot. "I wonder if Sheryl still owned any of these properties? And who is her heir? According to Marsha, Sheryl and her son Tony were estranged, so I wonder if Jazelle was her sole heir?"

"Even inheriting half of her estate would be a significant bump to a person's portfolio." April tapped a finger against her chin.

"We need to determine whether or not Sheryl still owned those properties."

"There's only one way to find out." April grinned.

"Pull up the county records?"

Her shoulders sagged at my suggestion. "Okay, two ways to find out." She glanced at the clock. "Too bad the county offices in Michigan are closed until tomorrow morning, and there's only a few minutes before ours closes. I don't think I can wait until tomorrow to find out. Don't you think a little fact-finding mission is in order?"

My mouth dropped open. "April Marie Carpenter! Are you suggesting what I think you are?"

She had the good sense to blush. "What's a good investigation without getting our hands a little dirty?"

I huffed. "Well, Evonne roped me into being in the play, so I have the gosh darn stinking choir practice tonight."

"Perfect. We'll go when you get done. With it being dark out, there'll be less chance of being seen by Shilo's prying eyes anyway." April's green eyes twinkled.

Chapter Twenty–Two

Katherine Johnson slapped a five-dollar bill onto the palm of Evonne's outstretched hand. "You win."

"What was the bet?" I asked as I approached them, plopping my purse down into an empty red velvet folding seat in the auditorium of the Emery Theater.

"Katherine didn't think you'd actually show up for practice tonight." Evonne smiled smugly while cleaning her glasses with her shirttail. "Clearly, she didn't know the power of a lifelong friendship."

"Clearly, she didn't know the power of a lifelong *guilt* trip." I tried to squeeze as much sarcasm as I could into those few words.

Katherine's laugh tinkled. "I wagered Evonne wouldn't be able to convince you to join the Whoville choir, but here you are, not even kicking and screaming." She opened her arms for a hug and came at me with the full force of her beaming smile.

Ugh. Here we go. Suck it up, Buttercup. Huggers never quite get us non-huggers. Over the years, I'd mastered getting in and getting back out of a hug in a split second, whilst patting the offender's back without flinching or letting on how I find the

189

whole routine distasteful. Katherine was another story. Her hugs were like a never-ending vise grip. While trying to breathe in her death clutches, I tapped out my obligatory three back pats, then suffered in silence until she finally released me. I'm pretty sure several hours passed. The second she turned her hugs onto the next arrival, I allowed myself a full body shake to reinflate my personal bubble.

Evonne smirked at me with one perfectly raised eyebrow. "You okay, there Miss Don't Touch Me?"

"Barely." I sighed. "Let's get on with the show."

"Not our turn yet."

Katherine must have finished hugging the entire crew to death, because she bounded up onto the stage and clapped her hands to get everyone's attention. Most of the actors waiting for instruction were kids, but there were a few adults scattered in. "Listen up, everyone. It's time to knuckle down and get our lines and steps perfected for opening night. All cast members with parts in Act One, quietly make your way to the stage and take your positions. I'll need my narrators in place downstage. Everyone else, remain seated and kindly give the actors your full attention."

Four kids—two girls and two boys—stood near the edge of the stage, evenly spaced apart. A few minutes passed while they all took their places, then Katherine called for silence. She pointed to the kid on the far left, who started reciting the beginning of the poem of the "The Grinch Who Stole Christmas." The next kid in line would take up the story at the beginning of each verse. Katherine had chosen the narrators well. All four kids had sweet lilting voices, but spoke up well and projected their lines into the audience. From where I sat, they were easy to hear and understand.

As play practice progressed, I looked around at the other people in the audience, either waiting our turns or watching their kids. I smiled and waved like the Queen of England, knowing nearly everyone in the audience.

"How long until we're up?" I whispered to Evonne.

She shrugged. "Beats me. Not until the end, I think. But the play is only about half an hour long."

"Not at this rate."

Katherine was doing her job well, stopping the action every little bit to give instructions on movement and articulation.

"I'll be right back." Staying hunched over in an attempt to be as undistracting as possible, I trotted up the aisle three rows and slid into an empty seat next to Oscar the mailman. "Hey there. Are your little ones in the play?"

He chin-pointed toward the stage. "Leif. My boy. Emma's not quite old enough yet."

"I suppose not. What part is Leif playing?"

"Max, the Grinch's dog." Oscar grinned, flashing a mouthful of straight white teeth. "He's super excited about it."

"And you couldn't be more proud."

"I'm so proud I might explode." He leaned forward and shushed me. "There he is now."

The little towheaded boy clambered onto the stage from the wings. He was on all fours and played the part of Max to perfection.

When Leif's scene was over, Oscar turned to face me. "How are you holding up with all the ridiculous rumors floating around town about you?"

"Are you talking about the so-called Carpenter's Corner Murders?"

He nodded.

"When I get my hands on Darlene, I'm going to wring her neck. You can count on that." I was half an inch from giving her boutique the boot, but had to consider my options before I flew off the handle. Winter might not be the best time to get another tenant in the building, and with my signature not even dry on my new loan, the last thing I wanted to do was shoot myself in the foot.

Oscar leaned sideways and nudged me with his shoulder. "Nobody believes the gossip, you know."

"I think several people might." Remembering a few icy looks I'd received this afternoon while walking to the laundromat, I wasn't nearly as confident as he sounded. "Speaking of...." I hesitated.

He raised blond eyebrows in a question. "Speaking of what? I've also heard you're trying to get Roxy off the hook, so don't be shy. Ask me what you want to know. I'll help if I can."

This town. I loved it dearly, but a person couldn't sneeze without making the six o'clock news. If we had a news station, of course. Our only news outlet was the gossip mill, and it was running overtime.

"Thanks, I appreciate it. With you out there walking those streets every day of the week…"

"And some Saturdays," Oscar added.

I nodded. "And some Saturdays. You must have a better handle than most on what was going on in Sheryl's neighborhood."

Oscar kept his eyes focused on the stage. "There's no way to do the job and not pick up on things, though I try to keep my head down and mind my own business as much as possible."

"You do see all the mail people get. Its got to be enlightening at times."

"Sure, I see their mail, but usually just in a vague way. There's a lot of mail to be delivered each day so I glance through to make sure I'm putting the items in the correct mailbox, but rarely notice who the sender is. I'm focused on the delivery address."

"There has to be a few exceptions though. Times when something stands out."

"Of course."

"People! Quiet out there." I glanced up to see Katherine standing on the stage, a hand shielding her eyes from the bright lights as she squinted into the audience. Satisfied her demand would be met, she turned back to the cast, her long skirt twirling around her legs.

Act One slid seamlessly into Act Two. Roxy's daughter, Makayla, took the stage as Cindy Lou Who's mother.

I lowered my voice to a whisper. "From what you've witnessed, who do you think might have killed Sheryl?"

"Good question." Oscar clicked his tongue. "The most obvious choice would be Marsha, given the bad blood between her and Sheryl."

I agreed. "Any juicy tidbits you can share about Marsha? I'm trying to build a better picture of all the suspects."

Oscar shot me a side-eye. "Not super juicy, but Marsha isn't nearly as frugal as she puts on."

"Oh, yeah? What do you mean?"

"Let's just say I carry a lot, and I do mean a lot, of packages to her address from a company specializing in 70s disco music and original posters."

I grinned, picturing stoic Marsha letting her hair down and getting her groove on behind the buttoned-up façade of her house. "Interesting, but I don't see how a love of disco relates to the case. As far as the murder goes, Chief Dallas doesn't think Marsha has the strength to pull it off on her own. She would have needed some help." I looked straight at Oscar to assess his reaction.

He didn't so much as flinch. "Sure, makes sense. Though Marsha did have a lot of simmering anger toward Sheryl, which could fuel an adrenalin rush. You'd be surprised what people can do when they're determined enough."

"I said the exact same thing. Anybody else you would consider?"

"Sheryl's daughter absolutely despised her."

"Jazelle? From what I've been told, the two of them were incredibly close, and Jazelle is torn up about Sheryl's death. Why would you think she hated her mother?" Of course, Darlene was my source of knowledge about the relationship between the Capri women. Not the most reliable contact.

"Like I said, sometimes it's hard to not notice things. Like the knockdown, drag-out fights coming from behind the doors of the Capri house, for example. Those two women screamed at each other like fishwives." Oscar leaned close and whispered in my ear. "You didn't hear it from me, but until recently, Sheryl was using Jazelle's social security number to work at the 7-Eleven in Greenwood."

I gasped and quickly covered my mouth so I wouldn't get another scolding from Katherine. "No way. Why in the world would she use her daughter's information?"

"Yes way. It was her way of bucking the system. She used Jazelle's information in order to continue to collect both her disability payments and a paycheck. It was fraud, pure and simple."

I stared at him, mouth hanging open like a cave. If Sheryl had all the assets from Jeff's death, why did she need to work? Her home was modest, and those properties should have provided a nice income. Even if she had sold them shortly after he died, she would've had a nice nest egg. Sure, they wouldn't have been worth what they were in current prices, but still, unless she was a complete spendthrift she shouldn't have been broke enough to have to work at a convenience store.

"Whoville Choir, please make your way to the stage," Katherine called out.

"Well, I'm up." I rose from my seat. "Oh, one more thing before I go. I understand that outside of your normal route the morning she died, you had words with Sheryl yourself. Rumor has it you gave her something in a manila envelope. What was it, if you don't mind telling me?"

Oscar blinked hard as a telltale blush crept into his face. "Sheryl and I have never had an argument, and anything I delivered to her was most definitely part of the mail service. Sometimes on heavy mail days, I end up making two trips around a block. One for packages, and one for small mail. Your informant was mistaken." He gave me a tight smile, unlike his normal big grin.

Seemed to me a manila envelope would be considered small mail, and not be delivered in the package circuit. There was something Oscar wasn't being totally truthful about.

Oscar glanced at me again. "Remember how I told you I didn't believe the rumors flying around about you? Thanks for giving me the same courtesy." He glared and faced forward.

My stomach clenched. "Oscar, I'm sorry." I wanted to say more, but I was holding up practice. *Way to alienate half the town, Dawna.*

"Hurry up." Evonne beckoned to me from in front of the stage. "They're waiting for us."

With a quick glance at Oscar, who continued to ignore me, I followed my best friend onto the stage. Katherine instructed each of us on where to stand, then queued up the music for

"Welcome Christmas." As the rest of the Whos from Whoville sang, I did my best to lip-sync along with them.

After two rounds of the song, Katherine flung her hands up in joy. "Fantastic. Let's run through it one more time, this time adding movement. Spread out across the stage, join hands, and sway back and forth as you sing." Katherine reached for two Who children and demonstrated what she wanted us to do.

I found myself between Evonne and Makayla, who pulled me in the proper direction when my body wanted to sway to the left when I should have been swaying to the right. They were my saving grace. We made it through two more rounds before Katherine declared the choir a success and ended practice for the evening.

"Same time, same place, Thursday night," she said.

Makayla squeezed my hand. "You weren't singing, Mrs. Carpenter. Don't worry. You'll do better next time."

I squeezed her hand back. "Thank you, honey. I'll give it my best try."

Folks were still milling around chatting, and parents who arrived to pick up their kids joined in the hubbub.

"What are you doing here?"

I turned to find Darlene, arms crossed and nose wrinkled, addressing me. I wanted to slap the snark off her face, but this wasn't the time. Instead, I tapped my chest. "I'm part of the Whoville choir. What are *you* doing here?"

"Picking up my friend's daughter, if you must know. The last thing I wanted to do was venture out in the snow, but she was in a bind, and I'm a good friend."

"You're so brave." I let the sarcasm shine in my voice. It had stopped snowing several hours ago and the city had done a nice job of plowing the streets. I started to walk away, but thought better of turning my back on her. "Nice rumors you've been spreading around town about me, by the way. Fortunately, I have good friends who have given me a heads up."

"Well...I...," she started to stammer.

"Well, I, nothing." I bobbled my head like a mad chicken. "You'll also be happy to know my building is no longer in foreclosure proceedings. I paid the bank in full yesterday. If I was you, I'd start looking for another place to hang your shingle."

Darlene's face turned red as she gaped at me, speechless for once in her life. I clenched my fists as I walked away. *Argh*. I hadn't meant to say anything about kicking her out of her retail space, but the woman got under my skin and I'd lost control of my mouth. Again. I caught a glimpse of Roxy coming down the aisle to pick up Makayla. While I wanted to find out how her father-in-law was doing, I needed to calm down first.

I nudged Evonne. "I'm going to hit the restroom real quick."

"Gotchya." She turned back to the woman she was talking with, and I slipped through an empty row of seats and up the side aisle.

As I took the last stall near the far wall, the main door of the restroom clunked shut behind me. I took care of business quickly, but sat there for a full minute with my eyes shut, trying to gain back some of the composure I'd lost. Once I got myself under control, I stepped out of the stall and washed my hands. I fluffed my hair in the mirror and swiped a finger under my eyes where my mascara had smudged, making me look like a racoon.

When I grabbed the door handle and pulled, all I ended up doing was smashing into it. Since I had expected the door to open like normal, I had already been in motion when I yanked on the handle. What in the world? I yanked again, certain the door had simply stuck and would open as it should on my next attempt. Nope. It was stuck good and tight. I pulled, yelled for help, and kicked the door. I was frustrated and about to burst into mad tears when the door opened from the outside and Evonne stuck her head in.

"There you are. I was getting worried. How did you manage to get locked in the bathroom?"

"Beats me. The door wouldn't open."

Evonne held up a broom. "That's because this was wedged into the handle."

I gawked at both my friend and the broom. "Are you kidding me?"

She shook her head. "Wish I was. Who did you make mad tonight?"

"Darlene, for sure. I don't suspect her of murder, but I wouldn't put it past her to lock me in here for the sheer meanness of it." I scowled.

"Whatever you said, I'm sure the girl deserved it." Evonne laughed. "How about Oscar? Were you interrogating him, too?"

I hitched my shoulder nonchalantly. "Maybe. He was fairly forthcoming, but he definitely held something back he didn't want to tell me. And he made me feel like a heel for questioning him." I didn't mention another one of the murder suspects had been in the theater when I'd gone to the restroom. Roxy.

"Well, whoever it was, they were trying to scare you." Evonne linked her arm through mine.

"It's going to take more than a few minutes in an old bathroom to deter me."

"They don't seem to know you very well."

Chapter Twenty-Three

By the time I got home at a little after seven, April had invaded my kitchen. Before I even opened the door, the tantalizing scent of red sauce and garlic washed over me. My stomach rumbled, but in order to earn my dinner I had to get through Thor first. The big dog blocked my entry, his tail slapping against the side of the cabinet. Lilac perched on top of the refrigerator, out of the dog's reach. She shot me a disdainful look before hissing and fading from view.

"Move it, friend. You need to let me come in and put my stuff down before I can give you proper pets." A good five minutes passed before the dog was satisfied and I could sit down at the table with a bowl of the delicious goulash April had whipped up. "Yum. This is so good. Thanks for having it ready. I was starving."

"No problem. It's a super easy dinner, and the clean up is a breeze since it's all made in one pot."

"I'm loving the heat. The sauce has a little kick."

"The spicy Italian sausage is what brings the heat. It's the only way to go."

I got up to refill my bowl. "I might end up eating as much as Smitty."

The elderly woman came over for dinner a couple of times a month. She was notorious for eating as much, if not more, than April and I combined. Where she put it all in that tiny little body of hers was anyone's guess.

"Speaking of Smitty, I popped over and checked on her when I first got here." April rose to get a second helping.

"Oh? How's she doing?"

"Good. Her son was coming to get her for dinner, so I didn't invite her to eat with us. She is adamant, though, that we need to go on the Christmas Light Trolley again, since we ended up missing the end of the tour last time."

"Because of a murder." I snorted. "No problem, though. There isn't Whoville practice tomorrow, so I'll see if I can get us on the tour tomorrow night. It's the middle of the week, so I'd be surprised if it was sold out. Are you wanting to go again?"

"Sure. With the investigation, J. T.'s working long hours, so I might as well."

"Gee, thanks. We're honored you'd lower yourself to hang with us peasants."

April laughed. "Not what I meant, and you know it."

"It's still fun to tease you." I carried my bowl to the sink, rinsed it, then found a container to put the leftovers in. "Well, if we're really going to do some digging, we better get it done before I chicken out."

Twenty minutes later, April and I picked our way by moonlight up the sidewalk lining Alpine Drive. The soft, new snow from this morning muffled our footsteps while wind whistled in the tops of the trees. We tried to keep to the shadows and avoid the bright lights of the streetlamps as we walked. Lucky for us, they were few and far between in this neighborhood. The blinds on the Kravitz house were shut against the dark night, though the light of a flickering television bled out around the edges.

"Let's hope they're watching a riveting show and Shilo doesn't feel the need to spy on the neighbors tonight," I whispered, pointing to their house.

"And they have it turned up loud enough to cover any noise," April added.

"I don't plan on making any noise."

My plans to be quiet went awry nearly as soon as I uttered the words. As I eased the gate open leading into Sheryl's front yard, the hinges squeaked loud enough to be heard in outer space. I winced and froze, expecting the neighbors to burst out of their houses with spotlights trained on us, and a helicopter to appear out of nowhere, blades whipping up a hurricane. All remained calm across the street at the Kravitz house, and the only light from Marsha's came from an upstairs window. When I didn't detect any human movement, I relaxed my shoulders. The light from Marsha's house rotated, throwing sparks of glitter out into the night. I grinned, picturing Marsha up there shaking her booty under her disco ball with Peaches & Herb playing on the turntable.

April shoved me from behind. "Come on. Go."

"What's our plan? How are we going to get inside?" I hissed through gritted teeth. We should've talked it out before we arrived, but it was too late now.

"Try the doors and windows." April disappeared into the shadows on the right side of the house, leaving me with the side closest to Marsha's house.

I had a sudden moment of panic, wondering if she had a security camera pointed at her nemesis's residence. I willed myself to get smaller as I crept onto the front porch and tried the doorknob, just for kicks and giggles. As I suspected, it didn't yield to my twisting. Keeping to the shadows, I circled around to the side of the house, yanking on each window as I came to them. All locked as tight as Fort Knox. A screeching noise froze me in my tracks. I swiveled my neck like an owl. There it was again. Relief flooded through me as I realized the noise came from a tree branch scraping against the roof of Sheryl's house in the wind. I tentatively moved forward again.

April and I came around to the back of the house at the same time. "Nothing?" she asked.

"Afraid not." I shook my head. "We might be out of luck." I found a bucket and overturned it underneath a small window I assumed led into a bathroom. Not expecting the window to budge, I stood on the bucket, stretched onto my tiptoes, and was shocked when the frame slid open easily. "April! This one's unlocked." I stepped backward off the bucket and pointed at the window. "You're younger and smaller than me. Have at it, sister."

She grinned. "Gladly. I used to be a master at climbing in and out of our bathroom window when I was a teenager."

I looked at her blankly. "What are you talking about?"

"You don't want to know." All I saw was a flash of teeth before she turned her back on my gobsmacked face and scrambled, head first, into Sheryl's house through the window.

A clunk and an "ow" filtered through the window.

"You okay?"

"Yep. Meet me at the back door."

I bolted onto the deck, following her command. April unlocked and eased the back door open, her left hand pressed to her forehead.

"What happened? Are you bleeding?"

"The toilet is too close to the window. Bonked my head on it, but I'm fine. It didn't break the skin." Her scowl kept me from asking any more questions.

We stood silently in the kitchen at the back of the house. The kitchen opened onto a small dining area, then into the living room.

"What are we looking for exactly?" April asked.

I stared at her. "This was your idea. You were all gung ho to come here tonight, so you tell me."

April glanced around, sucking air through her teeth as she thought. "Confirmation that Sheryl either does or does not still own the properties Jeff left to her. Paperwork of some sort, most likely."

"Deeds and financial documents," I filled in for her. "Though we're most likely on a wild goose chase, since I would think J. T. and his team would have found anything of significance."

"Unless they didn't realize the documents were important."

"True. Let's look for the obvious first. A desk or filing cabinet." I headed to the living room. "Oh, and a manila envelope. I'm curious to see if Oscar was telling me the truth or not."

The curtains were wide open, so April and I made quick work of pulling them closed before we turned on our flashlights and got to work. Two couches formed an L-shape, facing a brick fireplace with a flat screen TV mounted above it. The space had a minimalist feel, not what I'd expected from Sheryl. No clutter, no bookshelves, just bare surfaces. The only thing of substance was the impressive liquor cabinet taking up a good portion of the far wall. There was more booze on the shelves than behind the bar at Timber Creek Saloon.

"Uh, this is weird, isn't it." April formed her words as a statement.

I nodded. "I've never much trusted people who don't have books scattered around."

"Yeah, but that's not what I mean." April walked in a circle around the furniture. "For the queen of Christmas explosion outside, don't you think something is missing here?"

"You're right. I hadn't noticed until you pointed it out." There wasn't a single drop of Christmas inside the house. It could have been any month of the year. "More proof Sheryl's crazy display was done with the sole purpose of getting under Marsha's skin."

Even though Sheryl's house was neat and clean, the atmosphere felt heavy and oppressive. Icy fingers ran up the back of my neck and sent a shiver racing down my spine.

"Let's get this done and get the heck out of here. The house is giving me the creeps." I pulled two pairs of disposable gloves out of my coat pocket, handing a set to my daughter.

April headed down the hallway in search of a file cabinet in one of the bedrooms as I pulled open the drawer on a console table in the living room. After shuffling through an assortment of batteries, pens, phone chargers, an old cat collar, a remote control, cardboard coasters from various bars and restaurants, and a box of matches, I closed the drawer with a huff. Same old odds and ends everybody kept in a junk drawer. At least it was good to see Sheryl did have a bit of clutter, but she was good at keeping her mess hidden.

When I caught sight of myself in the round mirror hanging over the console table, I jumped about a mile high while involuntarily letting out a small screech. It wasn't my own face in the mirror that frightened me, but rather the wavering, grim countenance of the deceased homeowner. Sheryl jerked her head to the right, as if trying to tell me something. Her hair stood straight up all over her head, the ends smoking. I spun around but she was already gone. The smell of scorched hair filled the room.

"What's the problem, Mom?" April sprinted back into the living room at my yelp.

"Nothing to see here. Just another sighting of Sheryl's ghost, but she's already been and gone."

April flinched and cut her eyes around the room. "How do you know she's gone?"

"I guess I don't for sure, but I don't see her anymore, at any rate." I rubbed my forehead, feeling the pressure building.

She wrinkled her nose. "And what's the funky smell? Is something burning?"

"Uh...only Sheryl."

April gasped. "Mom! That's terrible."

"I wish I was joking." I waved my hand in front of my nose while my eyes watered. "Did you find anything in the back of the house?"

"Not really. She used one of the bedrooms as an office, but there isn't a file cabinet or a safe, only a desk. There were a couple of bills on the desk, one from Carpenter's Corner actually, and the other a utility bill, but nothing important. She probably did all her banking and paid her bills online like everyone else anymore."

"Most likely. Is there a computer?"

"Nope." April shook her head. "I'm guessing the police took it. But back to your visitation from Sheryl. Did she give you any hints?"

"I think she wanted me to search the kitchen." I told April about Sheryl's head jerk.

"Definitely worth a try. We aren't getting anywhere here."

We spent fifteen minutes opening every cabinet, drawer, and cupboard, and rummaging through them. By the time we finished, I knew Sheryl and I shared similar cooking habits. There were plenty of cans of processed soups, stews, and fake Italian noodles, but not a lot of healthy ingredients to be made into homecooked meals.

"I don't think there's anything here. I wonder what Sheryl was trying to tell me?" I huffed, ready to give up.

"Beats me." April put her hands on her hips and frowned. "I don't know where else to look."

For good measure, I rotated my flashlight around the kitchen one last time. As the beam swung past the refrigerator, a black orb floated through the ray of light. "Wait. Was that a ghost bubble?"

April gasped and bared her teeth in apprehension.

I swung the light over the same path again. There. The same ghostly bubble floated in the beam of light. My daughter and I stared at each other for a split second, before I tore open the door to the top freezer. I chucked out pizza, ice cream, breakfast sandwiches, burritos, and all manner of frozen concoctions, handing them to April, who dumped armloads of stuff into the sink.

"Jiminy Christmas. Still nothing." I slammed the freezer door in a tizzy.

April started placing the food back into the freezer, stopping to look inside the packages of anything already opened. "Shoot. Even the frozen waffles are actually waffles." She stuffed the last box back into the packed freezer.

I pulled open the main door of the fridge and stared inside. We weren't finding a single helpful clue. Did I imagine seeing Sheryl's ghost in the mirror? Was the supposed "ghost bubble" only a floating particle of dust? As I reached in to start removing things from the top shelf, I stumbled. The toe of my boot smashed against the kick plate covering the drip tray, shoving one side of the tray under the refrigerator farther and causing the other side to jolt out.

"Fo crimany sakes." I bent down to wrangle the pan back into place, but it wouldn't budge.

"You've got it all cattywampus." April knelt beside me. "Here, let me try before you mess it up worse."

When April didn't have any more luck than I had, we pooled our efforts. After some grunting and groaning, we finally popped the stubborn thing all the way off. April started to reattach it, but I grabbed her arm.

"Not so fast, missy. Let me look at one more thing before we put it back." I bent lower and shined my flashlight under the fridge. The drip tray on this particular model was a rectangular pan. "Here, hold the light."

I handed my flashlight to April, then gripped the drip tray with both hands. As I suspected, it was removable. I sat back on my heels. "Well, I'll be a monkey's uncle."

"Is that what I think it is?"

"Yep."

Only a small sheen of water was in the pan, a good indication the tray had been cleaned quite recently. Attached to the bottom of the pan was a Ziploc bag with several documents inside, including a manila envelope. I carried the tray to the sink, then pulled the bag out and shook it off. April found a kitchen towel in a drawer. She handed it to me and I wiped the bag dry before opening it.

"Ah. She had it double Ziplocked. Smart." I pulled out the documents and laid them on the counter.

April began to thumb through the loose papers as I skinned open the manila envelope.

"These are the documents from Sheryl's disability case. Why would she feel the need to keep them hidden?" April frowned.

"From what DeAnn said, there was something underhanded about the whole affair," I said, referring to our conversation with the waitress at the Stage Stop Café. I pulled the items out of the envelope and started to sort through them. At first glance, they appeared to be simple statements from the Social Security Administration for Sheryl's disability payments, but as I looked closer, a different story emerged. "Holy fright, will you look at this?"

April moved closer until we were standing shoulder to shoulder. "You're going to have to spell it out. What am I looking at?"

"Social security payment statements. Two years worth. The latest one is dated last week."

"Okay. What's the problem?" April asked.

I pointed to the name on the statement. "The problem is, these are mailed to this address but made out to Helena Dyer."

"Who is Helena Dyer?"

"Sheryl's mother."

"Oh." April blinked. "She must be fairly old."

"She's fairly dead, is what she is. And has been for a good ten years." I bit my bottom lip as I contemplated what this meant. "These statements are photocopies. I'd bet you my youngest child that this is the envelope Oscar and Sheryl had an argument about on the day of her death."

April placed her fists on her hips. "Mom, I am your youngest child."

"I'm aware." I grinned at her.

"You can't get rid of me that easy." She chuckled. "Do you think Oscar was trying to blackmail Sheryl?"

I shoved my glasses up. "Maybe. He doesn't seem like the sort who would stoop so low, but you never know. Whatever the case, we need to get this stuff to J. T. right away."

"How are we going to explain our little breaking and entering adventure?"

"We didn't break anything." When my daughter didn't laugh, I added, "Not to worry. We'll think of something."

We clicked off our flashlights and pulled the blinds back up, leaving Sheryl's house as we'd found it. We eased through the creaking gate, but only managed to get ten feet down the sidewalk before somebody yelled.

"Who's there? Is someone out here?"

I swiveled my head. Shilo Kravitz stood on her front stoop, shining a spotlight around the neighborhood. Her little dog, Elvira, joined in with some sharp-pitched barks. April grabbed my hand and the two of us dove behind a huge fir tree. I covered my mouth to stifle the fit of giggles threatening to break loose. A full five minutes passed before Shilo was satisfied no nefarious gangs were casing her neighborhood. She shut off the light and called for her dog to follow her back inside the house.

Chapter Twenty-Four

"J. T. will be here in a few minutes." April tucked her phone into the back pocket of her jeans, then got down on the floor next to my Christmas tree to give Thor a proper belly rub.

"Good golly, Miss Molly. You're a mess." I bent over and studied her face.

"What are you talking about?"

"Now that I can see you in the light, I'm not sure how we're going to explain away the nasty bruise on your forehead."

"A bruise? It doesn't hurt. I'd forgotten all about whacking my head." Startled, she reached up to rub at the offending spot. "Ow. I guess it does hurt when I press on it."

"Then stop pressing on it."

She fluffed her hair over her forehead. "Turn off the overhead lights and just leave the lamp on. I'll stay in the shadows."

I hit the switch and nodded. "Better."

While we waited for J. T., I pulled on another pair of disposable gloves, then took the Ziploc bag we'd found at Sheryl's house to the dining room and dumped the contents out onto the table. A small key fell onto the table with a clatter. I picked it up, turning it this way and that as I studied the key, then moved it aside and snapped pictures of each one of the documents. There wasn't time to review the paperwork from Sheryl's disability claim before I had to relinquish them to the police. I wanted to look through the documents at my own leisure and have the photos to refer to later.

At the sound of a car door slamming, Thor exploded off the floor. He raced around the house, bellowing his warning. Danger. Danger.

J. T. opened the door a crack to let Thor see who the intruder was. "It's just me, you big old lug." He stepped in, shutting the door behind him, and reached out to pet the dog.

Thor melted onto the floor in a puddle of both ecstasy and embarrassment.

Once J. T. finished reassuring the dog he was, in fact, a good boy, he sauntered into the dining room. "Hey Dawna. Where's April hiding?"

"In here," April called from the sunroom. "I'm enjoying the Christmas tree. Come join me."

I smiled to myself, knowing the real reason she didn't come out to greet him. No use getting him worked up over the bruise on her head. I gathered up the documents and headed in to join them. April sat in the rocking chair next to the tree, so, after dropping a quick kiss onto the top of her head, J. T. took a seat on the couch across the room.

He stretched out his long legs, crossing his feet at the ankles. Thor flopped to the floor and leaned against him. "What did you two find that is so important it can't wait until tomorrow?"

I handed him the Ziploc bag. "These are photocopies of social security checks. I think they're going to prove Sheryl was committing fraud." I leaned over and pointed out Helena Dyer's name. "This one is dated only a few days ago. The payment is made out to Sheryl's late mother, but sent to her address. Oh, and this was in the bag as well." I pulled the small key out of the pocket of my jeans and handed it to him.

He turned the key over in his big hand and studied it.

"I think it might be to a safety deposit box at the bank. It looks similar to mine."

"Good call. Probably where the rest of her important documents are we haven't been able to locate." He pocketed the key, then leaned forward and studied the documents without saying another word for a few moments. Then he sat back with a scowl, brought one foot up and crossed it over his knee, while his lips flattened. His gaze bounced between April and me. "Do I even want to know how you two happened to miraculously come across these documents? Did someone conveniently place them in your mailbox, Dawna?" He turned the full force of his sharp eyes on me. "Or did they thoughtfully leave them on your doorstep, April?" He swiveled his laser penetrating radar to her, then jumped off the couch and marched across the room. He gently took her chin in his hand and tilted her face up, swiping her bangs to the side. "And how, for Pete's sake, did you get this goose egg on your forehead?"

We both remained silent. Should have known Mr. Eagle Eyes wouldn't miss the bruise.

"Somebody better start talking right now or I'm going to haul the two of you into jail and throw away the key." He jammed his fists onto his hips and gave us the look. "Don't think I won't."

"The whole thing was Mom's idea." April thrust an accusing finger my way as if we were standing in front of the court at the Salem witch trials.

"Traitor!" My mouth flew open. "Are you flipping kidding me right now? You're the one who suggested our little side trip tonight."

"Maybe so, but you're the mastermind behind the whole snooping around thing."

"Because Roxy asked for help, and J. T. said I could." My voice was louder than I meant it to be as I defended myself.

"Whoa there. I absolutely did not," J. T. protested.

"Well, you didn't say I couldn't, and you did say my tips were useful."

Our illustrious police chief placed his hands on his hips, threw his head back, closed his eyes, and worked his jaw as if he was trying not to lose his temper. "I don't recall saying anything of the sort."

"Maybe not this time, but you did in the past. Remember? Back when poor Nate Durand was killed, you asked me to keep my eyes and ears open."

"What makes you think I wanted or needed your help this time? One invitation to assist isn't an open invitation to get involved in all of my cases. It was a one-time occurrence." He paused. "Remember when you asked me to help you get that sheetrock upstairs? How would you like it if I decided since you asked me for help one time, it gave me the right to take over all your projects? Every time you picked up a hammer, I'd jerk it out of your hand and do the project myself?"

"Now you're being dramatic. It's not the same thing at all." I shook my head. "Admit it, Chief. My observations have been useful."

He growled deep in his throat. "I'm not about to admit anything of the sort."

"Fine. Do you want something to drink? Hot cocoa? Tea?"

"I'm not twelve. You can't placate me with hot cocoa." J. T. plopped back down into his chair. "But yes, please," he added softly.

I smiled and raised my eyebrows. "Marshmallows?"

"Is it even hot cocoa without marshmallows?"

After the kettle whistled, I brought in three steaming mugs, each with two marshmallows melting into the chocolate, and a stick of peppermint for stirring. I'd brought along a plate of brownies for good measure. J. T. got his treats first, then I handed a mug and brownie to April with a glare. "This does, by no stretch of the imagination, mean I'm forgiving you for throwing me under the bus."

She sucked in her lips and dipped her chin. "Noted."

With tempers tamped down by chocolate, J. T.'s gaze landed on April. "Are you ready to tell me now where you came by this bag of documents?"

She stretched her neck back and forth before replying in a whisper. "From the drip tray of Sheryl's refrigerator."

"What?" He shook his head in confusion.

"You know. The drip tray. It's the thing under the fridge that catches the condensation." She raised her voice to a more normal level this time.

He sighed. "I know what a drip tray is, for crying out loud. You were talking like a mouse. I didn't hear what you said the first time."

Nobody had ever called my daughter a mouse before. She jumped up, her feistiness firmly restored. "I said, we found the documents in the drip tray of Sheryl's refrigerator." April scooped her bangs back from her face. "And I got the bruise, which is not a goose egg, by the way, from climbing in her bathroom window and whacking my head on the toilet."

"Are you admitting to breaking and entering?" His eyebrows had disappeared under the brim of his cowboy hat.

"There was no breaking involved," I spoke up. "The window was unlocked. We only entered."

He glared my way. "Semantics. It's still unlawful entry no matter how you look at it."

I waffled my head back and forth. "Semantics works for me. We didn't enter with the intent to commit a crime, but to solve one."

He held up the Ziploc bag. "And now how am I supposed to use this in my investigation when it was obtained unlawfully?"

April pointed vaguely toward Sheryl's neighborhood. "We could go put it back, then you can conduct another search and find it yourself. Or I could call in an anonymous tip and you could do a deep dive into Sheryl's finances."

The Chief of Police growled again. He downed the rest of his hot cocoa, then pinched the bridge of his nose before asking his next question. "In your unprofessional opinions, what do you think these documents prove?"

"It looks to me like Sheryl was committing social security fraud, and Oscar was aware of it. Maybe he was blackmailing her." I stirred my hot cocoa with the peppermint stick to blend the flavors. The candy slowly melted into the steaming liquid.

J. T. shook his head, a look of confusion on his face. "Why do you think Oscar knows anything about this?"

I started waving my index finger around in the air like I was conducting an orchestra. "Because he's her mailman. He would most definitely have seen these statements coming to her house for the last couple of years, since he's been working her route. Plus, rumor has it Oscar and Sheryl had a heated conversation the morning of her murder. He slammed a manila envelope down on her picnic table before walking away. This happened several hours before he came through the neighborhood on his normal mail delivery route. When I asked him what was in the envelope, he denied any knowledge of it."

"And for whatever wild reason, you've decided this is the envelope in question?" J. T. held up the package.

"Without a doubt. I think Oscar made photocopies of the statements and was threatening to expose Sheryl's fraud. What he did tell me was that, until recently, Sheryl had been using her daughter's social security number to work so she would still be able to claim her full disability benefits. So don't try to tell me mailmen don't pay attention to the mail they deliver."

"I think we're missing an important piece of the puzzle though." April grunted and cocked her head. "If Oscar was threatening to expose Sheryl, wouldn't you think he would be the one who would have wound up dead instead of her?"

J. T. and I both stared at her.

I noodled her comment around for a few seconds. "Good point."

"It's still worth taking a good hard look at Oscar," J. T. said through a yawn. He stood and stretched. "In the morning. It's getting late and I'm tired."

I pointed to the Ziploc bag. "There's paperwork from Sheryl's disability case in there also. Not sure how it's significant, but why would a person hide this stuff in the drip tray of their refrigerator if everything is all above board?"

"I'll look into it." He nodded. "We'll go through everything with a fine-tooth comb."

When April stood up, Thor roused himself, then indulged in a huge stretch, with his front paws extended and his hiney in the air. "Time for me and Thor to hit the road too," April said.

I stood at the window in the living room until both cars' taillights were out of sight, suspicious J. T. would end up at April's little cottage, and glad of it. I locked the doors, then ran a bubble bath. My bones still hadn't completely warmed up from our evening trek out in the December cold.

By the time I'd soaked in the vanilla-scented bubbles and read a couple of chapters, I was drowsy and ready for bed. Any more sleuthing was going to have to wait until the morning. Maybe it was simply an oversight on J.T.'s part, but for all of his grumbling, he still hadn't told me to stop snooping.

Chapter Twenty-Five

While Bill, Ernie, and Rick drank coffee and solved a good chunk of the world's problems the next morning from the comfort of Carpenter's Corner, I dialed Roxy's number.

"Hey there, Dawna. Your ears must've been ringing. I was about to call you," she greeted, sounding somewhat more cheerful than she had the last time we'd chatted.

"How are you doing? Are there any updates on Barry?"

On the other end of the line, Roxy sighed. "Not much. He hasn't woken up yet, but his vitals have gotten stronger."

"Well, that sounds hopeful, at least. Have the doctors figured out what's causing the problems?"

"Not yet. They're still waiting on labs to come back."

"Ugh. You'd think with modern technology things would move a little faster."

We discussed Barry's condition for a few more minutes, then I filled Roxy in on the discoveries April and I had made in Sheryl's murder case. "We're going to keep moving forward. Everything's fine here at the store, so don't worry about coming in tomorrow. I can handle things on this end."

"Absolutely not," Roxy protested. "I'll be coming to work at my normal time."

"Seriously, you don't need to worry about it," I argued. "You have enough on your plate. Consider it paid time off this week. Next week, we'll have to regroup."

"Listen, Dawna. I'm telling you, I *need* to come in. If I have to spend one more day locked in a hospital room with my ex, things are going to get ugly. There will be another murder, and this time I really will be to blame."

"Gotcha." I laughed. "We can't have that. See you bright and early tomorrow morning."

I hung up and strolled to the coffee klatch table to give the guys the update, such as it was, on Barry Dunsmuir.

Ernie rubbed his temple, causing his ball cap to rock back and forth. "Well, I sure hope Barry pulls through. There couldn't be a nicer guy."

"If he doesn't," Bill put in, "I'd be taking a good hard look at that Capri girl the kid has shacked up with. The rotten apple doesn't fall far from the tree."

"The kid?" I questioned. "Do you mean Brett? He's in his forties, for crying out loud."

Bill frowned. "Anybody under fifty is a kid to me these days."

Rick shook his head. "Can't fathom what Brett was thinking, leaving Roxy and his family for that piece of work. Mark my words, he's going to regret it. Probably already does."

Dramatic sighs sounded all around the table as the guys all scraped back their chairs and stood.

"I've got clean up today," Rick said. "See you blockheads tomorrow." Ceramic mugs clinked together and paper rustled as he gathered up the debris from their coffee session.

By the time the guys all shuffled out the door, a handful of customers had come into the hardware store and the normal bustle of the morning was in full force. I cut two keys for one customer, mixed four gallons of paint for another, helped a guy find a sheetrock patch kit, and rang up a fair amount of transactions before April came in at nine.

She gave me a quick break to use the restroom, then took over the register while I visited with customers and helped them locate the items they needed for their home repair projects. For lunch, I choked down quick bites of my turkey sandwich between customers. The day stayed steady until the middle of the afternoon. Once things slowed down, April disappeared into the back to work on one of her projects, and I flopped into the chair at my desk, glad to be off my feet for a few minutes.

I opened my laptop and transferred the pictures I'd taken of Sheryl's documents from my phone to the computer. The documents were a gazillion times easier to read on the bigger screen.

Not that I was an expert at sussing out anomalies in disability documents, but at first glance, everything seemed straightforward to me. The records stated the slip and fall incident Sheryl had while working at The Little Red Hen caused her to suffer a herniated disc in her neck and a spinal cord injury, leaving her permanently disabled. A doctor's report was attached to substantiate Sheryl's claim. The pain and suffering case ended with Sheryl receiving workers' compensation and disability benefits in an initial sum that made my eyes water.

To top it off, she also sued Clay Hopkins and The Little Red Hen directly, claiming negligence. According to Sheryl's testimony, Clay had mopped up a grease spill on the floor of the restaurant kitchen without putting out the proper "Wet Floor" signs. When Sheryl came to work a few minutes later, she claimed that not only was the hazard sign missing, but instead of doing a thorough job, Clay had only smeared the grease around the floor. Sheryl stepped over to the fryer to start an order of onion rings, and slipped on the greasy floor, causing her severe injuries. Between the lawsuit against Clay and the disability settlement, Sheryl had been awarded nearly a hundred thousand dollars up front, with lifetime disability payments of twelve-hundred dollars a month.

Holy fright. No wonder The Little Red Hen went out of business. Having to come up with that kind of money would knock the socks off of most small businesses. I whistled at the amount of Sheryl's compensation, then went back to the first image to study the documents a second time. The doctor who provided the medical report and signed the documents was Dr. L. Dyer with an address in Seattle.

"Dr. Dyer. Why is that name ringing a bell?" I blew out a breath and tapped my chin as the bell over the door jangled, effectively breaking my concentration.

"Hey there, Luther. How're things going for you today?" I shoved away from the desk and stood.

"Can't complain," the gruff, tattooed plumber answered. "Nobody'd listen if I did." He guffawed at the tired old joke.

"Nope, we sure wouldn't. What can I help you with?"

He whipped a small notebook out of the pocket of his leather vest. "Need to place my standard order, plus a few extras." He ripped a page out of the notebook and handed it to me. In handwriting neater than anyone would ever expect, Luther had listed not only the sizes and names of the plumbing parts he needed, but also the part numbers.

I took the page with a smile. "You always make my job so easy."

"That's my aim. No reason to make anybody's day harder than it already is."

"Amen, my friend." I glanced over the list. "We should be able to get everything from my usual supplier, so it'll arrive in a few days. I'll give you a call when it comes in."

"Sounds good." Luther leaned against the counter. He plucked a toothpick out of the breast pocket of his black leather vest, and popped it into the corner of his mouth like a cigarette. "Did you hear the Chief hauled Oscar Rudolf into the station this afternoon?"

A twinge of guilt for throwing Oscar's name into the suspect arena made my eye twitch. "Gosh no, it's been gangbusters in here today. I haven't heard a word. Did they arrest him?"

Luther shrugged. "Not sure. Chief Dallas brought him in, but Oscar wasn't cuffed or nothing."

"You were there when they took him in?"

"Yep. I've been over at the laundromat most of the day again. I was finishing up and loading my tools into the van when it went down."

"Went down? You make it sound like they had a shootout in the street."

"Nah, nothing as dramatic as all that." He winked. "Now, I know you're digging around, Dawna. I heard you trying to get info from Marsha yesterday, but let me tell you, nothing good ever comes from sticking your nose where it don't belong."

I jerked my head back. "Luther Voss, did you just threaten me?"

He chuckled. "Come on Dawna, you know me better than that. Of course I didn't. You're one of my favorite people and I don't want to see you getting hurt. Now, Sheryl Capri was no angel in my book, but someone who could do what they did to her won't think twice about protecting themselves if they think you're getting too close to the truth. Just don't let down your guard. That's all I'm saying."

I nodded. "I'll take your concerns under advisement. Thanks for watching my back." What was with all the men in this town thinking they had to protect me from myself? *Pretty sure I can hold my own, thank you very much.*

"Well, I'll get out of your hair." Luther tapped the counter with a beefy hand and headed for the door, but then turned back. "One more thing before I go."

"Yeah? Do you need to add something else to your order?"

"No, it's about Marsha. This morning, I overheard her on the phone with someone she called Clay. It was clear they were discussing Sheryl's murder. Marsha told this Clay fellow he needed to steer clear. Stay out of Pine Bluff until it all blew over. I can only guess what they were talking about. Anyway, thought it might be of interest to you."

So, I hadn't been making things up when I thought Marsha had been talking to Clay yesterday. "It is. I appreciate you telling me."

"No worries." He lifted a hand and left the store.

April strolled out of the warehouse, a splotch of white paint on her cheek. "Did I hear Luther?"

"Yep. Brought his order in." I got busy adding the plumbing supplies to my next order while I was thinking about it. The last thing I wanted was for people to get in the habit of driving to the big home improvement store in Greenwood because I'd dropped the ball on placing their special orders one too many times. Wasn't going to happen on my watch.

When I finished, I turned to find out what April was up to. She'd taken a seat at my desk and was looking through the images of Sheryl's disability documents.

"Well, what do you think? Do you see anything out of the ordinary?" I asked.

"Looks like Sheryl was bilking the system."

I frowned. "What do you mean? It all looked pretty clear-cut to me."

April shook her head. "I don't know. Just a gut feeling, and I can't help thinking about what DeAnn said about seeing Sheryl up at Wallowa Lake the same summer of her disability claim."

"Oh, right. I'd forgotten about that." My mouth gaped open. "Didn't she say she saw her riding a jet ski?"

"Yep. Riding a jet ski isn't something someone with a herniated disc in their neck and a spinal injury could do. If DeAnn's story is right, there's no way Sheryl had a permanent disability as severe as this document describes."

"Or any disability at all," I agreed. I filled April in on what Luther had said about Marsha talking to Clay on the phone earlier today. "If I was Clay and had to pay a huge settlement that put me out of business, only to find out the woman was lying about it all, I'd be madder than a wet hen."

"But mad enough to kill?" April questioned. "All these years later? Why wait so long?"

I shrugged. "Opportunity? What's the connection between Marsha and Clay? Between the two of them, maybe their anger fed on each other until they decided to combine all those years of rage and get rid of her."

"I suppose anything's possible. I do feel like there's something there. It's pretty coincidental to find out two completely different suspects know each other and seem to be talking on a daily basis." April glanced out the window, then suddenly straightened in the chair. "Speak of the devil."

"What?" I followed her gaze, only to see Marsha coming through the front door. "Hello, there," I greeted the older woman. "Did Luther need some more parts?"

Marsha flapped a hand, then glanced around the front of the hardware store. "No, he's all set as far as I know," she replied tentatively. "I thought I remembered you had one of those Giving Trees here in the store and was hoping there were still a few requests left to be filled."

"You're in luck. We do, and there are a handful left. Right over here." Not wanting to show how absolutely stunned I was at Marsha's, aka Mrs. Grinch's, request, I led her to the Giving Tree. "Are you looking for a particular age?"

Marsha shook her head without making eye contact. "Not necessarily. Just want to help bring a little cheer to someone's life. I've decided I've held onto my anger long enough. You helped open my eyes yesterday."

"Me?" My hand flew to my chest. "I didn't say much, only reinforced how people really do care about you."

"You might not have said a lot, but it was enough to give me a solid kick in the behind. It's high time I start thinking about other people and not just my sorry self."

Could this change of heart be guilt speaking from killing her ex-best friend? Or had Mrs. Grinch's heart really grown three times that day?

Marsha removed a bell-shaped paper ornament from the tree. "This breaks my heart. A sixteen-year-old girl whose biggest wish is deodorant and shampoo?"

I nodded, tears springing to my eyes. "It is heartbreaking. There's a lot of need out there."

"Well, she's going to get a whole lot more than toiletries from me." Marsha's pale blue eyes watered.

I smiled, surprised the stoic woman would feel so emotional over purchasing gifts for a teenager in need. *Miracle of miracles. Mrs. Grinch does have a heart after all.*

"You sell wrapping paper here, don't you?" Marsha glanced around the store.

I led her to our Christmas décor area, where Marsha chose a roll dotted with pine trees on a snowy white background. She'd looked at one bright red roll with jolly dancing snowmen, but put it back, apparently not ready to embrace the full joviality of the season. I took the roll of wrapping paper from her to free her arms as she continued to shop for clear tape, bows, and tags.

"Do you have anything a teenage girl would like?" She asked once she'd selected her wrapping supplies.

"Not much, but there is one thing." I showed her a basket of fuzzy slipper socks. "My girls loved these when they were that age."

"We still do," April yelled from behind the counter.

Marsha picked out a striped blue and white pair of socks and a pale pink pair with a fun cable-knit pattern. She then grabbed one of the small metallic flashlights from the display and deposited her selections on the counter beside the cash register. "It's a start. Where do you suggest I go next?"

April started to open her mouth with a suggestion, when another voice chimed in.

"A teenage girl? You're going to want to come to my place for a necklace and nail polish. And how about a nice sweater?"

Our heads swiveled around like owls at the sound of Darlene's voice. Unbeknownst to me, she'd entered the hardware store through the door between my store and Lipstick and Lace.

When Darlene realized it was Marsha she'd spoken to, the left side of her lip pulled into a snarl and she squished up her nose. "Oh. It's you. I haven't decided for sure, but I really don't think you're welcome in my shop."

"Do you ever have anything nice to say?" April crossed her arms and widened her stance as if she was getting ready in case a brawl broke out.

"Not when it comes to the likes of her." She flung a hand toward Marsha.

"Darlene!" I reprimanded her as if she was one of my own kids behaving badly. "What's gotten into you?" Not that it took much to make her snarly. And how dare she show her face in Carpenter's Corner anyway, after the rubbish she'd been spreading around town about me. The two of us needed to have a come-to-Santa meeting sooner than later. After all, he knew if you'd been bad or good, and she certainly hadn't been good.

"What's gotten into me?" Darlene pointed a manicured talon at her own chest. "I'm not the person who killed my best friend's mother. She is." She reversed direction and pointed the accusing finger at Marsha.

Marsha scoffed, but wasn't cowed in the face of Darlene's accusation. "I did no such thing. Though I'll admit I was tempted a time or two hundred over the years."

"Why should I believe anything you say? Jazelle knows you found out your husband was her biological father, not Roger Capri. She thinks you murdered her mother over it."

"My Doug has been gone for more than a decade. What would be the point of killing his mistress now?" Marsha's eyebrows knit together as she stared at Darlene.

"Aha! So you admit he was Jazelle's father." Darlene nearly jumped up and down with glee.

April and I jerked our gazes between the two of them as if we were watching a tennis match.

"I admitted no such thing. There's not a hint of truth in your accusations." Marsha's voice was calm and measured. "Where did Jazelle hear that rubbish from anyway?"

Darlene shrugged. "She's known since we were kids. There was always a rumor around town. Surely you heard it? I've never understood women like you, who bury their heads in the sand and refuse to see what's right in front of their faces."

Marsha cocked her head, amusement shining in her pale eyes. "And Jazelle's mother told her these rumors were true?"

"No," Darlene conceded. "Sheryl wouldn't ever come clean one way or the other. Jazelle's parentage was one more thing she liked to hang over her head."

Funny how Darlene's whole "Sheryl was the best person in the world" rhetoric had changed a bit with her admission about how Sheryl liked to push her daughter's buttons.

Marsha started to chuckle, then let loose with a full belly laugh. She bent over, grasping the counter with her hands and lowered her forehead to the counter, laughing so hard I thought I was going to have to get her a chair before she fell over.

Darlene crossed her arms and stamped her foot. "What's so funny?"

Marsha finally got control of herself. She wiped her eyes and straightened up. "Who knew those old stories would still be going strong all these years later. If you must know, I started the rumor myself. Never meant for it to spread like wildfire, and didn't know anyone still took them seriously."

I threw out my hands in confusion. "Alright, now you have to tell us the story. How did you start the rumor? And why? I've heard it myself recently."

"After Sheryl and I had our last big blowup, our friendship wasn't just on the rocks, it was officially over for good." Marsha leaned against the counter as she reminisced about the bad old days. "With us still living next door to each other, she went out of her way to do things she knew would get my goat. One of her favorite things to do that summer was sunbathe in her backyard. Nude. And in full view, if you happened to glance out of any of our back windows. In those days, we didn't have a fence between our two houses. Doug came home from work about six each evening. Sheryl was well aware he liked to relax in the backyard with a beer. At five minutes after six, all summer long, here came Sheryl. You could set your watch by her. She'd shimmy out of their house wearing nothing but a long T-shirt, settle onto her lounge chair, whip off the shirt and start slathering herself in suntan lotion."

"Oh my gosh," I said, appalled. "Did you say anything to her?"

Marsha shook her head. "Nope. I knew she was doing it just to ruffle my feathers, and I wasn't about to give her the satisfaction. Doug would raise his beer can to her, then turn his chair so he wasn't directly facing her. We planted a fast-growing hedge along the property line, but it took a good year before the thing grew big enough to hide her shenanigans."

"What about Roger? Sheryl's husband. He didn't care that she was out there flashing the whole neighborhood?"

"Roger worked swing shift at the mill, so he was never home when she was naked in the yard." Marsha shrugged. "The poor guy probably never even knew. Neither Doug nor I told him. And I'm just now finding out that if you're the subject of a rumor, people whisper about it to everyone but you."

"You still haven't explained how you supposedly started the rumors about Doug being Jazelle's father though." Darlene's voice was petulant, now the reason she thought Marsha was the killer was being dismantled piece by piece.

"I'm getting there. Simmer down." Marsha shot her a glare. "One of Doug's fishing buddies called one afternoon shortly after he'd gotten home from work. I told the guy to hang on a minute while I found Doug. Jokingly said he was probably out back with his girlfriend. It was a sarcastic throw-away comment, but when I went to call Doug to the phone, he wasn't out on the back porch. I looked around the house for a few minutes but couldn't find him. Told his buddy Doug would have to call him back, and said something about him apparently *really* being with his girlfriend because he was nowhere to be found. What I didn't realize, was this guy was the biggest gossip around. When Sheryl turned up pregnant a couple of months later, the rumors started to fly. I thought we'd shut them down, but obviously not."

Darlene crossed her arms and narrowed her eyes. "And where was Doug when you couldn't locate him? With his mistress like you joked about?"

Marsha scoffed. "He was in the bathroom. I hadn't thought to check there."

"Sure. Likely story." Darlene huffed and flounced back to her own store.

"And don't come back until you can be nice," April called after her.

I shot my daughter a disapproving look, though she hadn't said anything I wasn't thinking myself.

After April rang up Marsha's purchases, I suggested she check Fortner's for gifts for a teenage girl. I cupped a hand around my mouth in a mock whisper. "You'll find all kinds of gifts there without having to set a foot into Darlene's boutique."

"Good idea. They'll have all the toiletries, too. One stop shopping. I'll pop down there on my way back to the laundromat."

Chapter Twenty-Six

"With any luck, this time our Christmas light tour will be far less dramatic than the last one." Smitty settled into the front passenger seat of my Jeep and clicked her seatbelt into place.

"Fingers and toes crossed." I snorted. "Too bad we're going to have such a hard time seeing any of the lights."

Smitty looked at me in surprise. "What will be the problem?"

"Your snowsuit is glowing so bright, it's bound to outshine them all," I teased.

This time, Smitty had swapped out her psychedelic plaid suit for a school bus yellow ski outfit of a similar vintage. I was going to have to get a look into her closet.

"Good thing there hasn't been any zoo breaks in our area recently," April said from her position in the back seat.

"My lands." Smitty turned her entire little body to look at April. "You're talking such nonsense. What does a zoo break have to do with anything?"

"If a gorilla got out, you might be in trouble. He'd mistake you for a banana."

Smitty chuckled and playfully slapped at my wrist since she couldn't reach April. "Oh, you two. Always harassing me. I don't know why I put up with the likes of you."

"Because you love us." I grinned at her. "If we didn't love you right back, we wouldn't tease you so much."

Smitty smiled and settled back in her seat for the ride downtown. "If teasing is the indicator, then there's no shortage of love around here."

"No siree, Bob. There sure isn't." I put the Jeep in gear and headed for the trolley stop.

Being a weeknight, I didn't expect the Christmas Light Tour to be as fully booked as it was on the weekends. Boy, was I ever wrong. Even though we were fifteen minutes early, we weren't the first to arrive by a long shot. A dozen or more townsfolks queued up ahead of us waiting for the trolley to arrive. More people strolled up the street and began to line up behind us. I grinned when I spotted Roxy, Hunter, and Makayla headed our way.

"It's a nice night for a trolley ride, don't you think?" I called out to Roxy.

"Absolutely." She draped an arm around each of the kids, though Hunter shrugged out of her embrace in a hot second. "It's exactly what we need right now to cheer us up."

As they took their place at the end of the line, I faced forward and craned my neck to look around the man standing directly in front of me. I elbowed April. "Holy cow, Marsha's here," I whispered. "Can you believe it? Maybe she really has turned a new leaf."

April's head shot up and she stepped out of line to see for herself. "You're right. I wonder who the guy is with her?"

I leaned sideways at the waist to get a better view and accidentally gasped, causing Marsha and her friend to turn around.

She sent me a friendly wave. "Oh, Dawna. I didn't know you were coming tonight. I'd like to introduce you to someone."

After asking April to hold my spot in line, I stepped up to Marsha.

"This is my nephew, Clay Hopkins," Marsha said.

"We've met," Clay and I said in unison.

"I had lunch at The Nutty Goose the other day," I clarified. "He was nice enough to stop by my table and say hello." I turned to Marsha. "I had no idea Clay was your nephew."

She nodded. "He's my younger sister's son. Came to town to surprise me today." She shot Clay a somewhat miffed look.

Understandable, since I had it on good authority Marsha had advised Clay to steer clear of Pine Bluff for now.

I turned back to Clay. "Now when I had lunch in your restaurant the other day, and told you I lived in Pine Bluff, I'm surprised you didn't mention Marsha was your aunt." I pointed a finger at him. "In fact, if I recall, you said you didn't come here much."

The trolley pulled up, effectively cutting off our conversation. Though from the miffed look Clay gave me, I was pretty sure he had no intention of replying to my remark. I took my place back in line with Smitty and April. When it was our turn to board, I placed my hand on Smitty's elbow and helped her onto the bus. Marsha and Clay had claimed the first seat right behind the driver. *Good. I can keep an eye on them.* Even though Marsha seemed to be softening, I still wasn't convinced she was innocent of doing away with her former best friend. And now finding out Clay was her nephew made my suspicions grow even stronger. Sheryl had destroyed his business. I could only imagine the simmering anger building in his belly ever since. The way Sheryl was killed, then wrapped up in those lights and stuffed in the chimney screamed hate and revenge. A shiver ran up my spine as I thought about her awful demise.

Smitty, April, and I took seats near the middle of the bus, directly across the aisle from where we'd sat last time. Smitty suggested the change so we would have a better view of the opposite side of the street. The atmosphere inside the trolley was no less jolly than it had been at the beginning of our last tour. Colorful lights twinkled around the inside of the roof and Christmas tunes blasted from the speakers. My friend Judy from the Women's Service Club was playing the hostess-with-the-mostest tonight. She would deliver hot cocoa, apple cider, and sweet treats once everyone got seated.

Roxy started to slide into the seat across from us, but Hunter shook his head. "No, mom. We're going to the back." He barely rewarded us with a passing glance as he headed for the back of the trolley.

"He's not wrong," April quipped. "All the cool kids sit back there."

Roxy rolled her eyes and shrugged, then dutifully followed her offspring to the cool kids section.

I had a bit of déjà vu when the Rudolf family traipsed past us. When I spied little Emma with another candy cane in her fist, I dramatically threw my hands over my head and made a funny face at her. The little girl giggled.

"We decided we needed a do-over after the last trip," Oscar said as he deftly kept Emma's candy out of my hair this time.

"Same for us. I hope the kids weren't too traumatized over what they witnessed."

He shook his head. "No, they had no idea. They're fine, but they have been asking to ride the trolley again, so we decided why not?"

"To be perfectly honest, most of us adults didn't even know what we were looking at until we heard the news later," Freya, Oscar's wife, said in a quiet voice, before following her family down the aisle.

I held both my own and Smitty's hot apple ciders so she could get situated with her plate of sweets on her lap. Once I handed her hot drink over, I glanced up to find Darlene and Jazelle sashaying down the aisle. The seat across from us was still empty, but Darlene pursed her lips and frowned at me. "Well, looky here. If it isn't the Carpenter's Corner slayers."

Several people gasped and I heard a few murmurs starting up around us. The response was exactly what Darlene had been hoping for. She smirked with satisfaction and moved deeper into the trolley, dragging her friend along with her.

Bye-bye, buttercup. Apparently, she wasn't worried about holding onto her retail lease with me. Come January first, I was going to get serious about finding another business to take over her space. I turned and watched the two women flounce into the seat directly in front of Roxy and the kids.

Roxy threw her hands up shoulder-high with a look of complete disgust on her face. "Unbelievable."

"Do you have a problem, Roxanne?" Jazelle asked in a sickly-sweet voice while Darlene looked on with a smug smile plastered on her face.

My hand twitched. I'd never been a violent person, but right now I wanted to give those two catty women the smacks they had coming.

"Of course not. It's a free country. Sit where you'd like," Roxy replied through gritted teeth. "Everybody knows you take whatever you want, anyway. We wouldn't expect any less."

Hunter kept his gaze turned down, likely staring at his phone, while Makayla looked straight at Jazelle, her expression unreadable.

Jazelle flung her hair back over her shoulder. When her gaze fell on the Rudolf family across the aisle from Roxy, she flashed a million-watt smile and wiggled her fingers in hello. Oscar flushed as red as a holly berry, while Freya glowered. Little Emma was on Oscar's lap, their son by the window, and Freya in the middle.

"You better stay on your own side of the aisle, if you know what's good for you." Freya leaned forward across her husband's lap, delivering her threat to the other woman.

Oscar patted his wife's shoulder. "Sweetie, she's not worth ruining our night over. Pretend she's not there."

Freya sent Jazelle one more searing glare, then sat back and focused her attention out the window.

What is going on there? Could it be Oscar and Jazelle who were in cahoots to kill her mother? Maybe Jazelle had finally snapped at the way her mom treated her. We already knew, or thought we did, that Oscar was aware of Sheryl's social security fraud. Could he have been trying to blackmail her? Maybe the outcome wasn't what he expected, and he and Jazelle buddied up to do away with the vile woman. I turned back around and noodled the possibilities around. Freya might have found out Oscar and Jazelle spent time together, and suspected them of having an affair. Which wasn't out of the realm of possibility either, but Oscar didn't seem to be the kind of person who would cheat. In all my observations of him, it was clear he adored his family. I caught April's eye, wanting to toss ideas around with her, but now was not the time or place. She dipped her chin and nodded. The two of us were usually on the same page. Tonight's light tour was already proving interesting. We'd have a lot to discuss later this evening.

At seven sharp, Marvalene, tonight's trolley driver, started to swing the door shut, but reopened them when someone outside yelled. A couple jogged up the sidewalk and clambered onto the bus.

"Sorry we're late. I had a last minute client come in who was in a lot of pain. I couldn't turn him away." Laine Messina brushed flyaway strands of long dark hair out of her face. "Thank you for waiting for us."

"I hope you were able to help the poor guy," Marvalene said.

"Of course." Laine handed her their tickets with a smile.

After my last appointment with her, I wasn't so sure. If my experience was any indicator, the man probably left in more pain than he was experiencing when he walked through her clinic door.

Laine's husband, Mel, smiled sheepishly at everyone already seated and ready to go. He raised a hand in apology as they made their way to the empty seat across the aisle from us. Laine nodded hello to me as she slid into the seat.

"Aunt Laine," Jazelle called from a few rows back. "Why are you even here? Shouldn't you be in mourning?"

Laine stood and twisted around, a look of anger passing over her face before she tamped it down. "The same goes for you, darling niece. On top of grieving your mother, shouldn't you be with your new boyfriend? Word is, his father is touch and go."

Jazelle simply shrugged and tossed her hair. Behind her, Roxy blanched as white as a ghost. Laine shot her niece a final glare, then fell into her seat. I turned around in time to see both Marsha and Clay watching the scene with looks of pure disgust.

They shook their heads at each other before facing forward. The air inside the trolley virtually sparked with tension.

As soon as the Messinas were settled, and Judy had provided them with warm drinks and cookies, Marvalene pulled the door shut and swung the trolley away from the curb. We were finally on our way.

It wasn't lost on me that every single person who was a suspect on my murder list was on the trolley tonight. Yikes. What were the odds? I tried not to let them all take up too much room in my head. Instead, I focused my attention on the gorgeous lights outside the window and the delightful company of my own seatmates.

Just like on our first tour, we oohed and aahed over all the beautiful Christmas lights turning our town into a winter wonderland.

"The folks of Pine Bluff really know how to put on a show," Smitty said, her eyes gleaming like a young child.

"They sure do," I agreed.

"Look at the adorable woodland village." April pointed to a house coming up. "I didn't notice it last time. I love the little racoons and beavers. Aww. Check out the owl in the pine tree."

"You didn't notice this particular house because we were sitting on the other side of the bus." Smitty popped a piece of fudge in her mouth and chewed. "We have a whole new perspective this trip."

"We really do," I added. "It makes me want to take the tour twice every year. You really do see different things."

Across the aisle, Mel exclaimed, "Look there, Laine. It's Mama Dyer's old house. Those folks have really done a nice job fixing up the place."

The house he pointed at was a white, foursquare home draped in classic soft white icicle lights. A lit-up wire snowman waved from the front lawn, and a beautifully full Christmas tree, decorated with multicolored lights, shone through the front window. When Laine's parents owned the house, it had been covered in a drab gray asbestos shingle siding, most likely original from when the home was built in the 1920s.

"Ah. The place really does look good, doesn't it?" Laine said with a quick glance my way.

I nodded in agreement, while an elusive thought I couldn't quite grab a hold of niggled away inside my head.

The jolly Christmas light tour carried on throughout the town. It was with a bit of relief I noticed the route had been changed up enough to skip the street Sheryl's house was on. We'd covered most of the town and had started the final loop on a hill right outside of the city limits when someone seated behind us let out a loud yell.

"Stop! Stop the trolley!"

"Oh my stars, not again." The plate in Smitty's lap began to tremble as the trauma from a few nights ago came flooding back.

The trolley screeched to a halt, jerking us all forward and back in our seats, even though we hadn't been traveling at a high rate of speed.

Marvalene's normally soft voice boomed throughout the trolley as she eyeballed the riders from her rearview mirror. "What seems to be the problem here? We have ten minutes before I drop you back off downtown. Can't this wait?"

"No, it can't." Freya stood and pushed past Oscar. She reached out and grabbed a handful of Jazelle's long hair. "She's the problem. This wench right here."

Jazelle let out a high-pitched screech when Freya jerked down on her hair. After one tug, Freya let go, grabbed Emma from Oscar's lap, and held out her hand for her son to take. Roxy didn't miss a beat. In the confusion and screeching, I might have been the only one who was looking when her hand darted out and gave Jazelle's hair another tug. Roxy caught my eye, smiled and winked.

With both children in tow, Freya headed toward the front of the trolley. When Oscar scrambled to his feet, Freya whipped around. "Don't you dare follow me. This is as much your fault as it is hers. You stay right here with Miss Tramp."

Oscar dropped back into his seat, his face drained of all color. "Freya, honey. This isn't what you think it is. I love you," he called after her.

She didn't give him another glance as she and the Rudolf kids exited the trolley and started marching down the sidewalk.

"Are Freya and the kids going to be alright, Oscar? I could go with her to make sure," Roxy suggested.

Oscar pointed out the window. "We live two houses down. They're almost home already. Thanks for the offer, though."

In the rearview mirror, Marvalene's eye's flared and she let out a huff of breath louder than the hydraulic sound of the door's closing. "And I thought teenagers were bad." She shook her head in disgust. "Give me back my school routes any day."

For unfathomable reasons, Darlene decided this was the perfect moment to throw her weight around. "This is unacceptable. My friend and I have been treated abominably tonight by each and every one of you. You've all been nothing but rude, and the driver hasn't done a single thing to protect us. First thing in the morning, I'll be marching down to City Hall to file a complaint and get this whole Christmas light nonsense shut down."

"Oh good," I said to my seatmates. "We have another Mrs. Grinch in the making."

This time, Marvalene stood up and faced the riders, hands on hips. "You think we've all been rude, huh? Seems to me, the two of you have been causing trouble since the second you stepped onto this bus. And let me tell you, honey, I don't get paid enough to put up with the likes of you, so now I'm about to show you what rude really looks like." She threw open the doors and pointed out into the cold December night. "You either sit down and shut your mouth, or you get your sorry behinds off my trolley right this instant."

Darlene and Jazelle stared at each other, then Darlene sputtered a bit until she actually managed to get a few words out. "You've got to be kidding me. You can't throw us out there in the middle of nowhere."

Marvalene shot her a tight-lipped smile. "Try me. We're hardly in the middle of nowhere. However, it's a two mile walk back to downtown, and I don't think those shoes you're wearing are going to do real great on this ice, so I suggest you might want to really think about what you're going to say next. Capiche?"

After a quick, albeit silent, consultation, Darlene and Jazelle both nodded, then mimed zipping their lips shuts.

"Glad we could come to an understanding." Marvalene took her seat, closed the doors, and put the trolley in gear.

"Have Yourself a Merry Little Christmas" blasted through the speakers as we went on our not-so-merry way.

Chapter Twenty-Seven

April leaned over and whispered in my ear, "Well, at least tonight's drama didn't include a dead body."

"This whole town is going nuts. First the poor woman stuffed into the chimney, and now accusations of infidelity." Smitty shook her head, as if disgusted. "Seems like it's all interconnected, much like on my favorite stories. I don't even need to watch tonight. I got all the entertainment I can handle right here."

Smitty's voice was naturally quieter, but I still worried Laine had heard the comment about her sister.

April must have felt the same, since she tried to cover it up with a cough and a change of subject. "Speaking of entertainment, I'll have to decide what to watch tonight. Last time we took the tour, the *Christmas in Rockefeller Center* special was just getting over when I got home. *Jeopardy* came on after, so I was still able to watch it. I'm sure I won't have the same luck tonight and will have to catch the episode on repeat one of these days."

I cocked my head, finally grasping onto the comment Mel had made earlier on the tour that had been bouncing around in my head, then pairing it up with this new little tidbit. "They played *Jeopardy* later than normal on Friday night?" I asked April to repeat herself.

She nodded. "Yeah. Since the Christmas special was on for a couple of hours, *Jeopardy* didn't play in its normal time slot. I'm pretty sure it was nine-thirty before it aired."

"Huh. I'll be darned. How interesting."

April frowned at me. "Not really. I can think of a gazillion more interesting things."

"Not if you add it to something else I finally just realized." I angled my knees in so my back was nearly to the middle aisle.

"You're going to have to spell it out for me, Mom. I can't read your mind," April said. "And thank goodness for small miracles."

"Hey. My mind is a fascinating place." I took my small notebook out of my purse, opened it on my lap and wrote and underlined one word. "Dyer." I tilted the page toward April so she could read it.

She eyed me like I was a nut job. "Sorry. Still not picking up what you're trying to put down."

As soon as Mel had said the name out loud, it rang a bell. Dyer was Laine's maiden name. With a few minutes to mull it over, I'd remembered she had gone to school in Seattle and started her practice up there. It wasn't until her and Sheryl's mom passed away that Laine had come back to Pine Bluff. She came home to help with the funeral arrangements, but she and her new husband, Mel Messina, had ended up staying.

I wrote more in the notebook. "L's maiden name." I gestured subtly to Laine sitting across the aisle from me, but enough for April to pick up on the meaning. Next I scribbled, "Dr. D signed S's disability papers."

Her mouth formed a surprised "O." "Wouldn't that be a conflict of interest?" she hissed into my ear.

I shrugged, then scribbled some more. "Also lied about alibi."

April narrowed her eyes. "How do you know?"

This time, I leaned over and whispered in her ear. "She said she was watching *Jeopardy* when her sister was killed. Couldn't have been."

April slowly shook her head. "Nope."

I flipped to a clean page and wrote my daughter another note. "Text J. T. Tell him to meet the trolley at the post office."

April nodded as I stood and slowly made my way to the driver. When I got to the front, I squatted, protesting knees and all, beside Marvalene. We were passing the community center, only a few blocks from where the tour started and would end.

"Don't tell me something else is going on back there," she said.

"Fine. I won't tell you then. I need a favor though. Do you trust me?" I asked. Marvalene and I had gone to school together and had always been friendly with each other.

She nodded. "Yes, of course I do."

"Then I need you to drive slowly, and when we get back to Cedar Street, don't open the doors until Chief Dallas is standing there. Then let me off first, okay? Nobody else gets off until the Chief says so."

The whites of Marvalene's eyes shone as she eyed me like a spooked reindeer, but she nodded. "You got it. Can I ask why?"

"Not yet." I stood and patted her shoulder. "You'll find out soon enough."

Back at my seat, April showed me her text exchange with J. T. He was on his way as fast as his truck could go.

Marvalene slowed the trolley to nearly a crawl, then turned left down a residential street I was sure wasn't on the original tour plan. She cranked the music up and we rolled through the neighborhood with the whole group singing along to "I Saw Mommy Kissing Santa Claus." Well, all except Oscar, Jazelle, and Darlene. Oscar looked like he was ready to bolt, while the two women sat staring straight ahead, refusing to join in the fun since they hadn't gotten their own way. They were a couple of spoiled brats, if you wanted my opinion.

The trolley swung down another five streets, before Marvalene put us back on course and crawled to Cedar Street. J. T. was nowhere in sight when she pulled to the curb, so Marvalene took her time jockeying the trolley into position.

"Have you never parallel parked before?" Jazelle called, more than a hint of irritation in her voice. "The curb is wide open. I don't see what the problem is."

Marvalene glared at her in the rearview mirror as I chuckled to myself.

The trolley was finally lined up perfectly, but when our driver attempted to open the doors, the crank on the door glider didn't work. "Sorry folks," she grumbled. "There seems to be a problem with my glider mechanism. No worries, though. Go ahead and stay in your seats, please. I'll have it working, and you off the bus, in no time. It'll be a funny story to tell your family at Christmas dinner." She pushed and pulled on the handle until I thought her face would turn blue.

More people than Jazelle and Darlene were starting to grumble by the time J. T., dressed in full police uniform, stepped up and knocked on the glass doors of the trolley. Officers Everett and Bowman flanked him. Marvalene caught my eye in the rearview mirror, signaling to me it was my turn up to bat. I hurried up the aisle and waited at the front. This time, the doors slid open exactly as they should. Miracle of miracles.

I stepped off the bus and Marvalene slammed the doors shut behind me. The sound of protests from inside the bus reached my ears.

"What's this all about, Dawna?" J. T. asked, hands on hips.

He worked his jaw as I explained how I'd pieced the clues together until all the pieces fit.

"Laine killed her sister. I'm sure of it."

"You may be right, but filing a fraudulent medical report and lying about what television show she was watching isn't solid evidence Laine committed murder."

I sighed. "I suppose not. Shoot, I thought we had her." My face fell. I was fully convinced Laine was the killer. How could I get the solid evidence the police needed?

"I do think lying about her alibi is a good enough reason to bring her in for another round of questioning, don't you Chief?" Officer Samantha Everett held up her cell phone. "I just checked, and Dawna's right. *Jeopardy* aired in a later slot that night."

J. T. ran a hand over his jaw, then nodded. "Let's do it."

I motioned for Marvalene to open the door for us, then bounded back to my seat. I wasn't about to miss watching this go down.

J. T. climbed the three stairs to the main aisle of the bus, looked at Laine, and crooked his finger, as if beckoning her. "Dr. Messina, I need you to come with me."

Across the aisle from me, Mel shot to his feet. "What for this time? You've questioned her enough. My wife is grieving and this harassment has got to stop. I won't stand for it any longer." His voice thundered throughout the bus.

Laine held a shaky hand up, fingers splayed. "It's alright, Mel. He's just doing his job. You're right. I am grieving, but I'm also exhausted. I can't keep up this charade any longer. It's time to come clean."

I grabbed April's arm and squeezed. Was Laine about to confess to murder? It was more than I dared hope for.

As we all watched, her body seemed to sag and crumple in on itself. New lines emerged, elongating her face with grief and, I hoped, remorse.

Mel shook his head as if confused. "What are you talking about, Laine? Come clean about what?"

"About Sheryl." Her breath hitched in her throat as she continued. "I'm the one who did it. I killed my sister. I hope you can forgive me someday." A sob broke through as Laine covered her mouth with her hand. With a final glance at her devastated husband, she hurried up the aisle to surrender herself to J. T.

"What I want to know is if Laine is the killer, who locked me in the bathroom at the theater the other night? She wasn't even there." I frowned at my seatmates.

"That was me," Darlene piped up, her standard smirk on her face. "You had it coming."

April half rose, already in fighting stance, but I patted her arm. "Leave it. She's not worth the fight."

Chapter Twenty-Eight

A hush fell over the rest of the occupants on the trolley. For about seven and a half seconds, anyway.

Jazelle let out a high-pitched scream. "You killed my mother!"

As the rest of us stayed seated, she raced up the aisle in hot pursuit of her aunt. Jazelle's elbow came in sharp contact with the side of my head as she flew by.

"Ow." I pressed a hand to the sore spot while gawking after her as she ran off the bus.

Those of us still left on the trolley scrambled to cram together on the right-hand side of the bus. Wide-eyed faces pressed against the glass at the altercation taking place on the sidewalk. Smitty lowered the window at our seat so we could hear what was going on.

A shocked Mel had exited the bus after his niece and seemed to be pleading with J. T., who had already slapped a pair of handcuffs on Laine. Jazelle's eyes blazed with rage as she shoved her face as close to her aunt's as possible. She screamed obscenities while the spittle flew. Laine stared at the sidewalk and didn't respond to either Jazelle's fury or Mel's pleading.

Officer Samantha Everett approached Jazelle from the side. "Miss Capri, I'm going to need you to step back and let the Chief do his job."

When Sam touched Jazelle's arm to force her point, Jazelle spun, fists flying. Caught off guard, the first punch skimmed the officer's jaw, but Sam was ready for the second. She skillfully blocked the punch, then seized Jazelle's wrist in a blur of movement and had the woman's hands cuffed behind her back faster than you could say "Jiminy Cricket."

Inside the trolley, Darlene let out a sharp cry of distress, then hurried off the bus. Outside, she flicked a quick glance at her friend. I thought she was going to offer Jazelle aid, but instead Darlene threw her hands up. "This is on you to get out of your mess this time. I'm fed up with coming to your rescue," Darlene said to her friend, then darted toward Main Street and disappeared around the corner.

"So much for loyalty," I scoffed. I glanced between April and Smitty. "If either of you ever get arrested, I'll have your back."

"Where were you when I needed you back in 1969?"

"1969?" I blinked stupidly at her while racking my brain. "Woodstock?"

"Of course. They didn't take well to folks smoking whacky-tobacky back then. Called it 'the devil's lettuce'."

"Seriously? You were arrested at Woodstock?" April asked.

Smitty smiled sweetly and turned her attention back out the window without answering.

Laine was placed into the back of J. T.'s police cruiser. Jazelle kicked and screamed as Sam wrangled her into her car. The two women would be driven a block over to the police station. It was a fair assumption to guess Laine would be booked for murder and Jazelle for assaulting a police officer. It was looking like the self-proclaimed white sheep of the Dyer family had changed colors. Laine fit in with her criminal kin better than she thought she did.

"Seems to me it would've been easier to walk them over to the station," Smitty remarked.

April shrugged. "Probably protocol."

Once the cars were out of sight, frenetic chatter filled the trolley.

Marvalene placed two fingers in her mouth and shot out a high decibel whistle to cut through the noise. "Alright, there's nothing left to see here, folks." She gestured to the open door. "Time to head on home."

As everyone else exited the trolley, I hung back to have a final word with the driver. "Thank you for all of your help tonight, and for trusting me. I owe you one." I patted her shoulder. "We can all sleep easier tonight knowing the killer is off our streets."

"And knowing I'll be handing in my resignation to the city in the morning. This is far too much excitement for me. I'm going to go back to driving school bus." She let out a harried breath. "I thought driving the town bus would ease me into retirement, but you know what they say. The grass isn't always greener on the other side."

Chapter Twenty-Nine

"**G**ood news." Roxy pulled off her coat and hat the next morning, stowing them under the front counter. "Barry woke up last night. The doctor thinks he's going to be just fine."

We'd both arrived an hour earlier than normal. After the events of the evening before, I hadn't been able to sleep, and guessed Roxy's reason for coming in so early was the same.

"Excellent. I'm so glad to hear it." I placed the cash drawer inside the register tray. "Did they get the test results back yet? Any updates on what caused him to be unresponsive for so long?"

"They say it was a bad reaction to influenza. His blood work didn't show any signs of toxicity like the doctor first thought."

"Huh. I guess Jazelle didn't poison him then."

"Whoa there, Nelly. Whoever said anything about Jazelle poisoning Barry?" Roxy stared at me, her eyes as round as Santa's belly.

I looked at her, surprised. "Well, I sure thought I shared that theory with you." I headed to the coffee station to get a pot going ahead of the coffee klatch guys' arrival. "I must've forgotten with all the other hubbub going on."

Roxy trailed after me. "Apparently so. Feel free to share with me now, though." She crossed her arms and leaned against the counter.

I poured ground coffee into the filter without bothering to measure it. The guys' motto was "the stronger the better." My coffee tasted like pure sludge to me, and I never drank the stuff. I shuddered at the thought. "The speculation Jazelle may have poisoned Barry came about from talking to various people, including her Aunt Laine."

"Who turned out to be a murderer." Roxy shook her head. "I still haven't fully wrapped my head around her killing Sheryl."

"Me either. Her own sister?" I slid the basket into the coffee maker and pushed the button to start the brewing. "Anyway, I had a chiropractor appointment with Laine a few days ago. You know me, I couldn't bear to leave things alone, so I prodded her to talk about the loss of her sister. She indicated she thought it was possible Sheryl's last two husbands' deaths weren't as black and white as they appeared to be."

Roxy gasped. "No way! You aren't serious?"

"Yep. She talked about how Jazelle was exactly like her mother, and how the two targeted and used people. Laine went as far as to say how Brett would be lucky to make it out of his relationship with Jazelle alive. After you mentioned Jazelle had told Makayla the Dunsmuir ranch was going to be hers, I thought maybe getting rid of Brett's father was her first step in that direction." I waffled my head around. "Well, second step I guess. She's already reeled Brett in enough to be living out at the ranch."

"If Jazelle hurt either Barry or Pam, I'd have to kill her myself." Roxy pressed a shaky hand to her chest. "Thank goodness your theory was wrong."

I squinted and sucked air through my teeth. "Maybe, but I think she warrants keeping an eye on. I'm not fully convinced of her innocence."

"Neither am I." J. T. strode up to us.

Roxy and I both startled. Neither one of us had heard him come in. I glanced at the bell above the door, knowing we heard it so often, the melodic tinkle faded into background noise many times instead of announcing someone's presence.

"Mind if I join you?" J. T. reached for a coffee mug and poured himself a cup of the thick, bitter brew without waiting for an answer. He piled about six packets of sugar in his hand, shook them, ripped the tops off in one motion, and poured them into the coffee. A similar number of creamer packets later, and he deemed it worthy to drink.

I disagreed wholeheartedly. "Of course. What brings you by so bright and early?"

"And what do you mean neither are you?" Roxy asked. "You think Jazelle may have poisoned Barry?"

"No, I don't think she poisoned Barry. Yet." He parked himself in a chair at the coffee klatch table and crossed his long legs. "Thought you might like an update, and I do have some news about Jazelle, as long as you both promise it won't leave this room."

Roxy and I glanced at each other, nodded, then both pulled out chairs and sat.

"April's going to be miffed we didn't wait for her," I said.

J. T. winced as he took a swig of his coffee. "She'll be fine. I already filled her in."

"Well, now I'm the one who's miffed." I laughed. "We heard Laine confess, so we already know that part."

"The good news is, she didn't change her story during the official interview. In fact, she talked for two hours straight, finally getting all the diabolical stuff her sister did to her off her chest. We have her full confession on file now. Everything's properly documented." He set the mug back down on the table, leaving the coffee barely touched. "Laine says Sheryl coerced her into claiming she was fully disabled and filing the fraudulent report for Sheryl's disability hearing. From Laine's account, Sheryl spent all the years since threatening to expose her and get her license revoked if she didn't continue to give both Sheryl and Jazelle money whenever they demanded. The lawsuits that would have come about because of Sheryl's accusations would have destroyed Laine."

"I wonder what compelled Laine to give in to Sheryl's demands in the first place? Why she compromised herself and her license to lie for her sister?" I fiddled with a red stir stick on the table.

"Approval, apparently. Laine says she always felt like an outcast in her own family and was forever looking for approval from them." J. T. shook his head. "Beats me why. The whole Dyer clan were not much more than common criminals. I was glad to see the back of them when the last of their brothers skipped town."

"Poor woman. I actually feel a little sorry for her," Roxy said.

J. T. reached for his coffee, but thought better of it and pulled his hand back. "Can't say I don't agree. Laine said she was tired of living in fear of being exposed, and the anger kept building. A couple of weeks ago, Laine had finally put her foot down and refused to hand over any more money to Jazelle. The Messina's bank accounts were drained, and Laine was on the verge of having to tell Mel what had been going on for all these years. She was scared to death he would divorce her when he found out she'd sold their stock and had taken out a second mortgage on their house, not to mention how she'd compromised her career for her sister. With the money dried up, Sheryl amped up her threats, calling and texting every few minutes with her demands. Friday night, Laine finally snapped and killed her sister."

I frowned. "Snapped? Seems to me tampering with the power cord took at least a tiny bit of planning."

"Yep. The crime was somewhat premeditated, in my opinion, but that's for the courts to decide." J. T. nodded. "She says she was out of her mind the night Sheryl died, and while she remembers fraying the electrical cord and being so angry she wrapped her sister in the Christmas lights and shoved her in the chimney, she can't be held responsible. Some other energy took over and she plans on pleading insanity."

"An insanity plea feels like a cop out." Roxy knit her brows together.

"Do you think she'll get away with it?" I asked.

J. T. shrugged. "Not my call to make. The only thing I can do is submit my reports and let a judge and jury decide."

"True enough." I blew out a breath and pushed my glasses up. "Did you find out anything about Sheryl's real estate holdings?"

"Officer Bowman ferreted that information out late yesterday afternoon. It seems Sheryl sold the Michigan properties not long after Jeff, husband number three, died. She held onto the property in Greenwood, but blew through the money from the other sales in a handful of years."

"Blew through it how? She must have gotten a fairly hefty chunk of cash for those properties."

"Did you happen to take a peek in her garage while you were snooping around?" J. T. asked.

I shook my head. "No, I didn't have a reason to go in the garage."

"I'm surprised. You normally manufacture a reason to snoop."

"I most certainly do not." I crossed my arms over my chest and scowled.

"Do too." He met my scowl with one of his own.

"Can you two stop acting like children for a minute? I'd like to know what was in Sheryl's garage." Roxy crossed her arms on the table and leaned in.

J. T. threw both hands up, palms to the sky. "It was filled to the rafters with boxes marked with the SFYC logo."

"SFYC? I'm not familiar with that particular acronym," I said.

"The Shop From Your Couch network," Roxy supplied. "Don't tell me you haven't heard of it. The channel is on the air twenty-four hours of the day, with sales people who are great at convincing you that you can't live without the latest gadget. Tons of people are addicted to it."

"Oh sure, it sounds familiar. I only subscribe to a few streaming channels, so don't run across it. I remember the original shopping network, but it isn't something I think about very often." I shrugged.

"Well, looks like Sheryl was one of those people addicted to shopping from her T.V. screen. Much to the detriment of her bank account." J. T. rocked his chair back onto two legs.

"What about the storage units in Greenwood. She must've still owned those."

"Nah." He dropped the chair legs back to the floor. "By the time she had used up all her funds, she'd ignored the storage units too long. Poor management and neglect ran them into the ground. Sheryl ended up selling them a couple of years back for pennies on the dollar of what they should have been worth."

I whistled. "To be set up with income producing properties like she was, and then blow it all, completely flabbergasts me. What a waste."

"So, on top of being a terrible person, Sheryl was also a spendthrift. Got it." Roxy slapped the table. "Now, what were you going to tell us about Jazelle?"

J. T. clasped his hands around his coffee mug. He glanced between Roxy and me with a stern expression on his face. "What I'm about to tell you goes no further than the three of us. Do I have your word?"

"Scout's honor." I gave a three-fingered pledge.

Roxy nodded. "I solemnly swear."

The Chief of Police intently studied our faces for a minute before he must've decided we were trustworthy. "When I came in, I overheard you saying there was no indication Jazelle poisoned Barry, which is great news. It sounds like the hospital was thorough in the tests they ran, so I think we can be fairly certain they've covered all the bases." J. T. paused. "However, I'm not sure that was the case with Jazelle's late husband. Like I said, keep this to yourselves, but I had a call from the Chief of Police in Billings this morning. They've followed up on some accusations and have had some things come to light that throws suspicion on her husband's death. The family is having his body exhumed and a more thorough autopsy conducted. Montana law enforcement asked me to keep an eye on Jazelle for them. They want to make sure they know where she is in case they need to bring her in."

"Holy fright." I glanced at Roxy who had gone as white as a ghost. "Do you still have her in custody for punching Officer Everett last night?"

J. T. nodded. "Yep. Having her locked up in a jail cell is the best place I can think of to keep an eye on her." He blew out a short breath. "With any luck, the authorities in Montana will get back to me before I have to release her."

"Here's hoping." Roxy crossed her fingers on both hands and shook them beside her head. "If you end up letting her out, can you give me a heads up first? There's no way my kids are going out to the ranch until this is all cleared up."

"Can do." J. T. tapped his finger on the table and rose. "Time for me to get back at it. Dawna, thanks for your help."

He touched the brim of his hat and sauntered out the door seconds before the coffee klatch guys wandered in.

Roxy and I replayed the events of the night before for their benefit. I bit my tongue and kept the details about Jazelle to myself, as J. T. requested, but boy, was it ever a test of my self-control.

By the following Wednesday, Marsha had shared with me how she'd warned her nephew, Clay, to stay away from Pine Bluff because she herself hadn't been one hundred percent sure he hadn't killed Sheryl. He hadn't taken her advice anyway.

"I wanted to believe him, but that boy can hold a grudge. Thanks for your role in apprehending the real killer." She blinked her pale blue eyes and handed me a loaf wrapped in tinfoil with a red bow attached to the top.

"No thanks needed. I'm just happy our little town feels safe again." I brought the baked treat to my nose and sniffed, but couldn't smell anything through the foil. "What's this?"

"My famous fruitcake. I haven't made any for twenty years, but I think it's my best batch yet. I use my great-grandmother's recipe, you know." She winked. "The secret is applesauce."

Just the word fruitcake made me want to gag. "Can't wait to have a slice." My smile felt tight. "Thank you."

"My pleasure. You're going to love it." The bell over the door tinkled as Marsha left.

Earlier in the week, J. T. had let April and I know we'd been right about Oscar. And wrong. He had suspected Sheryl was collecting her deceased mother's social security, but he wasn't trying to blackmail her and had adamantly insisted he did not have an affair with Jazelle. Oscar admitted Jazelle had targeted him when he and his family first moved to Pine Bluff, to the point of nearly stalking him, but he'd made it clear in no uncertain terms that he was happily married and not interested. Jazelle didn't let his lack of interest deter her until she'd found another man to dig her claws into.

Recently, Sheryl had been trying to get money from Oscar, saying she was going to tell his wife he'd had an affair with Jazelle if he didn't pay up, and claiming she had proof. In retaliation, and hoping to get her to back off, Oscar had confronted her on the morning of her untimely demise with the photocopies he'd been making of her mother's social security statements. Instead of retreating, Sheryl had pushed harder. The manila envelope we'd found in the drip tray of her refrigerator was the same one Shilo saw Oscar slap down on her picnic table. According to Oscar, he had every intention of telling his wife about the harassment, but when Sheryl died, he thought the problem solved itself. Until Freya witnessed Jazelle flirting with him on the trolley and came to her own, incorrect, conclusions. The Rudolfs were a nice family. I hoped they would make it through this.

April breezed through the door with J. T. following in her wake. "Oh, what's this?" She grabbed the loaf Marsha gave me and quickly unwrapped it. "Fruitcake. Yum!"

I stared at her like she'd grown three heads.

She took out her pocketknife, cut off a slab, and stuffed it into her mouth. "This is delicious. Who made it?"

"Marsha," I said knowing I still had a look of horror on my face.

"Here, try it." April handed a chunk to J. T., then tried to give one to me.

I declined. "Over my dead body."

Not known for listening to her mother, my daughter attempted to shove a piece through my clamped tight lips. She failed, but a crumb managed to cling to the side of my mouth.

Without thinking, I licked my lips and...wait. "Hey, this isn't half bad."

"Told you. Ready for a slice?"

I shook my head. No need to go overboard.

"Are you two done with your shenanigans?" J. T. asked.

"Oh, yeah. Mom, listen to this." She pointed to J. T. as if to give him the go-ahead to speak.

"Is Roxy here?" he asked.

I shook my head. "Nope, it's her day off."

"Shoot. Well, I'll give her a call in a bit."

"Is this about Jazelle?"

He nodded. "The news will get out soon enough. This morning, Jazelle Capri was extradited back to Montana on suspicion of murder."

My hand flew to cover my mouth as I gasped. "She really did it? She killed her husband?"

"Seems so. Atropine overdose."

I pursed my lips. "Atropine? What is that?"

"A byproduct of the belladonna plant, though it has beneficial uses. Jazelle's husband had a prescription for atropine for digestive issues. He'd been taking the medication for years. From what they're saying, it looks like Jazelle crushed the pills up and put them in his food. With proper medical treatment, he would have recovered, but his kids are claiming that the week before his death, she wouldn't let them see him."

"On what grounds?"

"She claimed his kids constantly stopped by and were putting a damper on their newlywed activities."

"His kids must be as old as Jazelle is, if not older." I shuddered. "How'd they figure it out?"

"One of his sons lives and works on the ranch. After his dad passed, he went through the trash and found an empty prescription bottle. It had only been refilled nine days before his death, so shouldn't have been empty."

"So, Jazelle must not have been successful in getting his ranch deeded over to her."

J. T. shook his head. "Nope. She walked away with about fifty grand, but before they ever got married, the ranch was already in a rock solid family trust she couldn't touch. Must've been maddening when she found out there wasn't a way around the trust."

"I'd say so." I tucked my hair behind my ear as goosebumps dotted my skin. "Good night! The Dunsmuirs are incredibly lucky. They really dodged a bullet."

Chapter Thirty

A week before Christmas, my family descended on Pine Bluff in a rush of holiday excitement. Just in time to attend my debut performance as an unwilling participant in the Whoville Choir. During the practices leading up to the performance, I'd gotten a lot better. Okay. Maybe that's a bit of an exaggeration. A little better, anyway. But when it was our turn to dance and sing, I glanced into the audience. The sight of all three of my kids with their kids and spouses caused me to forget everything I'd learned. I couldn't remember a single word of the song or any of the choreography. When we were supposed to go left, I went right. When the rest of the choir moved right, you got it—I went left. The only thing I had going my way was the giant grin on my face from having all my people under one roof.

We celebrated the beginning, and ending, of my stage career by inviting half the town to dinner. At least it felt like half the town was crowded into my house, and I couldn't have loved it more. April made copious amounts of lasagna while I filled four extra-large Tupperware bowls with green salad. My daughter, Becky, and daughter-in-law, Sarah, sliced and seasoned scads of garlic bread. Evonne and Ernie arrived toting a dozen home-made pies. My stomach growled just looking at them. Every other person who came through the door brought something to add to our feast.

"Look at this spread. Nobody's going hungry tonight, and I hope you all brought leftover containers."

The second April pulled the first tray of steaming lasagna out of the oven, I filled a plate for Smitty and got her settled into the place of honor at the dining room table.

"All right, kids next." I clapped my hands and looked around. "Where have those little rottens gotten off to?"

I found five-year-old Hazel first. Becky's daughter sat beside the Christmas tree, holding an animated conversation with herself.

"There you are. Are you ready for some dinner, sweet Hazel?"

My heart overflowed when the little girl reached up and took my hand. Together, we went into the kitchen. With my arms around her waist, I held Hazel up so she could see while she told me what food she wanted on her plate. I put her down and started filling her plate.

"Hey, Bana." Hazel tugged at my sweater.

"Yes, love. What do you need?"

"Papa said to tell you he loves you."

I stared at my granddaughter. "When did you talk to Papa?"

She looked at me like I was an idiot. "Just now."

My eyes about popped out of my head. "Where?"

Hazel wrinkled her nose. "He's in the living room by the Christmas tree. Didn't you see him?"

You could have heard a pin drop as Becky, Patrick, April and I turned to stare at the little girl.

"Then he said to tell the rest of you to bugger off." Her namesake eyes sparkled. "What does bugger off mean, Bana?"

A clatter of boots echoed through the kitchen as my two grandsons raced up the basement stairs, breaking the shocked tension.

"Well, that was definitely Dad alright." April was the first to laugh. "Looks like Hazel may have inherited more than your little pug nose."

Before I could formulate a response, eight-year-old Wyatt flew at me like a rocket and wrapped himself around my waist. "Bana, Bana, Bana. Is it time to eat? I'm starving."

My oldest grandson, Patrick's ten-year-old boy, Robby, hung back, a little shyer than his cousin.

"Come on, Robby. Help me fill your plate." I beckoned to him with my hand. "Do you want to do it, or would you like me to?"

He grinned. "You, please." Robby asked for a big helping of lasagna, two slices of garlic bread, and not a single bit of salad. I happily obliged.

Once the younger kids were settled at the card table in the dining room, it was time for the rest of us to fill our plates. Roxy's teenagers would squeeze around the table with the rest of us. Before everyone got there, Patrick and Sarah had pulled the oblong oak table apart and added all three leaves to extend the surface. Even so, it was going to be crowded. Elbows good-naturedly flew as we jockeyed for space at the counter.

At the table, I glanced around at my family and most of my closest friends. I started to raise my glass of wine for a toast, but stopped mid swing. "Wait a minute. Where's J. T. and Chandler? I thought they were coming."

Chandler was J. T.'s tween daughter. She lived in Idaho with her mother, but was in Pine Bluff to spend Christmas with her dad.

"Nope." April scowled, then picked up her own wine glass and emptied it in one colossal gulp.

"Did he have to go to work? We should have brought Chandler here. She shouldn't be alone." Becky put her napkin on the table and started to stand as if she was going to rush out to J. T.'s house to get Chandler.

"Work is not the problem." April's words came out clipped and measured. "The daughter is the problem."

Bewildered, I glanced around the table, then back at April. "Chandler's the problem? I don't understand."

April huffed out a breath and let her fork clatter to her plate. "If you must know, Mother, Chandler has requested to spend Christmas alone with her father. They will not be joining us, and I will not be joining them. Now drop it, please, and let me enjoy those people who do want to spend time with me." Tears of anger and hurt sprang to her eyes, but she forced them back, refusing to allow them to fall.

"I guarantee you, and I'm talking from experience here," Rick Montgomery spoke up, "J. T. holds a world of guilt for being a divorced dad and not in his little girl's life every day. He only has a little bit of time with her and feels he needs to do everything he can to please her."

April glowered Rick's direction.

Rick waved his hands crossways in front of himself. "Right, wrong, or indifferent, it's the way it is when you don't have your kids full time."

"I can attest to that." Trisha pointed her fork at her husband. "The kids always come first, and believe me, there was a time when I wasn't sure I was going to make it through playing second fiddle to his kids. But it was all worth it in the long run."

Patrick had refilled his sister's wine glass, so April took another swig and sighed. "Time will tell."

"May I have seconds, please?" Smitty spoke into the silence.

I wasn't quick enough. Bill Wilder was up and had Smitty's plate in his hand before I got my chair pushed back. A minute later, he was back with a hearty second portion for her.

"Thank you, William." Smitty smiled, not at Bill but at the plate of food. "Now, if you'd all indulge an old woman, I'd like to take a moment to remember my late bridge partner. Sheryl may not have been everyone's cup of tea..."

You mean anyone's?

"...but she was sure one heck of a bridge player."

Evonne snorted. "She was probably one heck of a cheater."

Smitty ignored the comment. "And you all have to admit, she put on a fabulous Christmas light show. In fact, Sheryl's penchant for glowing lights reminds me of the time..."

Never sure of what Smitty's stories would entail, I sent a concerned glance to the kids table. The belly laughs coming from them made it clear they weren't paying a bit of attention to the adults. I turned my attention back to Smitty.

"...my sister and I were tasked with delivering a barrel of oil to a friend's cabin in Alaska."

"Alaska?" I interrupted. *Was there any place this woman hadn't been?*

She nodded. "Just outside of Ketchikan. Sissy and I were in our early twenties and up for any adventure, so when our friend radioed and said he was in urgent need of oil, we didn't hesitate to jump to his aid. It was late summer but a dark night. We needed to navigate the waters off the coast and get the oil to the friend's cabin on an island a few miles from shore, so we borrowed our uncle's old wooden dory. How hard could it be?"

"Wait a minute," Bill interrupted. "Two young women decide to take an old boat out into unfamiliar ocean water, and your uncle let you go?"

Smitty blinked at him. "Uncle was out fishing, so we couldn't ask. He'd told us to make ourselves at home and use anything we wanted while he was gone. We wanted to use the dory." She took a bite of her lasagna, chewing slowly while we waited for her to continue. "Like I said, it was a dark night in late summer. Cloudy, like the weather so often is in Southeastern

Alaska. Now, a barrel of oil is quite a heavy item, mind you. Nevertheless, Sissy and I managed to roll the barrel into the boat. We stood it on end so we'd have room for one of us to stand at each end of the boat. There was no such thing as GPS back in those days. All we had was a good sense of direction, a compass, and the stars."

"And a healthy dose of misplaced confidence," Bill grumbled.

"Sheesh. I'd be lost before I got the boat in the water," Roxy remarked.

"The old boat wasn't in the best of condition, but it still seemed to be waterproof, and that's all we cared about. Sissy and I each had an oar and determination, so we set out. It was slow going, and the night kept getting darker and darker until we could barely see each other. I will admit, we were getting nervous and beginning to think we'd made a mistake. Suddenly, the ocean lit up in neon blue sparkles. Pure magic surrounded us."

"It sounds amazing. What caused the colors?" I asked.

Smitty's eyes sparkled. "A bioluminescent plankton bloom. It's a phenomenon that happens in ocean waters all over the world. Needless to say, we were enthralled. So much so, that we forgot to pay attention to the boat."

Not a peep or a scrape of fork against plate sounded around the table as we waited with baited breath for the rest of the story.

"We were nearly two hours into the journey, with another hour or so to go, when I noticed my feet were cold. I looked down only to realize the bioluminescence was swirling around me, nearly up to my kneecaps. We were sinking!"

A collective gasp echoed around the table.

"Did you have a bail bucket?" Ernie asked.

Smitty winked at him. "It took a minute, but Sissy and I soon realized what the buckets Uncle had tied to the side of the dory were for. We bailed water out of the boat like our life depended on it." She tore off a chunk of garlic bread and popped it into her mouth. "Because it did. Uncle would have killed us if we'd lost his boat."

I nudged Becky with my elbow. "I don't think he would've had the chance. Not many people survive in the Alaskan waters for long."

"Did you make it to your friend's cabin?" Patrick asked.

"We sure did. Spent the night, then made the return trip in the morning, minus one very heavy barrel of oil."

"Whew. What an exciting adventure." I raised my wine glass, ready to try toasting to the health and safety of my friends and family once again.

Before I got one word out, little Hazel let out a wail as loud as a firetruck siren. I lowered my glass.

Becky shoved back her chair. "Wyatt! What did you do to your sister?"

Wyatt dropped his mouth open and shook his head rapidly, as if shocked to be accused of such a horrendous crime. "It wasn't me. I didn't eat her bread."

"Yes he did," Hazel wailed between sobs.

Becky picked her daughter up. "Wyatt, go to your room."

"I don't have a room."

"Go to the room where we're sleeping. Right this second, young man," Becky replied between gritted teeth. "I'll be there in ten minutes."

Wyatt stomped down the hallway, muttering to himself as he went. Becky took Hazel into the kitchen to get her another piece of garlic bread. When they came back into the dining room, I reached for the teary-eyed little girl and settled her into my lap. Becky sighed and headed down the hallway to have a chat with her son.

"Oh, hey, Mom," Patrick addressed me. "I meant to tell you the apartment looks great. You and April really did a nice job on it."

"Thanks. I'm really pleased with the transformation. I'm half tempted to move up there myself." I laughed.

"Do you have a renter lined up?" Sarah asked.

"A couple of people have inquired, so I've started a list, but I plan to be pretty picky, since whoever I choose will be living right over my head. I hope to have someone in there by mid-January at the latest."

Evonne placed her elbows on the table and tented her hands. "Speaking of your rental, I haven't seen your rental permit come across my desk yet."

"My rental permit? I wasn't aware I needed one." I shoved my glasses up the bridge of my nose and stared at my best friend.

Hazel squirmed in my lap and reached for my fork to help herself to some of my lasagna. Apparently my granddaughter had double standards when it came to eating food that didn't necessarily belong to the person shoveling it into their mouth.

"Of course you do, Dawna. Every rental property within the city limits has to be approved by the City Council. Don't tell me you haven't turned your application in."

I closed my eyes for a second and rubbed my temple. "We didn't need one when Alta rented the apartment," I argued.

"How long ago? Thirty years or more?" Evonne flung an exasperated hand up. "Things have changed since then. You definitely need one now if you don't want a hefty fine and a cease and desist order tacked on the door."

I took a deep breath. "Not a problem. Do I get the permit application at City Hall?"

Evonne nodded. "You know what, I'll email you one tomorrow. I'm sorry I didn't think to mention it sooner. I assumed you were aware you needed one."

"It's not your fault," I assured her. "Everything takes a permit these days. I should have realized. Once I fill out the form and file, I'm guessing a week or so to get the permit?" I shrugged. "It shouldn't affect my timeline."

Evonne sucked air through her teeth and shook her head. "You're looking at more like six to eight weeks, and that's not taking into account the holidays. You know what they say about the government, nothing moves fast."

"Holy fright! That puts me at the end of February. This is Pine Bluff, not the federal government, for crying in the buttermilk."

"Small town city government is still government." Evonne winced. "I'll see what I can do to try to speed the process up for you, but I can't guarantee anything."

I stroked Hazel's hair as she demolished the rest of my dinner. "I appreciate your help. It's good to have friends in high places."

"Are you going to be okay making your home equity payments if I can't rush the permit through?" Evonne studied me with a worried frown.

I waved away her concern. "Oh, yeah. The payment's quite small. I'll be fine." And it wouldn't be the first time I'd survived on packets of ramen noodles and hot dogs.

"Mom, have you had any luck finding out why dad took out the original loan in the first place?" Patrick asked.

I quirked my lip and shook my head. "Nope, most likely we'll never know. It's water under the bridge now."

"What do you say we cheer this place up with some pie?" Trisha rose from the table and started gathering everyone's dinner plates while Evonne and Ernie brought the homemade pie to the table.

April started a pot of coffee, Hazel helped me bring in the dessert plates, and Becky and Wyatt emerged from the bedroom. Wyatt apologized to his sister, then ran off to play with Robby.

I started with a slice of gorgeously pink and fluffy candy cane pie, knowing full well I'd sample all six flavors before the evening was over. Hazel climbed back into my lap. This time, she'd brought her own spoon along, which she immediately dipped into my pie. I laughed and snuggled her harder.

Clinking my fork against my ceramic coffee mug, I got everyone's attention and finally was able to complete the toast I'd been trying for. Instead of wine, I toasted my family and friends with coffee, which was more my style anyway. I held my mug high. "To be surrounded by all the people I love the most is the only Christmas gift I could ask for. Thank you for being here. You make me want to cry, now let's eat pie."

As we laughed and clinked our mugs together, Hazel's waving hand shot straight up, nearly colliding with my raised coffee mug.

"Hi, Papa!" she cried excitedly. "Look, Bana, there's Papa!"

Tears really did spring to my eyes when I turned to look where Hazel was pointing and found Bob leaning against the floor to ceiling bookcase across the room. He sent me a heartwarming smile and a goofy wave to his granddaughter. As I raised my mug in a toast to my dearly departed husband, Hazel bounced on my lap in excitement while the rest of our family and friends shared amused glances over our heads. All except for April, who nodded knowingly and squeezed my arm.

Acknowledgements

The biggest thank you ever goes out to you—the readers who have loved and wanted more of the Hometown Hardware series. Thank you for loving Dawna, April, and the whole Pine Bluff crew. You are the reason they keep showing up on the page!

Thank you to my local independent bookstores who have been so gracious and kind, having me in to help celebrate when a new book comes out. To Copper Bell Bookshop in Ridgefield, Washington, Lucy's Books in Astoria, Oregon, and Vintage Books in Vancouver, Washington. Thank you for your unwavering support of local authors. We couldn't do this without you and certainly wouldn't want to!

Thank you to my editor, Brittany Sumpter, for not rolling your eyes, too hard, at all my misplaced commas. Thank you to Rose Kerr and Kat Webb for reading and providing valuable feedback, even with all those typos still in place. And to my cover designer, Melissa Bourbon of WriterSpark for this delightful cover art! I appreciate you all so much!

As always, a heartfelt forever thank you to my family for supporting me, reading my books, and listening to my endless rambles about make believe people. Thank you for your excitement!

About the Author

When Paula Charles isn't writing, you can find her reading and contemplating murder under the towering trees of the Pacific Northwest. She is the author of the Hometown Hardware Mystery series, cozy mysteries loosely based on her grandmother and the hardware store she owned in a small Northeastern Oregon town. The first book in the series, *Hammers and Homicide*, was a Woman's World Book Club pick. Writing as Janna Rollins, she is also the author of the Zen Goat Mysteries series. Paula is a member of the national Sisters in Crime, and the Columbia River chapter. She lives in Washington state with her patient husband and a handful of furry and feathered creatures. You can find out more about her books, and sign up for her newsletter to receive a free short story in the Hometown Hardware world at www.paulacharles.com

Social Media:

Facebook: Rainy Day Mysteries

Instagram: rainy_day_mysteries